M000281557

COMMON BONDS

A SPECULATIVE

AROMANTIC ANTHOLOGY

EDITED BY

CLAUDIE ARSENEAULT
C.T. CALLAHAN
B.R. SANDERS
AND
ROANNA SYLVER

Common Bonds
Copyright © 2020 Claudie Arseneault, C. T. Callahan, B.R. Sanders and RoAnna Sylver

ISBN: 978-1-7753129-7-0

Cover by Laya Rose
Interior Illustration by Laya Rose
Interior Design and Layout by Claudie Arseneault

commonbondsantho.com

Short stories and poems copyrights

TABLE OF CONTENTS

CONTENT WARNINGS

The Aromatic Lovers: Mentions of misgendering

Voices in the Air: Drowning, human sacrifices, mentions of abuse

Moon Sisters: Controlling romantic partners

Cinder: Abusive parents

Not Quite True Love: Anti-aromantic sentiments

Dracanmōt Council of Human Study Report, Compiled by Usander Greystart: Alcohol, ableism, colonization allegories

Spacegirl and the Martian: Alcohol, animal abuse, roofie mention, PTSD mention, forced prostitution mention, abuse mention, thoughts of arson

Would You Like Charms With That?: Accidental misgendering, violence, injury, spiders

In the Summer A Banana Tree: Animal death

Remembering the Farm: No warnings

Fishing Over the Bones of the Dragon: Death imagery, alcohol

Asteria III: Alcohol, puke/vomit mention, Alzheimer, death

A Full Deck: Abusive relationships

Half a Heart: Animal death

Shift: Abuse mention, puke/vomit mention, mentions of species extinction

Seams of Iron: Animal cruelty, child illness

Not to Die: Apathy about life, death of loved ones, depression, mentions of nonconsensual relationship dynamics

Busy Little Bees: Abusive parents, forced pregnancies, puke/vomit

FOREWORD

Common Bonds is the culmination of three things we love: aromantic representation, speculative fiction, and platonic relationships. In its pages are nineteen different works which combine all three in wildly imaginative ways, from a pair of clones seeking the others of their batch to a pack of werewolves comforting one of theirs after a difficult breakup. Each of these stories approach our themes with different levels of explicitness, reflecting the myriad of ways we forge bonds with one another or relate to our aromanticism.

Everyone who belongs to a marginalized group knows how difficult it can be to find parts of yourself in fiction, whether through rarity or misrepresentation—or, quite often, both at once. When it comes to aromantic characters in short stories, the body of work available is also spread across various websites or buried within an anthology with several other stories. Part of our hope with *Common Bonds* is to create an easy starting point—something entirely dedicated to aromantic readers, where their stories are the heart of the anthology.

While aromantic people engage in a wide variety of relationships, including romantic ones, we chose platonic bonds because they impact our lives from beginning to end and their importance is often overlooked. We wanted to explore these connections—the joy and sadness, the new discoveries and long-lasting struggles, what they teach us about the world, each other, and ourselves—and the way aromantic people often redefine their relative importance, centering them in their lives.

As a final note, we call *Common Bonds* an anthology of aromantic speculative fiction because despite its nineteen different works, it only covers a fraction of the aromantic experience. In short, *Common Bonds* can never be *the* anthology of aromantic speculative fiction, and we hope it will be the first of many such projects—by us, for us, and about us.

Until then, however, enjoy this one!

Claudie Arseneault
C. T. Callahan
B.R. Sanders
RoAnna Sylver

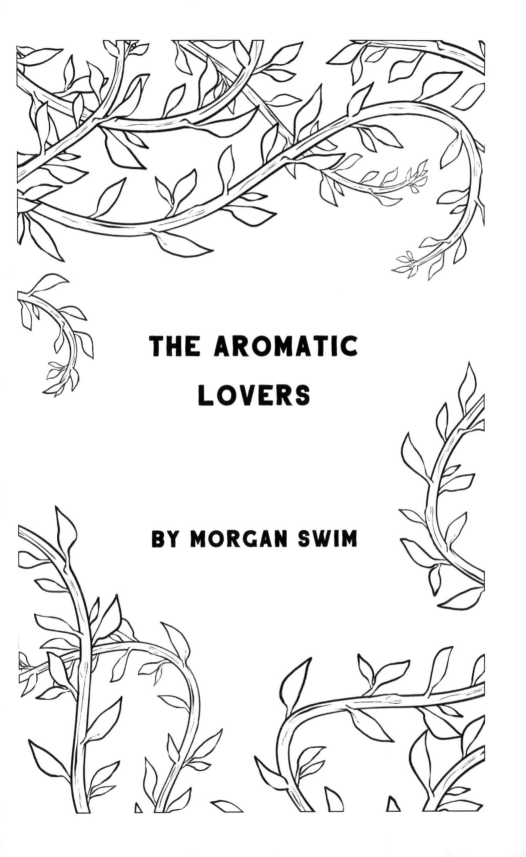

THE AROMATIC LOVERS

BY MORGAN SWIM

Temaste Square, fashionable and beautiful, was the idyllic heart of Karraine's shopping district. Thick strings of whisper vines trailed down from the second floor balustrades of the apartments that overlooked the square, their violet blooms like a blanket that obscured the brickwork. Floral scents mingled downward, competing and effusing into violent disharmony with the many barrels of spices, herbs, and potpourri that were piled high outside the shops. While floral and earthy scents beckoned customers into the potent and poorly ventilated perfumeries and aromatists' boutiques, yet more scents advertised meals offered within restaurants and cafes, heady coffee blends and hot curry wafted out into the greater miasma of the street. Even the square's central fountain poured not clean, sensible well water, but sweet tanmiss nectar, cloying and viscous as it oozed from a marble maiden's splayed palms.

In short, the city stank. Or so Matroise thought as they navigated the far-too-crowded-for-their-liking streets, one hand holding their oversized scarf to their nose in a vain effort to lessen the assault of scent.

They stopped short at the top of the stairway that emptied into the square to gather their courage, careful to stand to one side of the foot traffic to avoid the grazing touches of cheerful couples as they passed arm in arm.

Matroise gripped the vial of agrimovf oil with their unoccupied hand, a pained grimace hidden behind their scarf. Kita had to be lying about it. Had to be overselling her dire need for the scent, as Matroise knew very well it was not a key scent of Kita's gender. Had to be betting that Matroise's loyalty to her oldest and dearest friend would win out over their social anxiety and calculated avoidance of the city. Or at least a particular shop within it.

Matroise found Kita immediately, standing out from the crowd as always. She sat upon one edge of the fountain's base, enveloped in a voluminous white dress which gave her the appearance of an overgrown dandelion puff. Even from this distance, one could easily catch her scent. Hidden within Kita's airy dress were gauzy pouches of potpourri and fresh blooms sewn into its many folds of lace and cotton. Atop her head, a wide brimmed hat encircled with satin dill and peach blossoms framed her tightly coiled tresses and round face, her dark skin tinted with rouge, and her large eyes painted with white liner. She was the picture of feminine grace.

The smell of her made Matroise's hair stand on end.

Matroise themself wore heavy fabric and dark leggings, drab grays and faded forest-green cottons that were draped simply in pointed triangular layers. Their lank, brown hair fell freely around their long face, and their heavy-lidded eyes and sharp cheekbones were untouched by cosmetics. No oils or scented powders had been rubbed into their curl-toed leather boots or shoulder bag. No potpourri was hidden away in the inner lining of their tunic. Only the lingering scent of anoma powder and vinegar permeated their scarf, still draped high on their nose; another vain attempt to neutralize the odorous implications that seemed to cling, uninvited, to their identity.

As their eyes met, Kita rose from her seat and flitted through the square as if wafting on the breeze. Matroise looked down and then away, their hands absently brushing at their tunic, as if they could dust off their nerves.

"Matroise! How good to see you, as always. Oh, but that tunic with those shoes? No, never mind; I will be good today." Kita engulfed Matroise in a hug, arms thrown around their neck before Matroise could protest. After an agonizing few seconds in the cloud of Kita's fragrant hair, they extracted themself as politely as they could. As Kita pulled her arm back, the thickly applied hamariste paste on Kita's wrist smeared against Matroise's neck.

Kita had the presence to look apologetically sheepish as Matroise wiped their neck clean with a handkerchief.

"Sorry, dear."

Matroise wordlessly slipped the handkerchief away, then pulled out the bottle of agrimovf oil and handed it to Kita. She took it with a perplexed smile.

"What's this?"

"The agrimovf oil," Matroise said, mouth tight. Kita's face went pleasantly blank. "That you specifically asked me to bring you, frantically I might add, because you *accidentally* spilled yours all over your carpet yesterday evening. I made the two hours trip in from the farm for this. Any of this familiar?"

"Oh yes! Yes, of course!"

Matroise clicked their tongue. Kita tucked the oil away and then smiled innocently.

"Kita."

The smile lost its innocence and twisted downward into a pout.

"*Kita.*"

Having botched her gambit, Kita soldiered on bluntly. "Oh, Matroise, I can't bear it any longer! You were so morose last week, puttering around the edges of the drawing room like a rat trapped in a cellar, and I am not so moth-brained that I don't know the reason! I did my best then, dropping hints for everyone to pick up so you did not have to take the brunt of it, because no one knew how to address you!

Something *must* be done, and I just thought if we were to look together—"

Matroise took Kita's small gloved hands in theirs and took a deep breath. "Kita. You are one of my dearest friends and so I *know* you do not mean to do what I think you mean to do."

Kita's moue deepened, her little glossy shoes clacking out her displeasure on the cobblestone street. "But if I were to go in *with* you!"

"It would make not the slightest difference."

Their eyes locked. Kita cracked first, gaze flicking tellingly across the way, landing on the oak doors of an aromatist's shop. A very particular aromatist's shop.

"Oh, you really think you can pluck the sun from the sky, don't you?" Matroise hissed.

"But Dario is the best aromatist in all of Karraine! You know it!"

Matroise froze at the name despite themself. Kita's eyes narrowed.

"This isn't just about your scent, is it?" Matroise said nothing. "The three of us have been friends for years, yet lately you stiffen up like a wet cat whenever I bring him up. Has something happened between you two that I don't know? You seemed perfectly happy last week at my get-together, ignoring everyone else as you listened to him go on about his chemistry nonsense.

"It's not nonsense," Matroise interjected, despite their heart now threatening to beat out of their chest. "No one is ever interested in his experiments or his botany papers. You know, it's actually fascinating to listen to him, and *he* is the only one ever interested when I explain how we harvest agrimovf and turn it to oil. He's working on a paper just now about it now, actually—Kita don't look at me that way—but all anyone ever wants to do is ask him to make them a new perfume or about

6

fashion or—"

"Or ask him to dinner," Kita said suggestively.

Matroise turned and began walking back towards the stairs.

"No, don't you try to run off again—You're fond of Dario, aren't you?"

Matroise spun on their heel. "Keep your voice down!" they begged and grabbed Kita's plump cheeks between their palms.

Face smushed, Kita attempted a smile. "*Pleeease?*"

Matroise sighed. Kita dragged them along by the hand towards the shop's entrance.

Two little bronze carts laden with sale items stood invitingly to either side of the shop's open double doors, each elegantly formed with looping frames and thin metal wheels crusted with patina. The threshold gave way almost immediately to a maze of dark wooden shelves, every aisle capped by a circular table covered over in plush velvet and silk tablecloths that bore an assortment of palm-sized enamel cases full of scented powders and pastes. Several rows of shelves were laden with hand-blown glass bottles filled with perfume and oil elegantly and, Matroise thought, ridiculously shaped to the point of impracticality.

In another aisle, wooden boxes with fitted slip-tops were stacked three high, each packed with smooth creams and balms or rows of solid sticks of scented fat and pomades packaged individually in paper wrappings. Gatherings of dried leaves and fresh flowers hung above, arranged so thickly it looked as if a garden had sprouted from the ceiling. They too were arranged in rows, tied off in bunches that could be lowered with a series of pulleys.

With every step they took, a new scent accosted Matroise, each seemingly stranger and stronger than the last. Kita pulled out a paper fan and wafted the scents gluttonously into her nose with frantic flits of her wrist.

"Oh, isn't it divine?" she asked, as she looked back to Matroise.

"No," Matroise said. They covered their nose with the collar of their tunic. The scarf was not enough.

At the register counter, Matroise's eyes darted over the perfume labels. The words were clear, yet their meanings remained mysterious. *Carfasia's Afterbloom. Queen of the Morning. Damask/Demure in Jet and Weave. Fallow's Tip. The Half-day's End.* Meaningless signifiers that needled Matroise's sinuses.

Kita rang the bell, and after a moment, Dario materialized from the back room, a wide and easy smile on his lovely face. Matroise pulled their collar up further and ducked behind one of the shelves. Kita bounded up to him, balancing on her toes to greet him with a kiss on the cheek.

"Darling Kita!"

He was, if possible, more finely dressed than Kita. Always formal, his purple silk waistcoat was embroidered with curling emerald threaded fractals that complemented his warm complexion. Baggy sleeves that bunched at the wrists hid pockets stuffed with the dried petals of heliotrope and mazanti. His long black hair was oiled and tied back high on his head with a thin silver ribbon, ends hanging loose without a bow. And from his ears dangled the bright orange plumes of a Solareia, dipped in citrus scented paraffin oil, the color of the feathers a perfect match for his bright eye shadow.

Matroise risked a quick look towards them as Kita began one of her stories, content to let her take the lead. But even if they could dull the sights and sounds, Dario's scent was inescapable.

More exacting than most men, his perfume was riotously layered. Inflective and masculine, it was fashionably complex, cresting and fading over time, tantalizingly shifting into a new note just as one had divined the last. As it dispersed and mixed with the sweat of his skin, one began to detect, at last, the root scent of mimus flit extract. Quite suitable for a master aromatist.

Matroise approached him, unable to avoid the inevitable any longer when Kita's evanescent attention pulled her away to poke at a melt of cream wax half liquefied under an open flame.

"Now here's a rare sight," Dario said coyly. "Matroise, in my shop?"

Matroise squinted, as if the too-lovely smile on Dario's face was as painful as staring into the perpetual western sunset.

"Hello, Dario," they replied, eyes averted again now that they'd made the initial, required eye contact.

Kita looked back expectantly, pretending to appraise an advertisement rather than eavesdropping. Matroise blanched as Dario leaned over the counter towards them. When they said nothing, Kita tsked loudly, returning to loop an arm around Matroise's, and pulled them right up to the counter. Matroise endured their two expectant grins and overwhelming, intermingling aromas with a grimace. They had planned this, Matroise thought, possibly weeks in advance.

"The two of you are absolutely crystalline," Matroise said as they pulled a sleeve to their nose, defiantly.

"Oh, but come now," Kita whined. "You've had no luck finding a scent for ages and you certainly weren't going to go looking alone. What was I to do?"

"Mind your business, for one," Matroise mumbled nasally, embarrassed that Kita had said such a thing in front of Dario.

"If anyone can help you," Kita continued, undeterred, "it will be Dario. Why, he made Troust a lovely fragrance last week. You know Troust; e works down at the distillery and was having such a time getting the rose oil out of eir clothes. People were mistaking em for a girl every day after work! But Dario was clever enough to make em a perfume that layers on top of the rose oil! With one spray of it, the whole aroma changed, and now no one mistakes em anymore! Go on Dario, tell Matroise how pleased e was with that."

"E was rather pleased, yes," Dario said. He glanced at Matroise, whose distress was no doubtlikely obvious even half hidden behind their scarf. He gave Kita a measured look. "Though Troust came to me asking for assistance."

"Matroise wants help," Kita insisted. "They're just too shy to ask." Matroise said nothing, finding they were now unable to form words, their eyes downcast as they picked at the cuticle of a nail. Kita's lips pursed. "Don't you?"

"Kita, dearest," Dario said quickly, wearing the well-tailored expression of a salesman. "Do you see that square bottle on the top shelf next to *Painted Honey*?" Kita turned, her hair kicking up a fresh swath of merry rose hidden in her curls.

"That's the Brune Sands date extract I'd told you about—"

"Oh!"

"Yes, precisely. If you'd like to nab the tester and take it into the

10

back of the shop you can pour yourself an ounce of it. You know where the vials are."

"Yes, yes," Kita said, already halfway to the shelf, again taking to her toes as she reached up for the squat, navy blue bottle.

Matroise stole a glance at Dario then, only to find him looking back at them from the corner of his eye. Matroise suddenly found their shoes wonderfully interesting.

Bottle in hand, Kita made her way to the back room, pocketing a freshly picked bundle of ten-petal as she did. Dario rolled his eyes but allowed it, waiting until she finally passed through the diamond-shaped arch that separated the front of the building from the back. Frozen in place, Matroise said nothing as Dario walked around his counter to stand before them, arm extended politely towards them.

Matroise's heart skipped.

"It's too much for you in here, with all this." Dario gestured with his other hand, flippant as if he could wave away the thousand scents that surrounded them. "Let's find somewhere else to talk. We can take bets on how long it takes her to notice we've gone."

Now, with Dario right before them, Matroise could discern the individual notes of his scent, the electric coolness of sea mint, of abjer fruit and clay that draped Dario like heavy brocade. It suited him, unbearably so.

"Where?" Matroise managed meekly, torn between the appeal of escape and the risk of doing so arm-in-arm with Dario.

"You like the docks, no? They are quiet. Less people than the boardwalk, and the sea breeze dominates." Matroise couldn't argue; he was right on all counts. Still.

"But your shop?"

"Jeanette is upstairs," he said carefully, eyebrow quirking at Matroise's avoidance, "and I was going to close up soon anyway." He tilted his head in a way that made Matroise's face hot. "Shall we, or would you rather escape me as well?"

Matroise looped their arm with Dario's before they could process what they were doing, pulling him along as Kita had them just minutes earlier, and led the two of them towards the docks, their heart beginning to pound.

Dario sat to Matroise's right, just out of reach and with his back to the sun. Its rays played over the twilight waters, glinting off the well-waxed hulls of the hundred or so boats that bobbed on the horizon. Matroise sat facing Dario, tucked into the shadow cast by the little boathouse nearest them. They couldn't help but notice he sat downwind, considerate as ever.

In his hand Dario fingered a thin vial, as long and thick as his ring finger. His oil, Matroise guessed, the one he dipped his earrings in. He spun it back and forth with one hand as he spoke.

"She means well, of course," he said as Matroise looked away towards the water. "I think she sees it as her responsibility, as your friend, to help you with such things."

Matroise said nothing, but turned back to find Dario gazing at them, soft and patient, content with Matroise's silence. They inched their toe towards him, just close enough to touch the heel of his boot. He smiled at the gesture.

"You don't want my help then, I take it."

Matroise shook their head.

"I suspected as much." Dario sighed in what could have been a laugh, then tapped the heel of his boot against Matroise's toe.

Unable to find their voice, Matroise focused their gaze on one of Dario's earrings, not quite ready to risk eye contact again. Silence passed between them, though all around them were the sounds of sailors rigging their boats to the docks. The sounds of water sloshing on wood deck, of scraping and cutting and hauling up heavy nets. And the smells. Always the scent of salt and dredged up bottom-muck. Decaying seaweed. Smells that Matroise actually liked, though for themselves, not for what they could signify.

Dario moved suddenly, and the loss of his foot against Matroise's felt like a betrayal, but then he was sitting up and moving closer, his shoulder brushing up against theirs. He pocketed the vial and held his hand palm-up on his thigh. Matroise eyed the gesture and felt their face heat and spine prickle. They didn't move, eyes still locked on the vacant space where Dario had been.

"I could make you something unique, could use only a few scents. It doesn't have to be traditional."

"No, thank you," Matroise said finally, voice strained. They did not want to have this conversation. Not with Dario, because for him, they might actually explain.

Silence again for a time as they turned, feet now dangling over the side of the dock. They watched as a plume of mimus flits fell into the sea, their spinning wings melting as they hit the water's surface, not yet transformed by the heat of the water, not yet drawn down into the undercurrent to return as seeds to the other side of the Slatewater Sea.

"It feels like something, coiled somehow, inside of you?" Dario asked suddenly.

Matroise looked up at him, perplexed.

"That is what everyone says, at least. Some sort of mounting pressure that is, somehow, pleasurable." Dario's ease was gone, and there was a crease in his brow. Matroise had never seen him like this. "And when I say, 'I haven't the slightest idea what you mean' they all laugh and give me this knowing look. As if I'm being coy about it? I don't know."

"Dario... what?"

"Is it like that? Your thing. Your scent? Or your not-scent, I suppose. Everyone is telling you that you need to just go along with it." He scoffed. "That's what we're doing to you, isn't it? It's the same, sort of."

Matroise only stared, playing his words back in their head but found no sense in them.

Dario sighed. "You have feelings for me, yes?"

It felt as if Matroise had swallowed liquid mercury. Their throat tightened as an icy trickle spread down to their core. Expression blank, they froze in place; unable to move, even to run.

"That!" Dario said, gesturing at Matroise. "That right there. Whatever just happened to you? It doesn't happen to me." Matroise's heart was making a concentrated effort to climb up into their mouth and prevented them from replying. "People find me charming, and well, I suppose attractive, but I think it really is just that I dress well—"

You are *attractive*, Matroise thought silently.

"—and so they just. Assume. They make me out to be something out of a romance novel. An aromatist by the sea, in the fragrant city of Karraine where the sun never sets! Ah, picturesque, no? Surely I have a dozen lovers, at least."

A moment passed. And then Matroise understood.

"You don't have any lovers," they said slowly as they found their voice again. Dario nodded, his eyes and mouth hard, but not unkind. "And you have no desire for any, either."

Dario smiled. "This is why I like you, Matroise."

"But not like I like you," Matroise said without thinking. Immediately, they wished they could stuff the selfish words back down their throat.

"Yes," Dario agreed, but his usual ease and charm had returned. He took Matroise's hand in his and then, with only a moment of hesitation, lifted the back of their hand to his lips. "But that does not mean what you think it means."

"So this is what I've come up with," Dario said three days later as he stood in the back room of his shop, a skewed set of goggles crowning his head, and a terribly plain and soiled apron tied over his finery. Matroise sat watching him on a lopsided stool across the room.

With a handsome grin on his face, he held up a stick of balm for them to scrutinize. It looked like the shalaberry lip balm that Kita wore. Strangely, Matroise got no scent at all from the stick Dario held.

Dario closed the space between them. Matroise froze, eyes closed as he applied the balm not to their lips but just above them, a dab under each nostril.

"You might have to apply it a few times a day, but it should negate even the strongest perfume."

Dario did not withdraw, continuing to stand so close that Matroise could feel the warmth of his body. Without thinking, Matroise held their breath and closed their eyes to brace for the scent of him.

"Now, trust me here," he said, pulling the collar of his shirt back to expose his neck, "and tell me what you smell."

Matroise opened one eye and exhaled. With a stuttered intake of breath, their pained expression transformed into confusion. They took another breath. Then another.

"Dario, I don't smell *anything*." Matroise took his wrist and brought it up to their nose. Nothing. Matroise looked him directly in the eyes. "How did you do this?"

Dario grinned. "What can I say? I'm a master aromatist." With a tilt of his head he turned, cocked his hips, and walked back to his desk.

Matroise got up and began systematically sniffing every oil and paste in the laboratory. "Dario, this is... this is *amazing*."

"Oh, but I'm not done."

Dario produced a thin necked bottle with a wide base and walked towards Matroise again, this time stopping a meter short of them. "May I?" he asked as he held the atomizer aloft, one hand on the beaded bulb.

"Dario, you've more than proved that your balm works."

"Ah, but this is something more. Trust me once again?"

Matroise nodded and was enveloped by the mist. When the air settled, Dario made a circuit around them, sniffing the air, coming close and retreating as far back as the room would allow, and back in again.

"Yes, I think that will do."

Matroise stood feeling completely unchanged. With the balm under their nose, they couldn't smell it. They looked to Dario for explanation.

"With most perfumes, the bloom is telling within seconds. You can get pronouns from the bloom, but that's the easy part. Then, you get to the stem, and that's the nuance, the heart of the perfume, yes? Details. Personal quirks and preferences. Appearance can augment this, naturally, but it's the bit with the most variance. Fluid genders will have a lot of layers here, but you can still pick out a dominant one, if that's what the wearer intends, of course."

Matroise had a vague sense of what he meant. Kita smelled entirely different from her sister Asra, yet they were both undeniably women.

"But for you, I've anchored that variance to the root." Dario turned, fingers gliding quickly over his bookcase until he found a book, opened it, and turned to a diagram. "You see here how you're not supposed to use agrimovf as a root? Well, too bad, I've mixed it in a way with an aldehyde so that it's present in the bloom, totally absent in the stem, and then appears again in the root. And as you know, chemically, the plant is very interesting. Actually—I've been running a side experiment since the last time we spoke. The results are leading me to so many variable applications I can barely decide which to focus on first." He looked over his shoulder at a collection of conical flasks on his workstation. Several were bubbling merrily over flame. One suddenly turned sunburst yellow. Dario grinned.

"*Dario*," Matroise said fondly.

Dario swiveled back, looking apologetic. He clapped the book shut and put it away.

"Right, sorry. Anyway, the long and short of it is, no one note should dominate or last long enough for an actual sense of you; it will force one to consider. The bloom will provide just enough information for others to determine your pronouns when you first meet, but more than that, people will have to be politely in the dark as to your—" He paused, fingers flourishing in the air, "—essence."

"It really won't smell like any one scent either way?" Matroise doubted it, as much as they wished for it.

Dario gave Matroise a conciliatory look and clasped Matroise's shoulders with both hands. He leaned in again, his forehead nearly touching Matroise's. "You will remain an enigma to anyone to whom you do not wish to explain. I promise."

Matroise smiled, warmth blooming in their chest as Dario took their hand in his.

"And if anyone still troubles you, my dear," Dario purred, "I shall deal with them. Personally." He tilted his head down and their lips met.

Dario's newest perfume and neutralizing balm had been on display for three weeks without a single sale, though from Dario's mood and perpetual smile, one would never guess.

"You know, I'm still not used to you being here. Sometimes I'll turn around and see you and my heart will skip a beat from the shock," he said as he leaned over the counter, hands folded under his chin as he watched Matroise work.

"That's actually not far off from what *it* feels like," Matroise teased and laughed at Dario's sardonic smirk. "But no, I know what you mean. Kita keeps joking that the planet will start spinning any day now." Matroise moved down the aisle nearest the counter, rearranging the shelf of pomades by price and rarity rather than scent profiles. "Though she is happy that I show up to all her social engagements now."

"I hear her sister is absolutely crushed, though, given recent developments."

Matroise looked up to a coy smirk and eyebrow wiggle.

"Oh, don't tell me *she's* in love with you too?" Matroise sighed. "That would explain... a lot."

"Oh, no, nothing so ridiculous as that. She's in love with *you*."

"Oh, for heaven's sake."

"Um, hello?"

A plump person in a drab brown tunic and a scarf pulled high over their nose had entered the shop. They looked apologetic, and the faint scent of anoma powder clung to the air around them.

"My friend, welcome! How might I be of service?" Dario said warmly.

The person looked around to be sure Dario was not speaking to someone else in the shop.

"Ah, hello. I was referred here by someone and—" They stopped, expression crumbling into dismay. "Forgive me, but I'm starting to think this was a bad joke." They looked up at the dried flowers and herbs that hung from the ceiling and side-stepped as if afraid they might come crashing down upon them.

"Well this is an aromatist's shop, not a joke shop. I can assure you," Dario said with a wink.

The person seemed unconvinced. Matroise looked at them

closer; something about them felt familiar.

"Well you see, I'm told you sell a specialty product. Of sorts," the person said.

"You wouldn't happen to be talking about my neutralizing balm, would you?" Dario said cheerfully and produced a stick from his pocket.

"So you really have such a thing?" they asked, eyes wide.

"Newly made and still working on a series of variations but yes, we have such a thing."

"But how do you explain it to people? How would that work, if I didn't have a scent and couldn't smell anyone else? People would ask me what I meant by such a thing. How would they know what I *am*?"

Matroise stepped out from behind the shelf and could see the moment that their not-perfume reached them. Could see the threads of scent creeping close and then dissipating into indetermination. They couldn't place them. Matroise smiled at their confusion.

"Personally," Matroise said, "I'm more concerned with the 'who' rather than the 'what.' But if they must know, they can ask."

The person looked incredulous. "But that isn't *done*."

"Well, it's what I do." Matroise continued, their voice carrying a little louder, "So it *is* done."

Dario watched the scene with a lazy smile, hands on his chin as he watched. Matroise actually winked at him as their eyes met.

Overwhelmed, the person looked away to the table where Matroise's not-perfume was on display.

"*The Aromatic Lovers*?" they asked, reading the label.

"Bit of a play on words," Dario said, mirth barely hidden in his tone. Matroise gave him a deadpan look. "Oh, you think it's funny too, don't lie."

"What… what is it? You're wearing it, aren't you?" the person asked as they glanced back at Matroise.

"Tell me…?" Matroise began, fingers flitting towards them in question.

"Oh. My name's Tremian."

"Tell me, Tremian, what gender do you suppose I am?"

Tremian blanched at the question. It was an impossibly rude thing to ask. Dario chuckled.

"I know. It isn't done. But seriously, go ahead. Guess."

Tentatively Tremian considered. Matroise helpfully held out their wrist, where they had dabbed the not-perfume earlier.

"I haven't the slightest idea," Tremian said with trepidation.

"Precisely."

Confusion clicked home to understanding. Tremian picked up a bottle from the table and took another whiff of it. "Is there any way I could get this, but…" They hesitated, biting their lip and then, resolved, charged on, "Well this, but with just the *slightest* tinge of Marstan's bloom to it? And I really do mean just the slightest. Could you do that?"

Dario cracked his knuckles and then came out from behind the counter, retrieving his goggles as he did. He put them on with a snap, a wild grin spreading across his face as he stood before them, arms akimbo.

"Oh, you have *no idea* what he's capable of," Matroise said with a laugh as they led Tremian to the back of the shop. "He can definitely do it."

VOICES IN THE AIR

BY VIDA CRUZ

"Need to cross the river?" asked the fisherman in unaccented Kailog.

I opened my mouth to answer when a prickle jolted my back, the kind induced by someone else's intent stare. One hand on the hilt of Maragat's dagger, I whirled around and scanned the tree line. Sure enough, there was a wispy blue ball of flame, the skull outlined within turned in my direction. The moment my gaze landed on it, it disappeared.

A Bungom. Common enough where people have died; the river had likely seen more than its fair share of drownings. Perhaps it intended to lead me to my death? It wouldn't be the first time one had tried.

"Need to cross the river?" the fisherman repeated. I turned to him. He was what some would call attractive—tall and lithe like bamboo, smooth-skinned, and possessed of regular features positioned pleasingly equidistant from one another. When he smiled a warm smile, I realized that he'd been speaking to Tila, not me. But of course.

"What say you to a boat ride, Saha?" Tila asked me, in Ayurense. She was leaning against her mango wood walking stick—all that remained of my brother, Maragat. Her gaze held no trace of mischief, but whole and unbroken trust was there, like a jar freshly fired and left to cool. It made me uncomfortable that she could trust me so easily after all we'd been through. I adjusted the strap of the bag of mangoes on my shoulder and peered at the river stretching wide before my feet, its calm waters glinted under the late afternoon sun.

It brought to mind bluish, scaly skin, knobby fingers with nails sharpened to points, teeth like flint knives. My nostrils were beginning to feel pinched with the remembered pain of breathing water—

"No, no, and no. I would rather cross a thousand mountains!" I blurted a little too loudly in Kailog, my voice echoing all around as if it could dispel the creeping memory. There was nothing wrong with the fisherman's boat—carved of a light, solid wood, big enough to seat four people, its sides painted with blue and red triangles. But not even the possibility of Kailogan soldiers searching for us could compel me to board it.

The fisherman, whose gaze had been roving hungrily over Tila—not even ragged clothes, shorn hair, and skin burned from weeks of traveling unshielded from the sun could disguise her beauty, apparently—now focused on me. Me—small, swarthy, and wild of hair, Tila's complete opposite, and I could feel all that in the fisherman's appraisal. Then his gaze slid back to Tila, as if I had been no more than a fly.

"If she were my servant, maray," he said to her, "I'd have her beaten for insolence before she could exhale. The river will not bite, you know."

The seconds crawled by in my vision—the color in Tila's face dredging away, Tila opening her mouth to protest, likely to explain emphatically to this stranger that I was not her servant. I was a free woman, indeed, and I did not need Tila to come to my defense.

"Even so," I said, irritated that my otherwise firm voice bore a single trembling note. My legs itched to get away as soon as possible. "We will find another way over it. Even if that way goes *around*. Come."

"But Saha—"

"*Come.*" I snapped. Tila's head drooped, a flower wilting in acquiescence. Long ago, when beatings were earned by every little thing, I wouldn't have dared speak to Tila that way—at least, not aloud.

26

Though no one had been around to wield a rod for a long time, exhilaration at having done something once forbidden flooded my veins.

"You will walk a long way around!" the fisherman called after us as we trudged down the winding, stony path next to the river.

I did not spare him a glimpse. "We're used to that!"

"Saha," Tila muttered as she caught up with me. I had to remind myself that hers was a scowl of concern, not pity. I tried to smile at her; it felt like using cramped muscles.

"Don't worry. There will be other chances to cross," I said, to reassure the both of us. I said nothing of the flashes of blue between the trees that I'd glimpse from time to time. No point in spooking Tila.

The Bungom followed us until we reached a village upriver from where we encountered the fisherman. When we arrived, only a sliver of sun peeked over the treetops. Wave upon wave of welcoming villagers buffeted us. By the time I checked behind me, the Bungom was gone.

We were ushered inside a cavernous ceremonial hall, seated on either side of the village chief—a chatty man, much to my chagrin—eating generous helpings of roasted fish, imported Iriswani chili peppers, and fluffy rice. Though I was nearing my fill, my head swam with the remnants of hunger, with the bright firelight, with the aroma of roasting meat and chewed betel nut, with the deep boom of drums and the pounding of dancers' feet across the dark kamagong floor.

"Entertainers, you say?" the chief, Apu Namran, was saying in Kailog. He rubbed his wrinkled double chin thoughtfully.

"That's right," said Tila, nodding. "I dance and S—Puri here sings and recites poetry."

I glared at Tila. A month we'd been traveling under assumed names—just in case the princes of Kailog realized that they could spare soldiers from their throne wars to chase after two runaways who may or may not have caused the garden fire—and yet she'd been *that* close to exposing our identities!

"And there are only two of you? Where are your instruments?"

"We work better as a pair," I said. I focused on my plate. The fish was some of the freshest I'd ever tasted. "Loyang's feet fly to the beat of my voice. We need no one else."

"Impressive," said Apu Namran, as if he were testing how the word felt in his mouth. Then he clasped his hands over his mound of a belly. "Well, you're just in time! It is my daughter's wedding in two nights! Why don't you both perform at the celebration?"

The river and the Bungom twinkled in my mind's eye. "Thank you for your kind invitation, Apu Namran. But Loyang and I cannot stay long. We're headed north; we plan to cross the river in the morning. We shall pay one of your fishermen for their services, of course."

Apu Namran's face fell. "I'm sorry, but it is tradition in our village that no one go out on the river for three days before and after a wedding, including guests. Misfortune would hang over the marriage if someone were to drown."

"But Tayang, several have already drowned thanks to the Kataw," someone said. One of the dancers, a comely, plump young woman no taller than me and laden with silks and bangles had wandered over to our table. "Doesn't that mean there shouldn't be a wedding at all?"

Her voice had been a demure murmur and her eyes were

downcast, directed toward the food, but there was a defiant set to her jaw. From the way Apu Namran glared at her, she was probably his daughter.

"Awena, for shame! In front of our guests!" scolded Apu Namran. "We cannot very well turn your husband-to-be away when he arrives tomorrow!"

"Pardon me. A Kataw?" Tila chimed.

Awena turned toward Tila. "A water creature from the Eserasean Isles. It resembles a human but for its gills. It's been taking maidens from this village every month and eating them. Many have claimed to have seen it, but Tayang thinks everyone is hallucinating in their fear."

"That is because there is *no* Kataw! Why would one be here, so far from Eseras? The disappearances are just that—unfortunate incidents and nothing more!" snapped Apu Namran.

He spoke loud enough that the drumming died, the dancing ceased, and all eyes were on us. Whispers broke out. Awena had raised her head; she was unsmiling, but her eyes had acquired a triumphant gleam. Meanwhile, sweat slickened the gray hairs at Apu Namran's temples. He cleared his throat several times, probably to give himself time to get his bearings.

"Ladies," he said at length. He inclined his head toward Tila, who flinched in surprise. "It would be an honor if you could perform for us tonight."

Tila nodded a question at me. For someone who'd spent most of her life telling me what to do, she seemed to have a difficult time doing so on the road. I sighed and ambled toward the fire pit in the middle of the floor. Soft padding behind me indicated that Tila had followed, walking stick in hand.

A hush descended over the room.

I sat down with my legs crossed, never once looking at Tila as I raised my voice. "Apu Namran, honored guests, Loyang and I wish to thank you for our meal with this poem of my composing, called 'The Tale of the Mango Tree.'"

I beat the floor to keep time. It was the tale of a princess, her handmaiden, and how the handmaid's warrior brother fell in love with the princess. The warrior was killed hunting for the princess's dowry boar, and so, the handmaiden begged the Diwata of the Rice Terraces to bring him back to life. The Diwata planted the warrior's heart and up sprouted the first mango tree, a thing of magic and healing. When the handmaiden saw this, she was overcome with grief and threw herself over a cliff, while the princess renounced her kingdom and lived out her days under the shade of her love.

I kept my eyes closed all throughout, not because I was overcome with emotion or the poem's high drama, though I could very well pretend it was so with a well-placed crack in my voice. No, it was because I did not want to watch Tila dancing to it. Once had been enough.

When the poem and the dance ended and the audience surrounded us with applause, she was taking great care not to meet my eyes, either. The knuckles of the hand gripping the walking stick were white.

"You changed the ending again," Tila said in Ayurense, our own language, in the darkness of a room in Apu Namran's hut.

It was a statement of fact, not an accusation, but I was tired and in no mood for discussion. My shoulder ached from hefting the bag of mangoes, another headache was building, and the room we had been given was right next to that blasted river, which I could clearly hear through the window. I had expected that it would be behind us by now, not before. But Tila would not leave me alone if I did not say something. As I combed out my curls, I spat, "What of it?"

"You could have told me what you were going to do."

"I recite the same poem everywhere, Tila."

"That's what I don't understand!" Tila burst out. She clutched a blanket to her chest. "You know thousands of poems and songs, but you always choose to *recite* this one! I can't even remember the last time I heard you sing! Didn't Salayan herself once say that you sing as if a god has touched you? Why are you hiding your gift?"

Silence. And then I asked, "And your problem with this poem is?"

I could feel Tila's gaze burning into me. I would not give her the satisfaction of meeting it. She sighed her frustration. "You keep changing the ending. It never feels true. Changing the ending cannot change what happened in the past."

Not this again. I took my brother's dagger from its sheath—plain carabao leather, wholly unsuitable—and began to polish the blade. A useless endeavor, for the blade never tarnished, never dulled. Its hilt was its most striking feature, as it was wrapped in a spotless white cloth—fabric from the very dress of the Diwata Salayan, the lady of the northern rice terraces that we called home. The cloth was a promise of favor that often felt like a curse, especially now that I was too far away to ask for favors.

I said, "The real ending is too strange. No one will like it."

31

"But it is the *true* ending!"

"Then would you rather that the soldiers track us down more easily?"

"I told you before, the princes will be too busy fighting each other to send soldiers after us! It's a concern, but it's not the point, and you know it!"

"Then get to the point."

"Saha—" Tila ended my name on a choke. "—Am I not punished enough for you? It's my story, too!"

My headache weighed on my eyes and my jaw throbbed. I knew exactly what to say to end this. "Then make your own poem about it!"

Tila drew a hissing breath. Her eyes glassed over with hurt that threatened to spill down her cheeks. Despite having been the Awitana's daughter, heir to a treasure trove of epics and histories, Tila had no talent for either music or poetry. Her lack of it was the reason our tribe didn't listen to her pleas to flee as the Kailogan army approached and razed the village to ash. She spoke of her failures the night we met again in the palace of Kailog after so many years and not once since. I had promised to never remind, judge or blame her, and I had broken that over what?

"You're cruel," Tila whispered.

Nothing could erase what I'd said. I lowered myself onto the mat, tucked Maragat's dagger beneath it, and pulled a blanket over me. "Go to sleep, Tila."

I dreamed I stood in the rice fields of Iwakogan while a bitter wind blew. In the distance, a man stood with his back to me. I knew it was my brother before he turned, ever so slightly, revealing the familiar tattoos—a crocodile and a scorpion, the two linked by an intricate network of snake scales. And he smiled the nostalgic smile he wore whenever I sang. My name in his voice was everywhere.

I raced toward Maragat. I did not know what I would say, only that I couldn't again let him go.

And then he changed. His hair unfurled as seaweed, and the tendrils wrapped themselves around me. A cackle that did not belong to him—a cackle that I knew nevertheless—disturbed the air. I tried to run back across the field that was now a furious whirlpool. The weeds dragged me to him. Scaly blue hands clasped my face, nails pierced my skin, and I stared into eyes I hadn't seen since the palace of Kailog, eyes as black as the depths of the sea.

"Caught you, O Favored One," said the Diwata Tantirana. Her fanged mouth yawned wide enough to swallow me whole.

I screamed myself awake.

"Saha!"

I blinked. I'd raised the dagger high above my head. The moonlight gave the hilt cloth a spectral glow and the curved blade a deadly gleam. Tila watched me. Only, she wasn't on the mat beside me, but by the window, one leg swung over the sill.

"Tila, what are you doing?"

A shiver washed over her then. She shook her head and blinked, awareness dawning. She put her leg down, crept toward the mats, and settled in once more. "I—I guess I was dreaming, and your voice woke me. But I was sure I heard...*someone* calling me."

I could've bet all our belongings that I knew whom Tila thought

33

she heard. Maragat was the only person she could speak of with such tender notes. What weak, silly women we were, dreaming about the ashes of the past. I lay back down and said, "Try to get some sleep."

But Tila thwarted my advice. Not long after she settled in, her side of the room was filled with muffled sobbing. I turned over and prepared to reach out to her in the dark, ready to—what?

I withdrew my hand and shut my eyes, praying I would not see Tantirana behind them.

The next day, save for Apu Namran's inquiries over breakfast into the screaming, we did not discuss what happened. Not as we sampled the sweet, sticky rice cakes a few old ladies were pounding; not as we helped the servants douse a saya that Awena would wear at the wedding with a heady floral fragrance; not as we watched the solemn procession that signaled the arrival of Awena's husband-to-be, a juddering twig of a young man flanked by burly warriors; not as we wandered the village that afternoon, admiring the gaudy garlands of lilac and gold *ulan ng tala* being strung around veranda railings and over doorways.

There were about five nipa huts here and there, however, that remained bare. I was admiring from afar a deeply indigo blanket draped over the doorway of one such hut when I saw Awena herself enter it. Before I knew it, my feet were taking me up the house's veranda steps. Tila scurried behind me as I pulled back the blanket.

"Good day!" I greeted in a high voice.

There was a soft thud. Awena sat in the middle of the room, hands curled into claws, staring at me as if I'd grown horns. Across from her sat a woman whose soft tufts of hair barely covered her scalp. She huddled deeper into an indigo shawl when she saw me, the middle-aged lines around her eyes deepening with hostility. Between them, a cup rolled, its brown contents soaking into the mat. The room smelled faintly herbal.

"Maray Puri!" cried Awena. She quickly ducked her head and reached for the cup. Her hair slipped from a round, bare shoulder to curtain her face. "Did Tayang ask you to fetch me?"

"No," I said. "This house caught my interest. Good apu, may my companion and I come in?"

A muscle quivered in the older woman's jaw as she regarded me. She glanced at Awena, who whispered, "They're the entertainers I mentioned, Apu Sima," before nodding almost imperceptibly at me.

We seated ourselves on the mat, across from the two women, Tila fidgeting with the hem of her saya. Awena seemed smaller than the night before, hunched over the mat she wiped as if she wanted nothing more than for the floor beneath her to open into the soulworld.

"Maray Puri, Maray Loyang, this is Apu Sima, the best sailor in the village," Awena said.

"But no longer. Why does my house interest you, stranger?" Apu Sima snapped.

"Because it is one of the few that are not festively arrayed, apu. Indeed, rather than celebrating Maray Awena's wedding, it seems as if you're mourning the dead."

Apu Sima looked away. "My daughter. She drowned a month ago."

Awena took Apu Sima's veined hand in hers. "You don't know

that Hayani's dead, apu! We never found anything of hers, not even that anklet I braided for her! We could search again, she might still be—"

Apu Sima shook her hand free. "And who will search for her now? You, who shall be married tomorrow night? I, who can barely rise some mornings, let alone row my boat? I am tired of hoping, Awena. A Kataw now prowls the river, preying on our young women, and Namran insists on carrying on as if this is not so! He is hiding something, and don't tell me otherwise!"

Awena's mouth hung open. Tila had covered her own.

Apu Sima seemed to shrink after her outburst. She mumbled, "Leave me to my dreams, where I can still hear her."

The three of us rose—Awena to help her, Tila and I to leave.

On our way out, I heard Apu Sima say to Awena, "Pray to the Diwatas that your husband does not give you daughters, as you will only be feeding a monster."

"I know what you're thinking," I said in Ayurense as Tila and I started up the dirt path to Apu Namran's house. "You want to help these people. And the answer is no."

Tila regarded me with disbelief. "I don't understand how you can hear of a tragedy and not do something about it!"

"You can't fix every sad story you hear, Tila. That's not how your mother ruled the Ayuran."

"Oh, and I'm sure you've been dying to prove you can do better! That's your dearest wish, isn't it?"

She left me standing in the middle of the dirt path.

"When we get to the Ayuran Valley," I called, caring not that my Ayurense definitely marked us as rustic foreigners to all passerby, "you can rebuild Iwakogan by yourself. Clearly, two is too many!"

Tila didn't break her stride.

That night, I woke to low thundering from the floor. Firelight danced past the doorway, and shouts punctuated the darkness. I didn't know if the moon had not yet risen or had already set. I reached out to waken Tila but felt only air. Panic bubbled up my throat. I staggered to the doorway and hailed a servant boy running past with a lantern.

"Boy! What's going on?"

The fire cast a demonic glow against the boy's face. "Maray Awena is missing and her husband-to-be has fled in fear. Even Apu Namran believes that the Kataw lured her into the river. A search party is on its way now."

Gods, and that fool Tila probably went after her. "Could I borrow this light? I must get dressed."

The Bungom was the last thing I expected to see when I stepped out of Apu Namran's house. I'd nearly forgotten about it. This close, I caught the stench of burning bones.

Please come with me, O Favored One, sighed the Bungom. Its voice was young, female, urgent. *There isn't much time.*

The last time I followed a Bungom, it had led me to my brother's corpse. As I sprinted after it, enduring the scrapes the stones of the riverbank left on my bare soles, I prayed to whomever might have been listening that I would not be led to a lifeless Tila.

After what seemed like an eternity of running, the Bungom veered from the riverbank and hovered over the water. In its wake, I spotted three things: Apu Namran, lying unconscious among the stones, a mango wood walking stick not far from his outstretched hand, and a boat painted with blue and red triangles. This must have been the same spot where we had spoken to the fisherman.

I faced the river. There was a hissing in my ears that I was certain wasn't the water or the warm night air. Seaweed hair, scales, Tantirana's fanged grin, her sea-black eyes, laughter that could drown—

I took a step back. "No. I can't."

You can and you must, the Bungom said as it floated back to me.

"But—"

Someone grabbed my ankle. I cried out and searched for my would-be-attacker.

"Please, help me!" said Apu Namran in a feverish whisper. The light of the Bungom revealed dried blood at his temple, wild, red-veined eyes, tear-stained cheeks, and a mouth cracked and dry. His clammy, sweaty hand made me think of a dead fish, and he would not let go of my leg. "I tried to stop him—I never thought he'd take her—he promised he wouldn't—"

I stilled. "Who is *he*? The Kataw?"

Apu Namran nodded. "There was a drought months ago, and he came along, promised water and the freshest fish—as long as I let him eat maidens. What was I to do? We were all starving, so many had

38

died—I'd already lost my wife—"

Disgust roiled in my stomach. "And you never once thought Awena was in danger as well?"

"The wedding was supposed to save her!" Apu Namran cried in a quavering voice. "He was supposed to take your friend! But she didn't succumb to his song, so he took my daughter instead!"

The Bungom surged toward Apu Namran's face, aglow with wrath. *You let us all die! Begone, you foul, hateful man!*

Apu Namran screamed and scrambled back. He got to his feet and fled into the forest.

I apologize for this, O Witch of the Mango Tree, the Bungom said. Its skull turned toward me. Before I could scream, it engulfed my head with its flame and its voices and plunged me into the black, bitingly chill water.

After the Bungom released its hold on my head, I found myself hanging onto a frozen ledge at the lip of an immense cave of ice, taking great gulps of dry, frigid air. The Bungom had protected me from inhaling water, but I'd had to bear the burning bones smell and the panic frenzying my breathing.

I hoisted myself over the ledge. As the Bungom dried my clothes, I surveyed the room. Skulls, rib cages, pelvises, and femurs of ivory and decaying yellow littered the cave floor and filled hollows in the walls. Scattered here and there among them were stray bracelets, anklets, earrings, coins, blouses, and sayas. And in the middle of the cave were Awena and Tila, unconscious, suspended in midair within what appeared to be eggs filled with ghostly fluid.

Here he comes, the Bungom said before diving back over the ledge.

"You're late, O Favored One."

I'd heard that voice before. It belonged to the fisherman from two days ago—a glamor, I realized now. He leaned against a nearby stalagmite, legs crossed and arms folded over his bare chest. Green scales glittered all over his body while fine webbing connected his fingers. Gills fluttering at his neck compensated for his non-existent nose.

"Who are you?" I barked, cold anger lancing my tone. "How do you know that title?"

"You're slow for someone who has earned the favors of both Salayan and Tantirana," said the Kataw. "Anyone with two eyes and a knack for magic can see their marks on you. I want to know if your voice is really as good as they say—though with ugliness like yours, I'm sure you must be transcendent indeed if anyone is to bear your appearance for a second."

Tantirana had marked me? Gods help me. I unsheathed Maragat's dagger. "Then you must also know that I sing only for Diwata. Why should I entertain a lowly Kataw?"

An ugly scowl marred the Kataw's features. He swept the air before him in a diagonal motion. Breaking ice—a sound like thunder—echoed around the cave while the ground quaked. Ice rose around me and walled me from the hips down. My hands were free, but I'd dropped the dagger, which bounced down the ice mound and slid toward the Kataw.

"I am a prince of the kingdom of ice and pearl!" snarled the Kataw. "A prince in exile, but a prince still, and I will not be insulted by some

40

human who isn't even beautiful enough to grace my dinner plate!"

He crossed the cave, kicking the dagger as he went—it stopped near Awena and Tila—and grabbed my chin. "I meant to let you watch me devour your friends after you sang, but it seems that you singing for their lives is a better idea. I'm not so hungry that I can't put off eating for some fun!"

Then he nonchalantly tossed my chin aside with such force that the vertebrae of my neck popped.

Singing shouldn't have been a problem for me. Since I was a child, not even my mother's warnings or the jealous beatings Tila's mother subjected me to could keep me from singing. My voice made me into the heir Tila's mother never had, the Awitana my tribe should have had. My talent was such that Salayan, however unwilling, brought Maragat back as a tree for me. Tantirana threatened to drown Maragat from the roots and tell the lords of Kailog that I was plotting to kill them if I didn't sing for her. But ever since losing Maragat—twice—and escaping the palace of Kailog, only sighs and sharp words spilled from my lips. I almost believed I would never sing again—and some small part of me was relieved. Singing reminded me of Maragat listening smiling and eyes closed, the embodiment of a serenity I did not deserve.

Just then, there was a warmth at the small of my back. Directly behind me—so that the Kataw could not see—the Bungom was melting the ice. All I needed to do was sing for time. But could I?

You sing as if a god has touched you, Salayan had said the first time she heard me. If a Diwata believed in me, why shouldn't I believe in myself?

My first note was a sigh, as usual. The second was tuneless. The rest followed with the kind of musical feeling around of being weeks out of practice. But my voice grew in strength and relaxed into the right melody with every word. Despite being frozen in place, I was thawing from within and soaring over everything.

It was the song I always sang, the one about me, Tila, and Maragat. But as I neared the part where Maragat came to life again as a mango tree, I glanced at Tila and nearly faltered—Tila's right arm, which had been buoyed by her side, was now outstretched before her, toward me. Had my singing done that? What did it mean?

"Tired already?" asked the Kataw. He picked lazily at his fangs with a finger bone.

I glared at him and kept singing. For the first time in weeks, I sang the truth—that I ran from Iwakogan and spent ten years in a forest building a reputation as a witch thanks to the healing properties of Maragat's mangoes. That we were both taken from our home and transplanted within the palace of Kailog by greedy lords. That Tila joined the palace harem a year later, pregnant by one of them. That after I helped her get rid of the child, Maragat planned how we would escape—without him. That I failed to set fire to his trunk at the last moment, like he'd asked. That Tila had the strength to do what I could not.

A thud resounded throughout the cave.

"What—" began the Kataw.

Tila was free of her sphere and had fallen to the floor, coughing water, the dagger in her hands. At the same time, icy air caressed the backs of my legs. I tensed, ready to bolt.

"What did you do?" the Kataw roared as he rounded on me, fangs bared.

Go! cried the Bungom.

42

"Saha! *Catch!*" Tila yelled. She threw the dagger across the cave.

I dislodged myself from the remains of the ice mound, sprinted toward the dagger, caught it by the hilt, and swung it at the Kataw just as he was within arm's reach. Moss green blood welled from the long cut I dealt his face.

The Kataw howled as one webbed hand staunched the wound. The other attempted to knock me to the floor, but I blocked it and slashed the exposed arm at the soft flesh of the inner elbow. Then I kicked his leg out from under him.

The Kataw crashed to his side. Green blood flecked the white ice.

"How dare you!" he bellowed. He threw out his uninjured arm and crooked all fingers.

I barely dodged the stalactite that sprouted from the ceiling. It grazed my ankle as I leapt out of the way and sent me sprawling across the floor. I lay on my back, gasping at the sharp, ice-shot pain. The dagger had flown from my hand again.

Soon, the Kataw stood over me, his blood dripping onto my face. I shut my mouth but forced it open again after he pinned my neck to the floor.

"You're more trouble than you're worth, O Favored One," the Kataw snarled. "Since you're so determined to die in agony, it'd be my pleasure to grant you that!"

Then we both heard it. The wet hiss of punctured flesh. The Kataw's his eyes went wide. As he fell to his side, they began to dull.

Tila stood over us both, Maragat's dagger raised, half the blade bathed in mossy green blood. Not bad. I should teach her how to handle a knife one of these days.

As our gazes met, the dagger fell with a clatter, and she dropped to her knees, trembling. I sat up, gasping for breath, and wiped my face of blood.

"I heard your voice in my dream," Tila said. "It sang our story. I held onto it until I woke and broke the bubble.

"He called to me in Maragat's voice," she continued, eyes downcast. She held her saya in quivering fistfuls. "And I listened. I know Maragat is—you know—but I listened. I hated him for it."

Then Tila looked up at me with hard eyes. "But not as much as I hated myself."

Before I knew it, I was embracing her. I hated touching people. What had come over me?

Then from the far side of the cave, a thud.

Awena! cried the Bungom as it rushed toward her. It levitated over Awena as the girl retched water.

As soon as Awena was done, she wiped her mouth behind her hand and stared at the Bungom. "Hayani? You're—"

Never mind what I am, the Bungom interrupted. *What's important is that the Kataw is dead and the river has receded. You should all have less of a problem reaching the surface.*

Sad scrunched Awena's face. "So...you're gone after all..."

I did not know why, but I had a feeling that the Bungom, with its expressionless skull, was smiling. *Gone, but also free. It would make me very happy, Awena, if you three could give these trinkets to the girls' parents. I'm sure my mother would want to have my anklet back.*

"So what will you do now?" I asked of Awena by the docks of the riverbank as the morning breeze cooled us. We had just finished planting one of Maragat's mango seeds a few feet away—something I did for every place we stopped at. Behind us, a grateful crowd had gathered to bid us goodbye and ply Tila with all manner of gifts that we would probably barter or give away at the next village. But I would definitely keep the herbal brew that was guaranteed to put me to sleep. I wasn't about to brave the river awake.

"We're going to search for somewhere else to live," Awena replied. She smiled with a hint of bitterness. "We should've gone when the fish first disappeared, really."

"And your father?" Tila asked, having torn herself away from the crowd. Jewelry dripped from her ears, neck, and wrists; we would have to leave some gifts on the opposite riverbank.

Awena's smile flickered. "If we find him, I will put him on trial."

I couldn't imagine how heavy the burden of village chief was on a girl Awena's age. I had the urge to pat her shoulder but thought the better of it. Awena shook her head as if to ward off her sadness and continued, "I can't thank you both enough for what you've done for the village."

"Please, no—" I began, but someone cut me off.

"She's right. We cannot thank you enough." Apu Sima stepped forward from the crowd thronging behind us, her voice carrying far above the chatter. The skin beneath her eyes was puffy, as if she'd been crying, but she did seem haler that morning. Color was returning to her cheeks. Hayani's braided anklet circled her own ankle.

The wind carried Apu Sima's strong, full voice over us all. "If you will allow me to repay you both the best way I know, I would like to ferry you across the river."

I had been leaning heavily on Tila's walking stick. My ankle wasn't fully healed but it was strong enough to support my weight. I adjusted my grip, put one hand on my chest, inclined my head at Apu Sima, and murmured, "We would be honored."

MOON SISTERS

BY CAMILLA QUINN

Six days till the full moon, and already, Aja feels the wolf crawling beneath her skin. It hungers for a hunt, licking its chops and egging her to give chase to anything that moves. Anything she can sink her teeth into. She sighs down at her cell phone, breathing slow and even until the itch subsides.

Six days, she reminds herself. Six days until the pack carpools out to the national park an hour away. Darius and Payton will butt heads while trying to pick the best campsite. Mako and Molly will start roughhousing after the tents are set up. Santos will dog Summer's steps as she unloads supplies, pointing out squirrels and wildlife with one hand while stealing marshmallows with the other. Aja squeezes her hands, anticipation already swelling in her chest. Six days, and they'll be making smores until moonrise, shaking free the confines of these human forms, and tearing through the trails together, the wind in their fur, the moon rays on their skin, each other's howls loud in their ears. Her heart skips a beat just thinking about it. *Six days. Until then you can be patient.*

The wolf huffs, her ears twitching. Patience has never been Aja's strong suit.

Thump, thump, thump! A fist pounds on the wall behind her. "Yo, Aja!" Darius shouts through the wall between their apartments.

"Yo, Darius!" she hollers back.

"Wing Wednesday!"

She lets out a laugh under her breath. Since the pack discovered Druther's—the dive bar half a block down the road—and their Wednesday night special of ten-cent wings, they've made a tradition of it. Grinning slyly, she calls, "What?"

"Wing time!" Darius yells, his voice twisting into an excited screech.

"Say again, didn't catch that."

Thud! Something much bigger slams against the wall. "Asshole says what."

She chuckles. Looks like Darius is finally starting to catch on. "Wing time!" she parrots back to the wall. "Gimme a sec to put pants on."

In addition to throwing on a pair of leggings, Aja grabs a flowy tank top off her bedroom floor, the first shirt that passes the sniff test. Still, as she steps into her combat boots, she sprays herself down with Febreeze for good measure. After years as pack leader, Payton gets real touchy-feely when the group scent changes, and she'd be lying if she said she didn't live to mess with them. Besides, it's not like they're going anywhere fancy, just Druther's.

And if there's someone worthwhile holding down a barstool— someone with unconventional features and a nice laugh and an enlightened perspective on romance and her genuine disinterest in it— sure she'll grab at the opportunity to flirt it up, but tonight there's nothing particularly sexual about the itch under her skin. Not while the wolf is so riled.

More than anything, tonight will likely turn into Darius and Santos gorging themselves on chicken wings and one-uping each other to the point of nausea while Payton shakes their head and aims the boys towards the trashcans when their antics get the better of them. Really, if she wants to survive tonight and make it to tomorrow morning sober enough for her five a.m. shift at the bakery, she's gonna need some moral support.

"Summer!" Aja calls as she bangs on her roommate's door. "The boys wanna head to Druther's. Come with me so I don't have to drink myself under the table when I give up trying to keep them in line. I've gotta open tomorrow."

Summer doesn't respond, but when Aja presses her ear to the door, she hears sniffles and the mattress springs shifting. That's… odd. As the sweetest of their semi-dysfunctional found family, Summer's always keen to spend time with the pack. Or at least, she was before she started dating that Vera chick, a mundane woman with a perpetually puckered expression and a stick up her admittedly nice ass—Aja's been caught staring a few times.

Now that she thinks about it, she can't remember seeing much of Summer today. Or yesterday. She remembers hearing the front door open last night, remembers smelling Summer's soft rainy scent in the hallway when Aja finally crawled her way to bed, but after that, nothing. *Real odd.*

She knocks again. "C'mon, Summer, you slept away a beautiful day, but there's still a beautiful night to be had. I bet if you batted those pretty gray eyes of yours we could talk the boys into going by the dance hall later." Aja props her hip against the doorjamb then noses against the hinge. "That band you like is probably playing, and I think I'm real close to a breakthrough with that sassy bartender. The one with the Buddy Holly glasses and that gruff voice. Last week when I was chatting him up, he called me 'an absolute bumble-fuck', and I swear I went a little weak at the knees." She sighs dramatically. "He *gets* me."

A half-hearted laugh answers her. Aja perks up, bouncing up onto her toes, ready to spring. But when Summer answers, her normally bright voice sounds muddled and dull. Lackluster. "You should go without me. I'm not feeling well."

Aja stills, her inner wolf standing at attention. Something's wrong. Summer loves to go dancing, never passes up an opportunity to go dancing; even if she was puking her guts out and unable to stand, she'd still say she could pull herself together if she could just have a moment.

The door opens when she tries the knob. Inside, Summer's room is dark save for the pale moonlight peeking in through the curtains, and the air is heavy with the smell of a storm: ozone and refuse and rot. *Wrong. Very bad wrong.* Every inch of her on edge, Aja pads across the room, carefully sidestepping piles of sketchbooks and pulp thrillers and dirty clothes. There's a person-shaped bundle in Summer's bed, familiar brown and teal curls fanned out on her pillow. Without pulling her out from the safety of her blankets, Aja presses the back of her hand to Summer's forehead, waits a moment, and frowns.

"Feels alright to me. A little warm, but that's just how weres roll." Satisfied with her investigation, Aja waltzes over to the closet, scanning through the hanging garments for one of Summer's favorite sun dresses—the sleeveless one in an aqua floral print with a few buttons on the bodice. "The night is young, and the moon keeps flirting with me. Now, I'm plenty in touch with my inner goddess, but that's more woman than I can handle on my own."

A whine breaks through the room, sharp and pained and bitten off.

Aja flinches at the sound, her brow furrowing. "Sheesh, you sound worse than Santos when he's hungover." As she turns back to her dress quest, she snorts and calls over her shoulder. "What, did your human dump you or something?"

It's thoughtless and callous, and she regrets the flippant remark immediately. Especially when the Summer-shaped pile of blankets lets out a wrecked wail.

Oh goddammit, Perez, when are you gonna learn being an asshole always backfires on you? Scrambling across the room, Aja stops short at the bedside, one of Summer's hangers clutched in her hand. The wolf inside urges her to flop on the bed and wrap herself around Summer in a full body embrace. To kiss the tears from Summer's cheeks and bathe her in a familiar scent and never let her go, but... *Boundaries,* she reminds herself. Exhaling slowly, Aja tosses the hanger to the side, sits at the edge of Summer's bed, and awkwardly pats her shoulder.

Summer shakes and cries, and Aja curses herself for once again proving herself to be an absolute bumble-fuck. "Shit, I'm sorry, Summer. What happened?"

For several minutes, Summer just sniffles and sucks in harsh breaths and quietly counts down from ten. Twice, she gets tripped up and has to start over. By the time she reaches one, Summer isn't much calmer. Curled tight in her blanket cocoon, Summer mumbles a response so quiet Aja just barely catches her words. "She wanted me to move out."

Aja quirks a brow. Move out? Why would Summer ever move out? Even if the pack has settled in a shitty walk-up on the shady side of town, rent's cheap, and the building is warm, and from their living room, Aja can smell every member of the pack when they're home. Payton in their single on the first floor. Santos, his mate Molly, and her partner Jas—a human with a knack for witchcraft—in the corner unit on the third floor. Darius and Mako next door—though to be fair, most days their apartment reeks so strongly of pheromones that Aja is tempted to storm over and spray them with a squirt bottle before they can pollute the air any further. Yeah, there are plenty of downsides to economy housing, but the entire pack under one roof, close enough they can be at each other's doorstep in a heartbeat but still far enough apart to keep all their inner wolves from snapping at each other's throats? That's the dream. As close to perfect as they can get in this day and age.

"She wanted you to move in with her? After you'd only been dating for, what, two months?" She scratches at her jaw, her hands suddenly restless. Even for a were, two months is too quick for that level of commitment. At least according to conventional wisdom.

"N-no," Summer replies, poking her head out from under the blankets. Even in the dim light, her soft cheeks are red and blotchy and stained by tear tracks. "Not with her. Just... not here. Vee wasn't comfortable..."

Sure, that *sounds like something your average mundane asks their partner.* Aja leans back, trying to find some glimmer of sense in all this, but the harder she grabs for it, the more it eludes her. "I mean, sure, our landlady's plenty creepy, and there's the homeless guy who hangs out near our back alley, but Karl's harmless. It's not his fault people hear a German accent and see a wandering left eye and decide 'time to whip out my ableist bigotry'—"

"—It's you," Summer interrupts, fresh tears welling in her eyes before she turns and hides in her pillow. "She didn't like me living with *you.*"

The gears in her mind grind to a halt so fast it feels like the rest of her jerks to a stop a half-second later, leaving her with a wicked case of whiplash. *Me? What the actual fuck?* Aja stares, grappling for a response but coming up empty. Completely, totally empty. After ten long seconds, she regains control of her gaping lower jaw and summons her voice. "'Scuse-me-what-now?"

Wiping her eyes with the back of her hand, Summer pushes

herself upright. She hugs the blankets close around her shoulders like a shield against the world. This isn't Summer, the light of their pack. Isn't the woman who greets even the darkest days with a grin and a sly little joke. Seeing her shoulders hunched under a herculean weight, hiding behind the curtain of her hair, crying, leaves Aja's throat constricted and her hands faintly trembling.

Sniffling, Summer says, "Vera thought our group was too codependent. Too weird. And she thought you were…"

"Thought I was what?"

Hesitant, Summer curls in on herself, her voice coming out meek and thread-bare. "She thought you were a possessive ex trying to steal me away."

Aja just barely stops herself from laughing. Her? And Summer? *Gross!* "That's dumb," she says, rolling her eyes. "You're, like, my little sister."

"I know, Aj."

"Fucking mundanes," she spits out, distantly aware of the tremor in her hands. "They don't have any frame of reference. Of course, she thought we were weird. She's not anyone's pack."

"No," Summer answers, her head hanging. "She's not." Aja's hands clench. Now, she could be wrong, but that tone of voice makes it sound like Summer thinks her ex's lack of experience is somehow *her* fault. And that can't be allowed.

Aja growls with barely a thought to stop herself. How dare someone cause Summer pain? Who does Vera think she is, messing with Aja's pack? These people are the only family she's ever cared to call her own, the people who helped her master her nature when she was cast out of her home pack, who took Summer in when they found her at moonrise in the nature preserve, snarling and half-starved and frightened. How dare she?

Deep inside, the wolf bares its teeth, howling for blood. It nips at her heels, eager to storm out of the apartment and hunt down this good-for-nothing human who thought she could come between the pack and get away with it. But as quickly as the impulse rushes through her, Aja grits her teeth and squashes that ugly feeling down. Possessive and vengeful won't help her now. Not while Summer's hurting.

With a purposeful exhale, Aja banishes those thoughts and clears her mind. *What would Summer do,* she asks herself. *How would Summer respond if Aja was in need?*

The answer comes to her immediately—*kindly.*

So, Aja kicks off her boots and crawls under the blankets with Summer. Snuggling close, she wraps her arms around Summer's plush waist and holds tight. Summer hesitates for a split second, but another faint sob wracks through her. Aja strokes her back and hums into Summer's hair, praying she can be the comfort her moon sister deserves. "I'm sorry, Summer. I know you liked her a lot."

Summer sniffles. "You don't have to say that."

"Of course, I do. Just 'cause I don't get romantic love doesn't mean it's not important to you." She hauls Summer closer, easing Summer's head onto her shoulder so Aja can take her weight. She focuses on keeping each breath deep and steady, rubbing circles into Summer's back. "Break-ups suck, no matter your orientation, and it sucks so much more when you feel lost and alone. But you have the pack, Summer. You'll never be alone. Just say the word, and we'll be there."

Summer nestles against Aja, her rainy scent slowly turning sweet again. A few minutes more, and her breathing comes smooth and even, and her trembling settles. "Thank you," Summer whispers, not looking up from the crook of Aja's neck. "Thank you."

"Anytime, gorgeous," Aja says as she leans down and presses a kiss to Summer's cheek. Sweet at first, kind at first, but she can only resist her instincts so long. Before they part, Aja turns the kiss into a raspberry.

Summer yelps, squirming away, and Aja thrusts an arm in the air. "Victory!"

Laughing, Summer wipes her cheeks clean. "Asshole. And here I thought you had a sensitive side."

"Only for you. That shit gives me hives." She gives an exaggerated shudder even though she knows it's not distaste or irritation making her heart beat fast in her chest or draining the tension from her posture or turning her grin soft, knows it's something she's still not comfortable putting into words, something that swells when she thinks about this band of misfits she calls home. Exhaling forcefully, Aja shakes herself, blinking back an unbidden tear. "So, chicken wings?"

Summer curls back in on herself, toying with the frayed hem of a blanket. "I... I don't think I'm up for going out... Sorry."

"Hey, none of that." She squeezes Summer tight before rolling out from under the blankets. "You feel how you feel." But that doesn't mean she's gonna leave Summer to wallow in said feelings for the rest of the night.

And yeah, she can already feel tomorrow morning's headache welling behind her eyes, the kind she gets after a few too many nights without enough sleep, but screw it. That's a future Aja problem, and she knows herself well enough to know future Aja will agree—Summer's more important.

Lips twitching into a grin, Aja springs over to the bedroom

57

window. It slides open easily, a little cloud of dust puffing up from the sill. Batting the dust out of her face, Aja ducks her head outside and shouts, "Yo, Darius!"

In less than a minute, she hears another window opening, and Darius swings his head out, shaving cream still foamed along his cheeks and jaw, his dreads pulled into a knot. "Yo, Aja!"

"Rain-check on Druther's."

Darius gapes, visibly deflating. A rogue dollop of shaving cream drops onto his collar. "But Aj'... Wing Wednesday!"

"Sorry, bud, but I'm pretty sure chickens aren't gonna go extinct between now and next week."

"But Aja," he pleads. "Wing Wednesday." Like whining about it will change her mind.

Honestly, it's like he'll never learn. "Dude, Summer just got dumped," she shouts back. "Show a little sympathy."

"Aja," Summer hisses.

Just as she shoots Summer a consolatory grin, Darius calls back, "Oh, hell no! Nobody dumps our sweet Summer child!" He rubs his chin, smearing the shaving cream over his fingers. Darius squawks in surprise, scowls at the mess, and shakes his hand clean. "Okay, lemme grab food, Mako's Disney collection, and anyone else who's free. We'll be over in two shakes."

"Food?" Santos ducks out of a window on the floor above, bellowing. "Someone said food?"

Before she can reprimand him, a window on the first floor flies open, and Payton ducks out, their frizzy brown hair a mess of braids and plaits. "Santos, you inconsiderate hog, quit with the food talk. Your pack mate just got her heart stomped on!"

Santos barrels on, undeterred. "Can we get tacos?"

Aja hears Payton smack their head in their hands as she cranes back into the room to face Summer. "Tacos sound good?"

In lieu of answering, Summer chucks her pillow at Aja's head. Only Aja's quick hands save the pillow from a treacherous fate in the alley below. Smirking, Aja hollers out to the pack, "Summer votes pizza. She lost her taste for taco after what's-her-bitch."

"TMI!" shrieks Ms. Portia from the building across the alley.

"Sorry, Ms. P," Aja calls as she closes the window.

Still huddled on her bed, Summer buries her bright red cheeks in her hands and groans, drawn-out and heavy with exasperation. But when she peeks out from behind her hands, there's fire in her eyes. More fire than Aja's seen from her in a long while. "You're the worst," Summer says, climbing out of bed with all her blankets still gathered around her and hobbling into the living room. "Absolutely the worst thing ever."

Aja trails after, beaming. "You know you love me for it."

And the next morning, when Aja's alarm drags her into consciousness for her shift, she finds half the pack passed out in her living room—Darius and Mako spooning on the floor, Santos sleeping with his head pillowed on a stack of empty pizza boxes, Summer nestled on the couch with her head in Payton's lap. Even as her brain pounds against her skull, pride swells in her chest. Her pack. Her family. Her home. God, she loves these losers.

Padding carefully through the room, she gathers her half-charged phone and keys, throws on a clean t-shirt, and sneaks off to the bakery. And if she's planning on setting aside one of Summer's favorite raspberry scones to bring home later, well, that's no one's business but hers.

CINDER

BY JENNIFER LEE
ROSSMAN

So here I am, waiting for a prince I've never met to rescue me.

Now, before you start with the feminism stuff, let me say this: I'm *all* for women empowerment and it's awesome when princesses rescue themselves. I've rescued myself twice this year, once by discovering the antidote for a poisoned appletini and once when I was catfished by a creepy guy pretending to be a sweet old lady.

But there are times when your abusive stepmother literally won't let you leave your own house, when she punishes you by taking away your prosthetic legs even though you're a grown-ass woman, when it's just not safe or feasible for you to be the hero of your own story.

That's why I use Cinder.

Maybe it used to be easier to find princes, back when our grandparents were young and fairy-touched. Free love and all that, you know? You go to a love-in, have a little "porridge," fall asleep in someone else's bed, and in the morning, bibbidy-bobbidy-boo, you got yourself a soul mate and your true love's first kiss will break whatever curse ails you.

But it's the twenty-first century. We've got better things to do than sing into wishing wells and hope Prince Charming happens to be passing by. So we turn to Cinder. Just find a guy in your area with a foot fetish, swipe right, and he'll break into your stepmother's house and steal your legs so you don't have to.*

(*Happily ever after not guaranteed. But sometimes all you want is a "happily ever for the night." Just long enough break a curse. Or so I'm told. Being asexual and aromantic, those kinds of endings never really appealed to me. Give me a good friendship where they own an Itsy store selling artisan jewelry any day.)

My prince pings me when he's almost to the house; I pocket my phone and adjust my posture on the kitchen counter as I finish the dishes, surreptitiously keeping an eye out the window.

I know it won't be all singing mice and magical dresses. My stepmom will probably threaten him, I'll have to leave my meager possessions behind, and unless he lets me crash on the couch of his studio castle, I'll likely spend the night in a women's shelter.

But I'll be free. No more waiting for her to move me from where she's placed me, no more wincing when she raises her voice.

The sound of an engine sends competing jolts of excitement and dread through my body. This is it. Everything changes now, immediately and forever.

I turn off the water, glancing out the window as I dry my hands. A hideous car has parked in our driveway. I don't think VW Bugs ever came in that color orange, which would suggest someone did that *on purpose*.

But sometimes princesses can't be choosers. The guy getting out looks nice enough. A little skinny, some ink on his arm, gorgeous flowing blonde locks. I'll have to ask him what conditioner he uses because that man needs to be in slow-mo hair-flip commercials. For half a second, I almost think I'm attracted to him, but I think I just really want to have his hair.

My stepmother comes in, her mouth drawn into a tight line and her eyes narrowed behind her jeweled glasses. For too long, that look struck fear in me, but now I have to fight not to laugh. She has no idea it's over.

"Ashlyn," she says, her voice sharp and filled with warning. "Are the dishes done?"

She can plainly see that they aren't, but I don't answer her right away. By now the prince will have snuck in through the living room window like I instructed. I faintly hear the closet door creak as he fetches my legs, and now I can't suppress the laughter.

"The dishes aren't done, but I am." I raise my voice. "In here!"

The prince comes bounding in, triumphantly holding a leg in each hand. I swing my stumps over the edge of the counter.

In an instant, she realizes what's happening. And she is *not* pleased. She starts yelling, threatening to call the police. Once upon a yesterday, that would have scared me. The cops around here are all in the pocket of the wicked stepmothers union.

But as the prince helps me into the legs shaped to fit me and no one else, I can't find room for fear in all the hope, not even as glass shatters on the floor and she screeches like a rabid dragon. She can't harm a prince. That's the first rule of being a fairy-touched man: no mortal can hurt you.

Yeah, it's misogynistic and no, I'm not sure how it works for intersex or nonbinary people. (Though I do know a princess who was assigned prince at birth and after she transitioned—with a brief intermission as a frog—she retained some of the immunity while simultaneously being targeted by every witch in the tri-enchanted-forest area, so I'm inclined to think gender is Confusing.)

All I know is that she can't touch him.

The dish she just threw, though? That can totally touch him.

It shatters on impact with his skull and he crumbles to the floor, his beautiful hair splayed out around him in a steadily spreading pool of blood.

Well, damn.

I get my other leg on, my hands trembling as the fear surges back through my veins, and I run. I don't know where I'm going, I don't have time to grab a bag, I just run.

Should I stay to help him? Maybe. Okay, probably. But if he's dead, there's nothing I can do for him, and if he's not, I highly doubt she'd let me tend to his wounds. She's just escalated to physical violence. There's no going back from that; the plate that crashes against the wall just inches from my head confirms that much.

When I burst through the door, it hits me just how long I've been inside. The sun is warmer than I remember. Or maybe that's the global warming. Soon, magic mirrors will be talking about girls with hair black as smog and skin white as the politicians who deny climate change.

That hideous orange car is idling in the driveway. With nowhere else to go, I rush to it and throw myself inside. I don't know how to drive—most of my late teens and early twenties have been spent playing maid to my stepmother, in varying degrees of imprisonment—but it can't be that hard.

I shift into Drive and press a random pedal all the way to the floor. The car lurches into motion, and I see bits of grass and flowers spray up as my wheels dig deep grooves in her precious garden.

Then I'm on the road, and that sad little house with the gingerbread trim is shrinking in my rearview mirror.

I check the time on the radio clock. One minute after noon. It's a shame digital clocks don't chime; that would have made for dramatic background music to my getaway.

The prince's phone is on the passenger seat. I use it to call an ambulance for him, and as I go to set it down again, I notice a message from another match on Cinder.

A young princess being held hostage by a wigmaker downtown.

The prince had already agreed to save her right after me, and while I know she'd be able to find another prince soon, I can't put her through the agony of having her hopes dashed. It took so long for me to work up the courage to join Cinder in the first place... if he had cancelled, I might have taken that as a sign that I was doing the wrong thing.

No, I have to help her.

I spent a good ten minutes drawing tattoos on my arms with a ballpoint pen, and a further twenty messing with the various hair care products I found in the backseat. I thought it was important that I look as much like the prince as possible.

It turns out I needn't have bothered because Kavya is blind.

I find her in the back room of the wig shop, located at the top floor of a commercial building downtown. She's weaving strands of straight, glossy black hair into extensions, her fingers working quickly and nimbly.

It can't be all her own; real magic, the kind that made hair grow supernaturally fast and let princesses talk to woodland creatures, doesn't exist anymore. Her hair might grow a little faster than regular people's, but the tresses piled about her must have come from other girls, too.

I clear my throat, and she freezes like a bird hearing the footsteps of a booted cat. "It's not your stepmother," I whisper. "I'm your Cinder match."

Kavya relaxes so utterly, for a second I'm worried her spine has disintegrated. She makes a sound that I can't identify as a sob or a laugh;

I'm not sure if she can tell either. "I'm safe?"

Safe is a relative term. Her stepmother will be back from her cigarette break soon, we're in a building full of security, and even if we get out of here, we'll still be two disabled princesses in a world that sees us as little more than props for their Spinstagram photos. (Hell, the entire site was named because it started as a way for people to brag about the amount of gold their princesses can make on a spinning wheel!)

But I can't take away the hope in her voice. "Yes. You're safe." I close the door behind me and scan the room. Shelves of packaged hair, a small cot, and a radio. Nothing else. At least my stepmother pretended to give me a normal life. "We need to figure out a way out of here, Kavya," I say. "Can I take your hand?"

She nods and I help her up. "You don't sound like a prince."

"That's because I'm not. Long story. I'm Ashlyn; I'm covering for your prince today. How was he supposed to get you out of here?"

"The window."

I whirl around, checking every one of the walls. Highly unlikely I'd miss a window, but my adrenaline is still spiking from my own escape, so who knows. I might not be processing everything. Still, I think I know what a window looks like.

"There's no window."

"There used to be," Kavya insists, walking up to the wall opposite the door. She runs her hands along the concrete. "I used to feel the sunlight, but she covered it—here!" She taps one of the bricks. "Hollow. Just pull your cherrypicker around to the east side..."

"I'm staring at you in annoyance," I inform her, "because we don't have time for jokes."

But she isn't joking. "The prince didn't give you the keys to his cherrypicker?"

"He was a little busy... bleeding from a head wound."

Kavya nods knowingly. "Was he a Bluebeard in prince clothing?"

"Oh, I didn't—" But you know what? It's not actually worth correcting her. There's a sort of approval in her voice; she thinks I murdered the prince for wanting to marry and subsequently kill me, and she's totally cool with that.

I really like this girl. That's the kind of instant bond that best friends are made of.

Right? I don't exactly have much experience in that aspect. As soon as people learn you're fairy-touched, they tend to take advantage of you.

I almost had a friend once, in kindergarten, but she locked me in the playhouse and made me wash her dolls' clothes. Turns out she'd been told that items washed by princesses were blessed. Not an uncommon belief, sadly. She's going to make a terrible second wife to some single father of a princess someday.

But there'll be time to make depressing scrapbooks later. The sound of voices outside the door snaps me back to the present.

"My stepmother," Kavya whispers.

I go to the wall and start carefully prying the bricks loose. Sunlight pours in, illuminating dust motes like they're the kind of magical sparkles that can turn a sexy beast into an okay-looking dude. (I may be asexual and aromantic, but I can tell when people are attractive and most guys look so much better as anthropomorphic animals. This is fact, not opinion. Just look at teenage girls' art on Tumblrina if you need proof.)

Once it's fully exposed, I ease the window open. It's a long way down. Like, a beanstalk and a half at the very least.

I turn to Kavya to express my dismay, but she's hard at work, doing something that looks like hand crochet to make a long rope out of hair extensions. She moves so fast, I can hardly focus.

But… hair?

"I don't know about this," I whisper.

"Neither do I," she says honestly. "But it can't be any scarier than staying here, can it?"

She has a point. And seemingly minutes later, she also has a functional rope and harness made of hair.

Should I offer to go first, or let her go? Which is more chivalrous? I never learned about chivalry. When they split us up in middle school health class, I and the other got to watch a video called "Little Red Womanhood," about our changing bodies and how our hormones, not the full moon, turned otherwise calm werewolves into ravenous beasts.

Kavya doesn't give me the chance to decide which option is more chivalrous. Before I realize it, she's got the harness on and is rappelling down like a spider headed for whatever the hell a tuffet is.

Okay then. There's that problem solved.

Even as that thought is occurring to me, a new problem charges into the room: Kavya's stepmother, all rage and passive-aggressive mother-knows-best manipulation.

"She's lying," I shout out the window. "You're not better off here, the world is not a terrifying place. It's freedom."

I don't know if I believe what I'm saying. I just know that Kavya needs to.

I turn to face her stepmother, my back to the window. There's

70

nowhere to go; I'm trapped again. But I stare her down, because what else can I do? And when Kavya calls up to me, I waste no time scrambling over that window ledge.

I used to hate silence. Silence meant she hadn't found a reason to yell at me yet, hadn't decided what menial task I had screwed up that day.

But sitting here with Kavya in the VW van, Watching the setting sun turn the sky the color of my ugly pumpkin car? It's actually… nice. I'm not used to nice, to safety, to the feeling that I could close my eyes and trust that the person sitting next to me has absolutely no malice in her heart.

"What we do now?"

She turns her head my direction, her anxious hands never pausing in their delicate lacework. That old spool of thread I had in my pocket is steadily becoming a gorgeous doily. "What do you mean?"

I shrug. I know she can't see it, so I try my best to verbalize my helplessness: "Mmrrmph."

"Ah." She makes a sympathetic sound, but she's grinning. I like her smile. It makes everything feel okay.

"What's so funny?" I ask.

"You." When I don't respond, she elaborates. "You rescued me. You're supposed to be the one with the big plan. Rescue a girl, fall in love, have magical little babies who get kidnapped by witches and/or turned into amphibians and birds that sing showtunes."

I do an extremely classy snort laugh. "Yeah, I don't want any of those things. Especially the part about the showtunes."

"Oh, no one likes showtunes," Kavya informs me in a serious tone, then giggles.

God, this woman. Is there a platonic version of love at first sight? Because my heart is all warm inside and if so, I could make an A+ curse antidote right now.

"I don't want any of those things either," Kavya says with a shrug. "Maybe the rescuing princesses part. That seems kind of fun."

"It was." I lean my head against the window of the hideous Volkswagen. Not too hard, though, because some part of me is still convinced this is all an illusion, That it's all going to go away at the stroke of midnight. The ugly car will turn back into some rotting squash, my fabulous hair will lose its volume and shine, and I'll be back at my stepmoms house, cooking and cleaning and enduring her abuse miserably ever after. Alone.

"So," Kavya says as she finishes off her doily and begins making something else. "What do we do now? Whatever we want. We are free."

Free. What does that even look like for people like us?

"I don't know if I'll ever feel safe again," I whisper, so quiet that I almost hope she doesn't hear me. But she clearlydoes, so I continue, because I may have just met her a few hours ago, but I feel like my soul knows hers. "I'm always going to think twice before I eat an apple. I'm always going to be afraid every sweet old lady is a wolf wearing flannel." I wipe my eyes with the back of my hand. "I was never even under a curse, but I still feel like it needs to be broken."

Kavya is silent for a moment, frenetically tying knot after minuscule knot. "It may not be magic," she says finally, "Not the kind that turns us into ballet dancing waterfowl or anything, but abuse still changes us. It's evil, and it gets inside us and turns us into something we don't want to be. Scared. Tiny. Unsure of who we really are. But just because it isn't a magic spell, that doesn't mean there's no cure."

Before I can ask what she means by this, her hands are on my wrist. The physical contact brings a smile to my face. I don't know why anyone needs romance; friendship, if that's what this is, seems pretty great all on its own.

At first I think she's going to hold my hand, but then she ties a dainty little friendship bracelet around my wrist.

I don't know if it's magic or what. All I know is that something changes inside of me with that small, simple gesture. Everything is not okay. Not even close. But there's a tiny bit of hope, clinging to my heart like the last petal on an enchanted rose as the clock strikes its penultimate bell. An absurd and audacious notion that maybe, just maybe, if the fairies wish it so and the rule of threes is working in our favor, this poor little servant girl really could be a princess. And maybe she can live happily ever after.

"Thank you," I whisper.

She smiles. "So, I believe you asked what we do now. Are we are a *we*?"

I think about that for a moment. "I guess that depends on what you want to do next, now that we're free and all."

She has her answer right away, absolutely zero hesitation. "I want to rescue princesses and sell enchanted jewelry on Itsy."

"Sounds good to me."

I start up that ugly pumpkin car and drive toward our next Cinder match. Are we going to live happily ever after? I don't know. As long as we're together, though, it's definitely an option.

NOT QUITE TRUE LOVE

BY SYL WOO

"Finding your one true love is what makes life worth living.
Discuss."

While some may claim that finding your
one true love is the key to a happily ever
after, I beg to differ.

For one:

Have you ever dyed your hair purple and pink
And washed it off in a playground's sink?
But speaking of sinks, what do you think
Of summoning a fire in one?

20 minutes of walking in the cold, sharp rain to the Newton MRT,
Though certainly the joy is not in reaching
But the conversations along the way.

Does happiness not lie in dancing
Alone in an empty MRT station?
Too early for tourists, too late for locals,
Empty trains whizzing past amidst blasting music.

Have you ever sung along to music playing
From the floor above an auditorium?
Ever sat inside a theatre
Dark, empty, and echoing
And done nothing but eaten a Mentos?

"What makes life worth living" needs to be taken apart
As all good essay questions need to be
Does it mean what fulfills one?
What leads to self-actualisation?

In that case, I offer up that feeling
When you work at a complex problem long enough
And it suddenly comes apart at your fingertips.
Could it feel like finally getting recognised
For work you've spent ages doing?

Does it feel like finally understanding that you don't need to ever be okay?
That it's alright to just take care of yourself?
It might feel something like making a friend you just click with,
Whose mind and yours are on a wavelength that no one else can touch.

I have 15 minutes left to finish this essay.

Love. What is love?

What does it mean to have one true love?

I have many true loves,

Too many true loves that push at the walls of my heart

Surging and stretching; whispering and inspiring.

How am I supposed to choose a single one?

(Or am I supposed to wait

Months, maybe years, maybe decades, maybe a lifetime

For one to come find me?)

Am I supposed to choose my love for fantasy?

Am I supposed to surrender my love for politics?

Am I supposed to decide which of my friends I love?

5 minutes left.

To conclude, I…

I feel that the number of narratives that have to deal with a girl giving up everything for a guy she feels romantic attraction for is ridiculous and…

To CONCLUDE.

I disagree with the claim that finding your one true love is what makes life fulfilling.

That will be all.

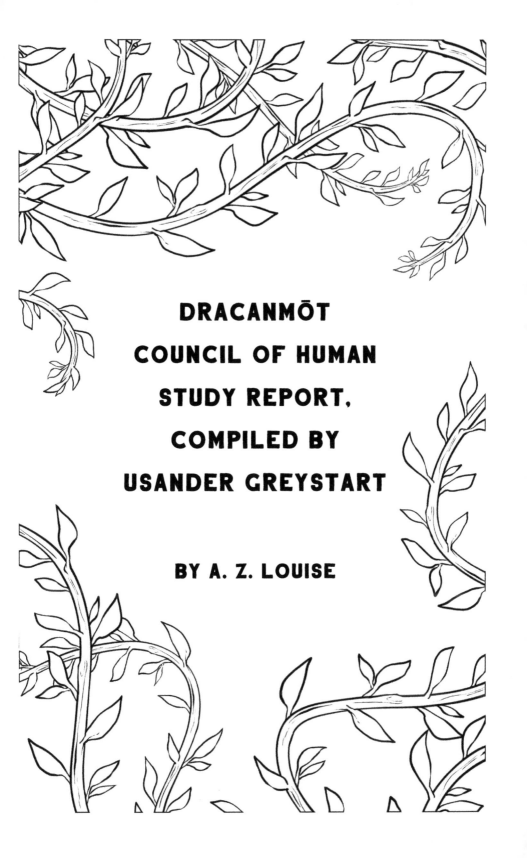

DRACANMŌT COUNCIL OF HUMAN STUDY REPORT, COMPILED BY USANDER GREYSTART

BY A. Z. LOUISE

DRACANMŌT COUNCIL OF HUMAN STUDY REPORT
Compiled by Usander Greystart

Day One

I arrived in Luvoda early this morning. The inn is passable, and I have engaged a room for the next two weeks. The gold the Council has allotted will be more than adequate, though I did need some help counting out the coins. I have made notes as to the values and names of each coin, which will be useful as I continue my study, though I have learned that every country has a different currency. Borders have likely changed since our last contact, and I will endeavor to find a map to learn more.

Thus far I have only interacted with the people at the inn, so that I might know how best to talk to people in the town and avoid making myself seem strange. I have already made two mistakes, the first of which is that I chose the wrong skin color. The people here have dark skin, and mine is light, and I cannot change it now. The second is that they seem baffled by my choice of gender; they are too polite to ask, but they stumble over their gendered tongue when I speak to them. I will certainly be making a formal complaint about the thoroughness of the scouting reports about the area.

It took little time to learn that most of the people in town spend their idle hours at the tavern, which is next door to the inn. The innkeeper informs me that he does not allow the sale of wine or ale in his common room, because when people drink them, they become too rowdy and break the crockery. There will certainly be more to follow once I discover what wine and ale are. I recall some mention in my readings over the years, but they never made much sense.

In any case, the innkeeper and his daughters have decided that I am rich (I suppose that by their standards, I am), perhaps a lord of some kind. In the words of the eldest daughter "I suppose lords need to travel often for wars and things." She's quite sharp, which could be helpful, as long as I manage not to give myself away.

Day Two — Entry One

I have now eaten a few meals in the common room. Human food preparation is interesting and uses many herbs and spices. The innkeeper's clever daughter laughed when I commented on it and said she would not expect an outlander to know about seasoning. I don't know what that means, except that I should like to go to these other places to learn about their food, too. It will surely reveal the joke.

The daughter—whose name is Elitt—asked me many questions. I tried my best to divert her attention by asking her the purpose of wine and beer, and thankfully she was so surprised by the question that she forgot to be curious. Both are beverages, and the latter is intended to render bad water safe to drink. These drinks, with the exception of "small ale," have added pleasurable effects, but Elitt has warned me that too much will make me ill. Now that I have had some interactions with humans, I shall go to the tavern and see what all of this is about.

Day Two — Entry Two

I am at the tavern and have had wine. It is very fun, and the patrons are singing human songs, which I have attempted to transcribe. Quite warm and a bit dizzy.

Day Two — Entry Three

Had too much wine and mentioned the Dracanmōt. Have fled the town and will return in a better disguise in a few days.

Day Six

I have returned to the inn, and there has been much talk about the strange outlander who came through a few days past. They are all convinced that he was quite mad, and some have apparently discussed finding him to get him help with his affliction. Elitt was especially worried, to the point that her sisters began to tease her about having a fancy. I tried to lift her spirits with humor, but she didn't laugh until I told her that I had seen a rich man on the road, who looked perfectly healthy and whole. Once I had eased her mind, she mostly laughed because I am exceedingly unfunny.

Still, I believe I have gained Elitt's trust. We went on talking long after the kitchen was closed, and she confided in me that her sisters like to tease because she has no need for romance. She claims that they don't mean any harm, but I admit that I find myself feeling rather protective over her regardless of whether it is my business. She is an interesting person, and I think she has much to teach me about humans, especially the ways in which social bonds form and are maintained.

But I digress. It is important to note that my new disguise is much better. In my first stay with the humans, I noted that they will look right past one of their own given the following details:

- ❖ The individual is an adult: easy enough, as I am an adult and did not consider a child-form. The societal differences between child humans and the adults are akin to ours;
- ❖ Looks similar to the locals: I am now a shade of medium brown with dark curly hair;
- ❖ Expresses gender in a predictable way: I have chosen an approximation of woman-form, because I prefer their clothing choices, and;
- ❖ Does not have any noticeable ailments: Given the talk in town about my previous attempt, it is safe to say that differences in mind can call attention to a human. I do not know whether it is the same for physical differences, but I will endeavor to find out.

From now on I will avoid drink (entertaining as it may be) but the tavern seems to be a good place to continue to learn. The decrease in inhibition makes humans just as talkative as it did me, making the place the center of most rumors in Luvoda. Within a two-hour span I have transcribed twelve of their songs and learned that there is an alleged witch in the scrublands outside town. I will investigate him further tomorrow, though the town may have larger concerns than witches.

Word has come from a nearby town that raiding parties of orcs have been driven off. This could be a good way to learn more about human ways, especially regarding war, but it could also prove deadly. More reports to come, of course.

Day Seven

A party has been formed to help protect the town of Reveda, and I have volunteered, as has Elitt. She has a wicked-looking spear, which she says she has used to kill orcs several times before. I don't doubt her in the least, for she holds it as comfortably as she does a dinner tray. As I came unarmed, she has given me an old spear and a whetstone for sharpening.

It was not a long walk to Reveda, but it is a considerably smaller town, so we have had to camp. Humans do not simply sleep outside, instead bringing many tents and supplies, starting a fire for comfort, and cooking even though the weather is hot. Some of the townsfolk came to talk to the Luvodans and plan the defense.

Elitt and I were chosen to stand watch for a few hours while the others slept, and I asked her how long her people had been fighting orcs. She assumed that I was from the nearest city, where a wall kept the creatures out, and went on to say that nobody remembered a time without orcs making raids for food or to push back the humans. When I asked why the orcs wanted to destroy human towns, she said it was their way to take over as much land as they could hold.

According to Elitt, orcs value land over all else, though they do not grow food. The humans suppose that it is the orc religion, this belief that they are promised the land by their god-given superiority of physical strength and will. Money is only of use to them as a way to obtain resources like weapons, which can then be used to claim more land. I believe it would be interesting to go among the orcs to see what they think about the situation, but I suppose that is outside the purview

85

of this report. I would, however, urge the Council to engage in further study to better understand the humans and their ways.

As far as research into human ways goes, when I suggested that humans value money more than anything else, Elitt said that was more the way of dragons. She also claimed that her great-grandmother had once seen a dragon, but that they are gone now. The legends are of the wildest kind, curses and eating virgins and so forth. I asked her why dragons liked virgins in particular, and she posited that it must be some sort of magic.

So far, she has laughed off all of my strangeness as the ways of a city person, but I did not want to risk saying that dragons in stories love these things because they are what the storytellers value most. Those stories always seem to involve a human tricking a dragon out of its treasures, because the humans want to believe that they can win gold from larger and more dangerous beings through cleverness.

Instead, I asked Elitt what she values. At first, I thought she was changing the subject when she asked me about the outside world, but after some consideration I have decided otherwise. This place is isolated, and news is almost as valuable as currency. I have given her some small details of home, knowing that she would not know the difference between our cities and human ones. I fear that I am beginning to grow rather fond of her.

Day Eight — Entry One

There was a raid in the night. Several orcs came into camp while I slept after my watch, but it was hard to tell how many. In the dark, enemies seemed to be everywhere. I comported myself well enough in human form, but there were several injuries, and a fire was set at the edge of Reveda, which burned down a goat barn that had been emptied of its residents. The orcs are likely having a very nice goat breakfast as I write this.

Since then, there has been a great deal of argument; half of the Luvodans want to find the orc encampment and exact revenge, and the other half wish to bring the injured back to Luvoda for safety. I regret that I cannot register my opinion that the injured are more important than vengeance, but my responsibilities to the Council are more important than my opinions.

Day Eight — Entry Two

On the way to the encampment, walking while I write, so the Dracanmōt will excuse my penmanship. Human war songs have been transcribed. Many end in death of the heroic figure or total obliteration of the armies. I will have to learn more of these traditions, but I for one would like to hear of a happy ending or two.

Day Eight — Entry Three

I have been captured with a few humans, including Elitt, who has been injured. I fear that she will die if nothing is done, but my friend is of little importance when it is clear that we were tricked. The orc leader, Glaatch, was quite smug about the fact that we were chasing down a diversion. It is crucial that one of us escape and warn the townsfolk. It would be easy enough for me to do it, but I would compromise myself a second time, and possibly ruin our chances to continue study in this area. I know the rules of the Dracanmōt require me to remain hidden, but I am not sure whether that would be ethical, or if I could forgive myself if Elitt should die. Hard to write in these conditions.

Day Nine — Entry One

Early morning, and there is precious little light, so my penmanship will remain messy. Elitt has survived the night, but her leg injury still has not closed, and some bleeding continues. The other humans have told me that the wound needs stitching, or it will never heal. I think that cautery may help, but we have no access to fire as long as I remain in this form. It is likely that Reveda has already been raided. If not, the time is near.

Day Nine — Entry Two

Have spoken to Elitt. Told her there may be a way for me to get us out of here, but that our friendship would surely be at an end. She agrees that it is more important that the people of Luvoda and Reveda are safe. I have said my farewell. She stood to embrace me despite the fact that her leg must cause her pain. She smelled of burnished-copper pain and fear sweat, and she whispered that orcs are canny, and will try to test my plan in any way they can. She told me to keep to the plan, not even knowing what my plan is. Her trust in me is a light in dark times, and completely undeserved, as I have lied to her from the start. More reports to come if I survive.

To the esteemed members of the Dracanmōt,

I would like to begin by apologizing for my actions, but I will not express regret for them. I will explain them here and pass these pages to a courier to be delivered to Council of Human Study. After that, you will not hear from me again. It will become clear through this explanation that I am neither able to fulfill my duty to the Council or the Dracanmōt, nor am I inclined to do so.

I told the orcs guarding us that I knew of a cache of weapons hidden in Luvoda and would tell them where it was if they agreed to release me. They took me to Glaatch so that I could give her the location, but she was far less gullible than her compatriots. She took me back to the tent where I had been kept with the other Luvodans, meaning to hurt the others to determine whether I had told the truth.

Knowing that we were all concerned for Elitt, Glaatch singled her out to be tortured. It seemed to be the end of my plan, and I prepared to say the word to transform right there in the tent; there might be injuries if I did, but I was willing to gamble for Elitt's sake. Elitt and I met eyes, and she winked. She was telling me to stay to my plan. For the sake of everyone in Reveda, I did. I stood and I watched, and I am not ashamed to say that I prayed, that I wept.

I will not say what transpired in that tent save that Elitt managed to convince Glaatch that there was indeed a treasure in Luvoda. We were soon on the road, some of the other prisoners struggling to walk with their injuries. Elitt had to be carried by one of the orcs, her body hanging limp over his shoulder. I thought that my beautiful human friend had given all that she had. I had to be willing to do so, too, or her death would be for nothing.

I kept to the plan. I knew that was what she would have wanted me to do. Keep to the plan and keep Luvoda and Reveda safe. I fell behind, trying to play at fatigue. One of the orcs stopped, turning to tell me to hurry up with quite a few colorful curses. I assumed my true form, the orcs and humans growing small and frantic beneath my wingbeats. I thanked the Great Wyrm that the humans and the orcs ran in opposite directions.

I blew smoke at the orcs to confuse them, and most were easy to catch, frightened and rubbing their eyes in pain (they tasted exceedingly gamey, and I do not recommend a meal of orcs for any dragon you might choose to study humans when you receive this report). It was Glaatch who gave me trouble, smashing me in the wrist with her mace. I tried to crush her, tried to snort fire and smoke into her face, but she was persistent. Another orc, one I was sure I'd killed, stabbed me in the ankle, and I went down like a hamstrung deer. I snapped at her, but Glaatch danced away. The other orc stabbed me with its spear again, and I snapped, and he stabbed, and I snapped, until I was tired and could no longer fight. Glaatch raised her mace to bash my head in, but at least I had the comfort of knowing that I had helped save scores of human lives.

As I watched, steel budded in Glaatch's chest, and from it blossomed a glimmer of reflected sunlight. I had never seen anything more beautiful or horrible, and I likely never will again. Glaatch fell, and behind her stood Elitt. She pulled the spear from Glaatch's back and dispatched the other orc, then sat down next to me, falling into my side. Her tender human flesh felt strange and vulnerable against my feathers, and in the silence, I could hear her breathing. It was the best sound I have ever heard.

We have since returned to Luvoda, where the injured are now recovering. I believe that Elitt and all her friends would have died had I not taken matters into my own claws, and doing so sooner would have saved them suffering. I see now that conducting this study through deceit is unethical. I have accepted a better position, anyhow, and should you send another dragon to study the people of Luvoda, I will see them off with extreme prejudice. These are my people now.

Yours in flight and flame,
Usander Greystart

SPACEGIRL AND
THE MARTIAN

BY CORA RUSKIN

You know that bit in a superhero movie where the villain kidnaps the hero's girlfriend/high school sweetheart/everlasting love and puts her in grave peril to taunt said hero? I always thought it would be easy enough to avoid those situations, given the way I'm wired. But at this moment, my nemesis is dangling Josie from the bagel shop (who always gives me extra chilli sauce, and *possibly* remembers my name) from a height of about 300 metres.

Yep. Poor, sweet, generous-with-the-chilli-sauce Josie hangs in mid-air, directly above the icy, bacteria-infested waters of the Thames. She has stopped screaming now and drags air into her lungs with a horrible scraping sound. Her feet are still, like a character in a Tex Avery cartoon who hasn't looked down yet. The fact that gravity isn't working on Josie is nothing to do with her and everything to do with the woman whose hand is wrapped around the back of her neck.

The Martian.

I don't use her other name.

A black mask obscures the top half of her face so that only her eyes are visible, shining coldly like chips of ice. The skin of her face and hands is ruby-red. I don't know if it's some kind of greasepaint, or if she just happened to turn scarlet on a whim, or if she uses the blood of her enemies as foundation. I also don't know where the hell she gets her clothes from, because they make her look like a Disney villainess—all black and purple, with a long, swirling, impractical cape.

What I do know is that she has the same power as me. The ability to halt the effects of gravity is how I am able to swim up into the night sky. High above the pavements full of gawking, shouting onlookers. Above the buildings, above the skyscrapers, towards The Martian, whose vicious nails dig into Josie's neck. She doesn't have super-strength, as far as I know, but anything she touches becomes gravity-immune too, so Josie is weightless in her grasp. If she lets go ... My dinner becomes gravity-immune at this thought and threatens to come back up. I swallow and rise the last few metres until I'm level with Josie and The Martian.

"Good to see you, Spacegirl," she says, in a tone of voice that makes it obvious how stupid she thinks my name is. "I was just wondering, how long have we been doing this little dance?"

"If by *dance*, you mean one-sided psychological torture that puts the lives of innocent people at risk—" she tips her head back and laughs "—I'd say about five years."

Josie struggles to get her breathing under control. When she speaks, her voice shakes, and I've never felt a stronger urge to wrap her in a blanket and feed her biscuits.

"L-look, I don't know what's going on here, but it looks like I'm in the m-middle of something that's got nothing to do with me. So, if you just put me down *safely* on the ground, I w-won't call the police."

She doesn't recognise me. My face is obscured by a Zorro-style mask, (It is actually part of a Zorro fancy dress costume. Budget cuts, you know) and there must be any number of women with cropped, dark hair and blue eyes in this city. Besides, she's only ever seen me in my civilian uniform of jeans and tee-shirts, which is a world away from my superhero costume.

"You know how to end this," says The Martian, ignoring Josie. "Just hop the fence over to my side. The grass is much greener, trust me."

"No way in hell."

"Oh, come on, it'll be just like the old days."

96

Her voice is calm and coaxing, but this is when she's at her most dangerous. Balancing shiny, happy promises in one hand with violent death to everyone I care about in the other. I watch her eyes.

"No," I say, and let gravity take me down. I am falling because Josie is falling. I stretch my arm through the rushing air but can't reach her. If she hits the surface of the Thames at this speed, it might as well be made of concrete. She's screaming, or maybe I'm screaming, or maybe it's just the sound the air makes when you tear through it. She flings an arm out, and I grab it and switch the gravity back off. We are about a metre above the river.

We just hang there for a moment. Then I take her by the shoulders and swim through the air, dragging her over the river. I set her down on the bank and try to ascertain that she's okay-ish before people start crowding around, wanting to understand what just happened.

"You're not hurt, are you?"

"What the fuck?!"

"I'll take that as a no."

"Who the fuck are you?"

"Spacegirl. Do you have someone you can call? I just want to make sure you can get home safely."

She pulls a phone out of her jacket pocket, still staring at me like I didn't just save her life. Charming. "Hey, babe," she says into the phone. "Yeah, um, don't freak out, but … I think somebody spiked my drink." She's not even looking at me anymore. She's got the phone sandwiched between her shoulder and her ear and is looking down at her hands, which are shaking violently. People come towards us, crowding in on us. So, I switch off the gravity, and it's up, up and away.

My shift is over, so I head towards The Seven Stars—the local superhero watering hole. It's not exactly a *friendly* pub. Most superheroes are pretty cagey with their secret identities, so the emphasis is usually on drinking rather than getting to know each other. Still, there's comfort to be had in getting pissed in the company of people who are all in the same boat. I trudge through the back alleys, feeling conspicuous in my costume. I am in a thoroughly shitty mood.

When I first started out, I didn't think the loneliness would be a problem. I had no interest in relationships, anyway. I tried having a boyfriend once, but when he told me he was falling in love with me, I felt like peeling my skin off, and so I dumped him as kindly as I could and finally accepted I was aromantic. Close friendships were easy enough to avoid as well, since I keep unsociable hours, and I'm shy in a way that's often mistaken for stuck-up. So, it's not like I have a bestie, or a tight little circle of friends who could end up as collateral damage in the musty old superhero-supervillain conflict. But tonight has made things more difficult. Apparently, it's not enough to avoid friendships. Anyone who smiles at me or treats me like a real person is now at risk.

What's the point of it, anyway? Why not just say yes to The Martian? Be a supervillain. Avoid all this drama. Obviously, working with her would bring its own kind of drama, but still…

On the morning of my eighteenth birthday, when I woke up hovering half-way between my bed and the ceiling, I knew what to do because I'd watched enough movies. I was supposed to wear a catsuit and give myself a cool-sounding but non-threatening nickname, then use my superpower to rescue people.

That's what you're meant to do. Whatever you've got, you're supposed to use it for good. If you're one of the clever kids at school, you're supposed to study quietly, get good grades, keep your head down, and don't make anyone else feel stupid. Definitely don't make complex, evil plans about how you'll take over the world one day. Be a nice girl and people will like you. If people like you, you won't be alone.

God, the bullshit people feed us when we're young and impressionable. I storm into The Seven Stars and head over to the bar through an ocean of spandex-clad, work-weary bodies. Bernard is sitting in his usual spot, hunched over what is hopefully a beer, not a whisky. He drinks too much, but like many superheroes of a certain age, he's seen enough to give him pretty major PTSD, and alcohol is his way of keeping the shakes under control. I once tried suggesting therapy, but he said that's for rich people and millennials. I can't convince him otherwise on account of being a millennial (albeit a poor one), so I just let him do his own thing. He'll be okay. I hope.

"You're up," I say, tapping him on the shoulder.

"Greta!" He beams through his salt-and-pepper beard. He's drinking beer, but something tells me it isn't his first one. "You're just in time. I'm gonna prank call Mechaniman."

"Your shift is starting," I point out, tapping his watch.

"Are you forgetting I can manipulate time? I'll just turn the clock back in a bit."

"I wish I had your superpower."

"I wish I had your costume."

He pinches the stretchy fabric of my sleeve, and I wonder if he used to snap bra straps when he was a kid. I'm not all that keen on my costume. The fabric is nice (it's an inky blue-black with a swirling pattern of stars on it), but really, a catsuit only looks good on you if you're made out of silly putty. If you're an actual person, with lumps and bumps and bones, it's bound to be less than flattering. Still, looser clothing tends to get caught in things, much like long hair. Practicality is the name of the game when you're fighting crime and villainy.

"When are you actually going to get yourself a costume instead of fighting crime in corduroy trousers and a David Bowie tee-shirt? And when are you going to come up with a superhero name, for that matter? No offence but Bernard doesn't sound very heroic."

"Captain Bernard?"

"Lazy. And not good."

I order a large white wine, while Bernard dials Mechaniman's number and holds the phone up to his ear, waiting and grinning. After a few seconds, he mouths "voicemail", then speaks in a gravelly, Batman-ish voice.

"Mechaniman, this is Thomas from the High Council. We've been looking over your portfolio and are seriously considering offering you a position. Of course, we'll need to see a presentation, so if you could come to Headquarters first thing on Monday morning, that'd be great. Now, I'm a fan of your work so I'm going to give you a little tip. The council tends to respond best to presentations with *flair*. So, don't be afraid to really make an entrance and throw in a few fireworks. Not literal fireworks, of course. Unless you want to. Right then, I'll see you Monday, at 9am. Best of luck."

I shake my head at him as he hangs up. "Prank calls? Seriously? What's your deal with Mechaniman?"

Bernard takes a long drink of his beer, then wipes foam from his beard with the back of his wrist and says "Funding".

"Funding?"

"Funding. You know Mechaniman's loaded, right?"

"Yeah, I heard he's on the Forbes rich list. I mean, I don't know which guy on the list he is, but he's one of them, apparently."

"Well, my point is, he's a bloke with a metric fuckload of money and no superpowers. Now, imagine you've got that much money and zero superpower."

"I'll take that deal."

"What do you do? Do you use your obscene wealth to fund actual superheroes? Help the people who have the powers and skills to keep the world safe by giving them resources, training, stuff like that? Or do you waste money on a fancy, inspector-gadget style suit that doesn't even work properly in order to make *yourself* a superhero?"

Despite his bitterness and his grumpy old man shtick, Bernard is actually an incurable optimist. He thinks that Mechaniman's choice is between a good thing and a slightly less good thing. It doesn't even occur to him that Mechaniman could use his money for evil means.

"If I had a load of money and no superpower, I'd build myself a chocolate mansion," I say, honestly.

"It'd melt."

I sip my wine in silence for a moment. There's a question that's gnawing away at me, and Bernard doesn't look like he's planning on leaving the pub any time soon, so I might as well ask him. "Bernard, how do you think people become superheroes or supervillains?"

"Genetic abnormalities, lab accidents, radioactive spi—"

"No, I don't mean how do people get superpowers, I mean ... You get superpowers, and then you either go down the hero road or the villain road. So, what's the deciding factor?"

Bernard rests his hairy chin in his palm. "Interesting question. I suppose it all comes back to the nature/nurture debate. Are good and evil genetically pre-determined, or are they the result of our background and upbringing?"

I hate it when he answers a question with another question. "Which do you think?" I prompt.

"Honestly, I think it's a combination of both. Some people are naturally pre-disposed to anger, just like some people are naturally pre-disposed to be gentle or brave or whatever. But people are moulded by their upbringing too. You can't raise kids without morals and expect them to choose the right path when they're grown."

"But there must be more to it than that. I mean, what about families? They're genetically similar, at least, and they're living in the same environment, but every family has a black sheep."

"Growing up in the same family doesn't mean having the same experience of life. And we haven't even got onto the topic of free will and personal choice yet."

"Christ, I'm not drunk enough for that."

Bernard laughs his crackly laugh, then drains the dregs of his beer. "Get some rest, kiddo," he says, squeezing my shoulder. He leaves the pub, and I turn back to my wine.

By the time I leave The Seven Stars, I'm a little the worse for wear. I stumble tipsily through the backstreets, taking one wrong turn, then another one in a failed attempt to turn back. It's drizzling now, soft and cold. I pause, trying desperately to get my bearings.

Across the road, there is a pub. Lighted windows and noise. I gravitate towards the possibility of human contact, rather pathetically. The pub is called The Tipsy Crow, and the bird on the sign looks evil and wasted and makes me smile. I peer through the window and see a strangely familiar crowd. The clientele of The Tipsy Crow looks like the clientele of The Seven Stars would look in some kind of alternate universe. There are capes, but in dark colours rather than primary ones. There's a lot of unusual facial hair and ostentatious headgear. Slowly, so bloody slowly, it dawns on me. This is where the supervillains go to get pissed.

I could come back when I'm sober—with gasoline and matches—and burn this place to the ground. London would be a hell of a lot safer if I did that, but it scares me, how vivid this fantasy is. I close my eyes and hear everything, from the rasping strike of the match, to the last dying screams. When I open my eyes again, I see The Martian.

She is settling herself in an empty booth, not far from the window. She holds an indigo-coloured drink in one of those hipster-ish, jam jar glasses. As she sits down, she takes a swig of her drink, and it paints her lips purple. Then she takes off her mask, throwing it on the table like she's kicking off uncomfortable shoes.

With the mask gone, I can no longer pretend she's just The Martian. Because that's my face, stained red on the other side of the window. My blue eyes. My sharp, thin nose. My twin sister, Frieda. Frieda, who used to pull the legs off spiders when she was six, and hated the world and everything in it by the time she was twelve, and once broke a boy's nose because he called me a frigid bitch. My mind swirls with love and hate and fear and envy.

She turns towards the window and our eyes lock. It freezes us both–we are still as dolls. Everything seems heightened, somehow. Rain in my hair. Watery light cascading out of the window. I watch her stand and weave through the crowded pub. She comes outside and leans against the wall.

"Hey, sis," she says, grinning like the cat that got the canary.

"Hey."

"Want to come in, out of the rain?"

I imagine waltzing into The Tipsy Crow and decide that being beaten to death by a crowd of drunk supervillains is not a desirable way to go.

"Would you stop trying to kill me for five minutes? We're off the clock."

"I'm not promising anything, but I'll try," she says and swallows the dregs of her drink.

"Come for a walk with me."

"Why?"

"Why not?"

She shrugs and chucks the empty glass against the wall of the pub where it shatters loudly. We melt into the darkness before anyone comes outside to investigate the noise.

We walk in no particular direction, with no particular purpose. "Does this mean you're on my side now?" Frieda asks. Casual, like it doesn't really matter much whether I'm good or evil, but it would be more convenient for her if I were evil.

"Piss off," I say.

"Hey, I was only asking. So, did you get a cat? I remember you saying you were going to get a rescue cat."

"Yeah, his name's Domino. He thinks he's a dog, though. Always wants to play fetch."

It's about midnight when we find the mugger. At the entrance to a narrow alley that smells faintly of curry, I hear the sounds of a struggle and fling an arm out, stopping Frieda in her tracks. I peer into the gloom and see a tall but scrawny man in a hoodie, trying to pull a clutch bag from the grip of a woman in a pale pink dress. He's growling "Gimme the bag, bitch!" at her. She's telling him to fuck off and wrapping herself protectively around the clutch bag, obviously drunk enough to disregard personal safety. I have maybe three seconds before he punches her or smashes her head against the alley wall.

"Wait here," I hiss, and charge into the fray.

There is a large quantity of wine inside me, so I deal with the would-be mugger rather clumsily. I grab him by the waist and rise up into the air, dragging him with me. He gives a yelp of shock and releases the woman's clutch bag. But then he panics and starts kicking his legs, trying to get away. One of the kicks collides with the woman's face and she stumbles back against the wall of the alley, pressing a hand to her nose.

At the alley's entrance, Frieda watches the shambolic rescue unfold with an expression of mild interest. "Oi!" I yell at her, struggling to keep a tight grip on the wriggling criminal in my grasp. "Come here, and make yourself useful, would you?

I persuade Frieda to keep hold of the mugger, dangling him high in the air, while I float back down to the ground and check on the woman. Her nose is bleeding messily. Above us, the mugger shouts and swears in Frieda's grasp.

"Are you okay?" I ask the woman.

"I thick he broke by dose!"

Some cautious poking and prodding reveals that it isn't actually broken. But the poor girl is still bleeding all over her chin, so I help her rummage around in the clutch bag for a packet of tissues. She's almost done cleaning herself up when I hear a sharp cry, followed by a thump.

I whirl around and see the mugger lying on the ground in a crumpled heap. Above him, Frieda hovers with her arms folded. I shoot her a questioning look. "He called me the c-word," she says, almost primly. "He'll be fine, anyway. Nothing worse than a broken ankle."

We leave the mugger in the alley and help the woman into a taxi. "I'm hungry," Frieda announces, slamming the taxi door, and my stomach growls suddenly in agreement. This used to happen a lot when we were kids. We'd get hungry or thirsty or sleepy at the same time. Our minds might have been on two different planets, but our bodies were perfectly in sync.

We find the nearest McDonalds and order fries and chicken nuggets. Frieda demands extra ketchup and the server gives her six of the little packets without a second's hesitation. We eat (Frieda drowns every bite in ketchup) and reminisce about Happy Meals, back before they got ridiculous with their carrot sticks and apple slices and organic milk. You knew what you were getting, back then. Junk food was junk food. Healthy food was healthy food. Everything was simpler.

"Thanks for your help, back there," I say cautiously, licking salt off my fingertips. "Though dropping the guy was a bit unnecessary."

Frieda snorts. "Excuse me, who was responsible for that girl getting her face kicked in? You. And who made sure that guy will never try stealing another handbag? Me. That was my first time saving someone and I did a better job of it than you."

My guts twist in resentment, and I briefly remember those Maths tests in Year 8, when she always did better than me even though she never studied. But behind the jealousy, there is something like hope. She just took a step towards my side. Accidentally, and on her own terms, but that doesn't matter.

"I s'pose so," I say, in a grudging tone of voice. "Maybe you wouldn't make such a terrible superhero."

She frowns, her scarlet forehead wrinkling. "You do realise that guy's a junkie, right? He'll stop stealing handbags, but he'll have to score somehow. Maybe he'll try burglary. Or sucking dicks for cash, or something."

That fragile sense of hope shrivels up.

"Though, I guess sucking dicks for money wouldn't be so terrible," she continues, chewing meditatively on a French fry. "It's providing a service, at least. Wouldn't be my first career choice though. And that guy didn't look like he'd be any good at it."

I glare at her, jaw clenched. "What?" she says, eyes wide and innocent. "Look, it's not my fault that the world's broken. It's not my fault that you're trying to fix it with Blu Tack and string like a little kid."

"I'm a little kid? You dress up like bloody Maleficent from Sleeping Beauty and keep breaking things. Maybe the world's already broken, but you keep smashing it up into smaller and smaller pieces and then jumping up and down on the pieces and setting them on fire!"

I can feel my face heating up. It's probably almost as red as hers now. Frieda takes a long slurp of her milkshake, then says "Let's go and get some fresh air. You look like you need it."

The rain has stopped, and the night has a freshly-washed smell. We wander aimlessly, down residential streets lined with sensible cars and neat little front gardens and hanging baskets full of petunias, their colours muted in the dark.

"We should nick a car," Frieda says, trailing her fingers casually over a Nissan Micra. "We could drive out of the city and go wherever we fancy. Somewhere like the Scottish Highlands, or deepest darkest Wales. A wilderness-type place. We could get away from all this bullshit for a while, and just hang out." I can't see her face clearly, but her voice sounds wistful, like she really means it.

I start to wonder what it would be like if we went somewhere remote, where I wouldn't have to be Spacegirl and she wouldn't be The Martian. We'd just be Greta and Frieda again. Maybe it would be like that time when we were eight years old and went camping with Mum and Dad. Building campfires and toasting marshmallows together. Lying under a sky full of stars, snuggled up under a ratty, woodsmoke-scented blanket and trying to spook each other with ghost stories. Or maybe it would be like that time when we were thirteen and went hiking. Frieda took the map, then ran off while I was having a wee behind a bush. I got hopelessly lost and ended up spending a whole night in the forest, shivering and terrified. Perhaps the two of us have been on opposite sides for longer than I thought.

I'm so wrapped up in my own thoughts that it takes me a moment to notice that the Nissan Micra is floating about a metre above the ground. I stare at the car, then at Frieda who giggles. Frieda doesn't usually giggle–her laugh is too loud and sharp to be called a giggle–and I wonder how much she had to drink at The Tipsy Crow before I showed up.

"I have an idea," she says, floating up into the air and taking the car with her. "Let's stack up all the cars on the street on top of each other. We can make a big tower. It'll be like playing Jenga!"

"Why the hell would we do that?"

"Why the hell not?"

I can't help but laugh — it's the lingering effect of the wine. Also, the car looks absurd, floating in mid-air like a big, silvery balloon. My laugh comes out as a mad cackle, shattering the peace of the silent street.

Placing my hand on a nearby Toyota Yaris, I float it up into the air and manoeuvre it into position above the Nissan Micra, which Frieda has positioned above a Ford Focus. "Ready?" she says, suppressing another giggle. "Okay, let go!"

There is a groan of compressing metal, then two loud smashing sounds as the windshields of the Ford Focus and the Nisan Micra shatter, spraying glass over the road like sharp-edged confetti. Shit, I wasn't expecting that. I look at Frieda, expecting to see her grinning malevolently. But no, her smile is soft, and she's looking at me like she's proud of me. Like she loves me.

A couple of lights come on in the upstairs windows of the houses. I think of the owners of the cars trying to explain this to their insurance companies and of dogs cutting their paws on the broken glass and of someone else having to clean it all up. I grab Frieda by the arm, and we scarper.

By 3am, I am more than ready to sleep. Frieda and I are floating side by side in the sky, high above everything. The air has that sharp, pre-dawn chill, and I lean against Frieda, wrapping the edge of her cape around me and stealing some of the warmth from her body.

I'm not sure who won. It's hard to tell whether she's on my side or I'm on hers, or if we have somehow created our own side. I don't really care, right now, though I should. The fate of this city—hell, the fate of the world—could be at stake. But at the end of the day, I suspect I'm no different to anyone else. I always cared more about being loved than about anything else.

Frieda takes out a cigarette and lights it. She offers me one, but I just shake my head and watch the smoke curl away into the night. It joins the thicker smoke that billows up from The Tipsy Crow, which burns as brightly and cheerfully as a campfire below us.

WOULD YOU LIKE CHARMS WITH THAT?

BY E. H. TIMMS

My brain had been bugging me for a good half hour to run down and check the doorstep. I'd figured it was just my anxiety playing games again until I had to go down and open up for the day, but I unlocked the door and saw Kit hunched on the step, so, yeah, it had been prescience all along. Not the first time that'd happened. Sometimes it was hard to tell which channel of my brain—anxiety or prescience—was insisting I do something for some unrevealed reason. I'd learned to roll with the ones I could do and let the ones I couldn't yammer. Most of the time, at least.

I braced myself for whatever had brought him here this early in the day. Callie and I were the closest thing Kit had to a set of parents. The kid had hung out around the shop on and off for years since he'd been kicked out of his birth home for being queer. Not so much of a kid any more actually, more the age of the youngest adventurers who came into the shop for their first swords and scrolls.

He looked up at me and got quickly to his feet. "Robin! Hi…" It wasn't much of a challenge to guess what he needed. He'd been grieving a breakup with his closest friend and once-roommate for months. Sometimes he leaned on his cuddle-friend Jenny for comfort—though that'd been harder, I understood, since he'd started couch-surfing there—and sometimes, on us. I sighed and opened my arms in wordless consent. He flung himself into them and buried his face in my shoulder. His words were half-muffled. "Is breaking up with a friend always this hard?"

"Yeah, mostly." I drew him inside out of the drizzling rain and closed the door. "Is this about the usual one or a new one?"

"Usual."

"Want to talk about it?"

He pulled away long enough to shake his head. "I'd rather have a distraction. And a bed for the night."

"Something wrong at Jenny's?"

"She wants my bed for her main partner. The long distance one. Tonight and maybe tomorrow."

"All right." I reached out a long arm and retrieved the feather duster. "Dust the weapons off, would you? And the armour? We still have a shop to run."

Upstairs, Callie took one look at Kit, checked the teapot, and reached for a third mug. I slid into my usual chair—built to fit my width—and reached for the nut butter. "Kit's hoping for a bed tonight, too," I told her, slathering my doorstep of dark bread and taking a bite.

"As long as you're all right with a bed roll on the floor, we can manage that," Callie told Kit, as she brought the mugs of tea to the table and settled to her own breakfast. "Have you eaten?"

Kit nodded and cradled the hot mug close to his face. "That much I managed."

I slid the nut butter along to Callie, and she grinned and began slathering her own doorstep.

We're an odd pairing, Callie and I—she with her slender wiriness and lack of height, and my almost dwarven proportions, if dwarves grew to be six foot two. Adventurers hear that we're a mage and warrior pairing or guess it from the "Fire and the Sword" name of the shop. Then they look at us and assume that I'm the warrior, and she's the mage. It's actually the other way around.

Kit sat there and watched us, and I could feel an unasked question itching at me. I raised my eyebrows over the rim of my own cup.

He darkened and put his cup down for a moment. His thumb darted up and down the handle in a self-soothing pattern. "You taught me that there are words for what we are." He pronounced them carefully, still holding onto a touch of the cascading, eye-opening joy that discovering the right label brought, "Aromantic. Asexual. That it varies from person to person. And that relationships don't have to be built with romance as a foundation. I just wondered… I mean, you're so close? How do you get there with someone?"

"Long story," I told him.

"*Very* long story," Callie corrected with a wry smile.

She raised an eyebrow at me in turn, invoking the old double check. We'd got into the habit of checking in with my prescience before launching into anything major when we were still taking on adventuring jobs after I'd convinced myself it was just anxiety one time and been wrong. That crossing had dumped us in a whole stinking mess, and neither of us wanted to make that mistake a second time. Which was why it was a double check. If I couldn't tell prescience from anxiety all the time, why force through something against a major bout of it unless we absolutely needed to? I consulted my brain. For once it wasn't yammering on either of the main channels—for a moment, at least, because of course the moment I realised that, anxiety shot out of bed with a yelp and flailed for something to latch onto. I shrugged minutely and took a bite of bread, using the rhythm of chewing as my own self-soothing pattern. "Prescience for his being here, nothing else either way."

"And if we tell him some of it? The better bits?"

Anxiety jittered at first but was soothed by the limitation to the better bits. Prescience, on the other hand, opened an eye and fairly purred in satisfaction. Callie must have read my response off my face. Her smile widened. "Bits it is then. Between customers, of course."

Callie liked her outfits to be both pretty and functional, and now that the shop was doing better, she got to indulge. A little, at least, like the leather armour she wore in today. Tooled leather boots, armoured skirt in blue and silver (blue leather, silvery steel) and a boiled-leather bodice over a blue shirt (embroidered with tiny white flowers). As she said, it's the cut and shape that mattered for moving and fighting, not the colour or the decorations. I liked trousers better than skirts, but my crimson tunic had a subtle woven pattern of feathers, like the bird I was named for. Plain white shirt under it, grey trousers and boots tooled with lightning bolts down the outside.

Downstairs, she leaned on the counter, Kit leaned against the wall, and I lounged on a bench with my legs sticking out.

Knife-hilts gleamed in Callie's bun like hair-decorations. Their steel almost matched the silver at the roots of her hair. Colour-change cantrips made a half decent hair dye, if you're patient, but there wasn't much they could do for the lines on both our faces.

Kit asked tentatively, "How did you meet?"

I kept my voice carefully light. "Oh, we grew up next door to each other."

I was barely five when she moved in. She was almost six. My mother introduced me as, "This is Robin, she's just your age, dearie. Why don't you play together while the grown-ups move furniture?" Then my mother vanished, as always.

Callie clapped her hands together. "I didn't know there were any girls my age here!"

"I'm not a girl." My voice came out stubborn, somewhere between tears and resignation. "I'm a kid who uses she."

Brittle, frozen, silence filled the two paces between us.

Then she shattered it by clapping her hands together. "I didn't know there were any kids my age here! What shall we play?"

To Kit, I went on, "After I finished my training, I was looking for somewhere to live, and she had an advert up for a room-mate."

Callie laughed. "I didn't realise Robin was the kid-next-door until after I approved her application."

"Sounds like something out of a bard's tale!"

"Sure," Callie agreed, "except the bards would mess up and get romance all over it."

We were saved from going further down that path by a customer pushing open the door. He was human, and brown, and familiar. One of our regular customers, Joe Wood by name.

He nodded to me and joined Callie at the counter. "Nipper says he got your note about his new shoes?" he said, referring to his sentient pony friend.

I reached up to the order shelf, found the package of horseshoes marked with Nipper's name and set it on the counter. "They arrived yesterday and this time none of them were missing. They're supposed to fit themselves to the hoof, but he might want to get a farrier to check them anyway. Better safe than sorry."

"Thanks. Hopefully we'll be able to get them fitted before we take the next batch of youngsters out on the road." Joe heaved a bag of coins onto the counter and all four of us bent to count out the correct sum.

I grinned as we got the last of them into place. "Thanks for that, and best of luck with the youngsters."

Joe pulled a face. "Thanks, we'll need it."

Kit looked at the door closing behind Joe. "Don't they know either he or Nipper could take on the entire party single-handed and come out on top?"

"Their parents do, and they pay Joe extra to make sure their little darlings get safely to the next town without bruising the kids' egos too badly," Callie explained.

"A lot of young adventurers have giant egos and fragile hides. They don't take criticism too well. That's why they 'run off' or 'leave home' in the first place."

"We certainly did."

Kit gaped at me, eyes wide. "You did?"

"Not the way you had to, but, yes. We were young and foolish adventurers once."

Callie chuckled. "Those were the days—luckily we survived them."

A medley of scenes flickered through my mind.

The time, very early in our career, when she was checking one pile of rubbish, and I was checking another on the far side of a cavern. I had a sudden feeling I ought to ask her if she'd found anything and turned just in time to see an enormous spider lowering itself towards her back. All I could do was yell her name and hurl a dart of magic. The dart hit and knocked the spider sideways so it hit the floor. Callie whipped her swords out and skewered it before it could try anything more.

The time when Callie managed to duck through a gap in the massed webs, as did our two companions, but when I tried to follow, last of all, I got stuck in the web. It brought the swarm of spiders out of hiding, and Callie came back to cut me out once they'd taken out all the spiders. We carted home the body of the companion who died of a poisonous spider-bite.

The time when the bandits surrounded me, and Callie came

running at full glorious charge, red hair streaming out behind her. Firelight glittering off blood-streaked swords. Then she was through the circle of them, and we were back to back, trusting each other, making a new inner circle of her blades and my staff.

The time when the dragon we'd been hired to deal with turned out to be bigger, older, and stronger than anyone had told us. I flung a mage net to slow it. Then we dropped our pride and our egos and ran for it, legs burning, lungs burning, too frightened to stop. And the look on her face when we finally reached safety, and she told me, "I am never doubting your prescience again."

"We became shoulder friends," I said carefully. Alarms jangled through my head at random, set off by the memories. "Decided we liked each other's company and stuck around. And here we are."

Callie left the counter and joined me on the bench. Our shoulders just touched. A comfort touch for both of us. "Home," she murmured, and I caught the aftershock of memories in her eyes too. "We made it."

I laid my hand over hers. An open hand, because right now I knew all too well that a grasping hand—anything that closed around her really—could set off her fight reflexes to get free. "All the way to the shop."

Kit shuffled over to the bench too, and I tucked in and made space for him on the side away from Callie. Better that than risking him getting hit by Callie's reflexes. "Shoulder friends?" he asked.

"Shoulder friends are the people you trust to stand at your shoulder or guard your back," I told him, buying time for Callie to recover. "Did I ever you tell the story about the dancing fountain?"

"No! Did it really dance, or was it just a metaphor?"

"It really danced—the fountain was actually run by a water sprite. Xie had a dozen or more rock blowholes to shoot fountains up through and thought we wouldn't be able to guess which one it would come through next. We wanted to come past, but xie challenged us to catch xer water first as xie sent it up randomly through one hole or another."

"And did you?"

"It took a few tries," I told him. The first spout had splashed me, but I hadn't caught any in my hands. In the end I'd closed my eyes and let my prescience take over, moving as it wanted me to. "Water suddenly shooting up left, right and behind you is just a little distracting." I felt Callie's tension ebbing and continued lightly, "Xie wasn't exactly pleased about losing xer challenge. Thought it was a washout." The little sprite had brought the water up virtually under my feet and drenched me.

Callie chuckled, almost light enough that I believed it. "You looked like a drowned cat."

Not long after I finished the tale, the door opened and a pair of dwarves came in, one old and one young. I narrowed my eyes to try and pick out the pronoun markers braided in their beards. Dwarvish languages don't generally have gendered pronouns, but most dwarves pick a pronoun to use in more gendered languages as part of their coming of age. Used to be that all of them defaulted to "he/him" whatever their actual gender, but in more recent years they'd branched out. I liked that dwarves didn't see pronouns and assume gender. They stuck to gender neutral terms, and if you were wise, you did too when you were dealing with them.

Sure enough, the older one had he/him markers braided in his silver beard. The younger one still wore the unchosen/undecided markers of a pre-coming of age ceremony in a glorious (if short) red beard.

The older one looked from me to Callie and back again, with only a glance at Kit. I saw the recognition of Callie's armour spark in his eyes, and he chose to approach her. "My grandchild here wishes to choose a first axe, and I wish to support the decision and purchase the axe," he informed Callie in a rich alto rumble.

Callie bowed slightly. "I am honoured that you chose our shop. If the young warrior would like to step this way..." She led the pair over to the racked axes, and I went the other way to prepare the testing pells. We had two—one six feet tall, and one three feet tall—with arms in proportion. The younger dwarf was almost three feet square, the older almost a foot taller and broader. I brought both pells out into open floorspace. I'd learned over the years of shopkeeping that some customers liked a pell close to their own height; others preferred variety. Kit came over to help me, leaving Callie to discuss the relative merits of single-headed versus double-headed axes with the dwarves.

Or with the younger one anyway. I felt the tingle of being watched and looked up to see the older dwarf gazing at Kit and me.

He murmured, "Is this your child?"

Kit stepped forward and bowed before I could reply. "She is my honoured elder," he said, "but we are heart-kith, rather than blood-kin."

I rested my hand on his shoulder in thanks, caught for a moment without words for the complex mix of pleasure and anxiety that I felt at his statement.

The dwarf considered that for an endless moment, then returned Kit's bow. "You have an excellent elder."

My gaze locked with the old dwarf's for a long moment, and we both smiled, recognising kindred spirits. Then the younger dwarf bounced over with an axe to try out. I broke the locked gaze and stepped clear of the pells.

Finally, when the pair had chosen, paid, and departed, we pushed the pells back into their usual place and retreated to the bench again.

Callie picked up the thread of the tale by saying, "Once we'd had enough of adventuring, we pooled our resources, bought the shop, and moved into the flat above it."

"As simple as that?" Kit looked disappointed.

"Oh, it has its ups and downs, like all things."

I quipped lightly, "And that's just the stairs between the shop and the flat."

Kit laughed.

Callie grinned and flicked my arm with a finger—it was a very old joke for us.

"And here I thought it was getting up early and not crawling down into bed until late!"

I chuckled. "That too." There hadn't been much left after we stocked the shop, and dragons were easier to defeat than poverty. Furniture for the flat came a long way behind furnishing the shop. Other people saw the shop. Only we saw the flat. It had been bedrolls on the floor for both of us and whatever food was cheapest.

One time I came up after locking up the shop to find Callie crying quietly in the dark. I muttered a cantrip that set a dim light floating in the air and crossed the bare room to join her huddled on our bedrolls. "What's up?"

"Sky's up," she sniffed and leaned into my side.

I sighed and dug in my pockets for a handkerchief. "OK. What are we eating today?"

She took it and blew her nose. "We've got pease pudding left from yesterday. Pease pudding cold. No firewood left." She sighed in her turn, her breath warm against my neck. "Robin, I'm *so tired* of peas. And because of the firewood, we can't even have toast, or tea, and my monthly cramps turned up and..." The words dissolved into tears again, and all I could do was hold her and let her weep herself out on my shoulder.

These days, we could afford fresh bread most of the time, instead of stale day-old bread that had to be toasted. The first time we'd scraped up the coin for some (as Callie's birthday gift actually), we'd inhaled that fresh-bread smell like we could hang onto it forever. It's fun—or at least 'an adventure'—to sleep in bedrolls on the floor and eat scant food for a few days when you know there's an end to it. It's much less so with no end in sight.

"We had our advantages though," Callie pointed out. "We know each other. We trust each other. We already knew how to work together to get things done, and we enjoy each other's company."

"It takes time to get that close to someone," I put in, not joking this time, "but it's worth it. Your partner is going to be there come good days and bad. If you don't like that they're there, why are you with them?" I left it unsaid that we also knew each other's pain points. The mental bruises and scars that you warned for, covered for, or worked around, as appropriate. That trusting Callie also meant believing her when she said she needed something—and also when she said she was OK. It meant asking and offering and not expecting old wounds to vanish overnight. And holding each other in the ways that made your partner feel safe. Which for me meant that I always left a route for Callie to bolt, and I didn't take offence when she used it. She almost never did use it, she just needed it to be there. And it also meant that I got to be held and listened to, instead of being the person everyone else leans on for support without ever having space to lean on someone else.

Kit sighed. "But I didn't grow up with anyone. Does that mean I'm never going to be close enough?"

Callie shook her head and offered an arm. Kit leaned his head on her shoulder, and she held him for a long moment. "Most folk don't pair up with the kid next door. They get to know each other as adults. Like you and Jenny."

I added, "Not everyone wants a partner. Some people like being on their own, and that's fine too. Don't feel you have to pair up just because all the bards go gooey over it."

Kit mimicked gagging. "If I wanted sweet and gooey, I'd buy a jar of honey."

"So, what do you want?" I asked.

Kit considered that, staring up at the ceiling. "I want something more substantial. Solid. Lasting. I want someone I can lean on in hard times and celebrate with in good times. I want someone who accepts me as I am—accepts all of me as I am, ace, and aro—all my queerness together, without picking the bits they want and the bits they don't."

"Sounds like you need a shoulder friend first and foremost," Callie suggested. "If you're shoulder friends, you can get through almost anything, and sometimes it shifts over to a partnership as well. You'll find someone, if you want someone."

I sensed rather than saw movement outside our door. "Customers coming, I believe."

Callie stiffened. "Thanks for the warning."

Kit jerked upright out of the circle of Callie's arm, and all three of us slapped business expressions onto our faces. A breath later, we were ready, just in time.

In the Summer a Banana Tree

BY THOMAS SHAW LEONARD

Imagine the banana tree,
  swaying in the corner of the garden,
  leaves sprouting, hands opening
  outwards, in reach of embrace.

Now picture the mound,
  from which has sprung green,
  upwards into the sky, a body
  growing from its patted earth.

I know that here was once a friend,
  that I can now only call departed,
  a turning from the grieving of flesh
  into the departure of bloom.

I recall the canopy and shade,
  and remember the distant barking,
  the trampled grass and paw marks,
  a begging of eyes for a final gesture.

Perhaps the difficulty of goodbye
  lies in the inability to speak of moments,
  that all that remains are remains of memory
  and seeds of time grown into banana hearts.

And in the morning sunlight,
  I will picture you basking in the corner,
  your head in my father's lap, paws on his legs
  while I hold back the urge to call your name.

REMEMBERING THE FARM

BY THOMAS SHAW LEONARD

Here in the sunlight the scenery dissolves
into a man amongst dried up fruits, a cluster
of apples, overripe pears, and berries
from a farm across the sea, closed down
years ago.

Here I imagine you sweeping a chimney,
picture ash floating in columns of grey,
vanishing into the seamless skies
of Hersham enduring a season
only you know.

All these things I can only dream. Wallpaper
yellow and crumbling, shattered teacups,
broken plates, scattered glass. The irony
of a home I envision as broken,
a farmhouse grown destitute in longing.

I have never visited. Maybe a signpost
now lingers, a whisper of foreclosure,
wood rotting alongside the sign's
insides. Maybe the illusion remains simply
an illusion.

Perhaps this has always been the story
of my father. A traveling of distance,
a click between phone call to receiver,
a voice that echoes through memory
before returning to a home not mine.

Before the image disappears, I continue
forward, stepping over remains,
over broken fences, turned-over wheelbarrows,
parts that remain in place
of the whole.

Here I will point at the pitchfork
by the gate. I see you in overalls,
tossing hay under the sunlight. Alone,
I recall your story of the fruit market,
smiling at the image of abundance.

In returning to the Autumn that preludes
Winter, you return to me, a man
before departure, before parting
with the first of his families
to be left behind.

FISHING OVER THE BONES OF THE DRAGON

BY JEFF REYNOLDS

We took the boat out at dawn, like we had the last time we went fishing, over a century ago.

Father rowed us to a spot he loved beneath an immense, ancient sycamore that leaned over the water so that the branches formed a bower. It felt like a cathedral of green above our heads. The air here remained still, even when the weather on the lake raged and stormed. I'd always smelled something like the scent of winter, or heartbreak, here under the old tree. That had been when I was young. Now I knew the truth of those scents, and the air under the sycamore smelled like loam and mold and sap, nothing more.

Father dropped the anchor into the lake, disturbing the smooth surface. When the ripples stilled, I looked down through the glassy water. The dragon lay there as she had since he'd first brought me here, her bones bleached white as though she'd died in the desert and been stripped clean by years of sand-driven wind and sunlight. No silt clung to those bones, no weeds grew from them, as though the lake kept her clean to maintain her dignity in death. Fish darted through gaps in the skeleton, drawing on the remaining vestige of her fearsome reputation to protect them from dangers that swam out beyond the sycamore branches.

I reached for my pole and he his. I used a lure beat from a scrap of tin, painted with yellow and red spots. My father used worms he'd dug up in the back yard yesterday, kept under the middle seat in a brown, ceramic jar. He hadn't complained when I told him I didn't want to use worms. He didn't ask me to explain why I couldn't bring myself to kill anything, not even a worm. He'd just nodded and taken the spade from the shed and left me standing there watching as he went to work.

I dropped my lure in first with a short cast. I let it sink for a few seconds, then turned the reel, pulling it back towards the boat. I heard the plunk of his hook entering the water, glanced over to see the wooden bobber floating on the surface. He didn't use a reel, preferring to cast and doze while waiting for a bite.

"Fine day for it," he said. "Should start raining in a bit. Make them more active."

I nodded in reply. Didn't say anything. That was the most he'd said to me since I'd come home a few days before. A year and a day gone, and we'd barely talked at all.

He'd stood there, passive, staring at me. Mother had been aflutter, holding my shoulders as her eyes roamed over me as she searched for some change, some indication that a year of absence had altered her son, though I looked exactly as I had when I'd been taken. There was no time in the other place, no sense of growth or change. I left at eighteen, returned at nineteen, but I was the same physically despite the passage of a year and a day.

A year and a day for them. A century and a day for me. No, I wasn't the same, not in my head. My thoughts were different.

"What did they do to you," she'd said, hugging me. I felt the damp of her tears through my shirt, and I flinched from her as she brushed my hair away from my eyes. "What did they do to my boy?"

"Nothing," I said. "Nothing at all, mother, I'm fine."

Not true. They'd done everything to me.

"Oh, my sweet boy," she had said. She pressed her hands to my cheeks and pulled my head down to her, kissed my forehead, crying the whole time. I pulled her hands away, tried to be gentle, but I saw the pain in her eyes when I left her standing in the kitchen and went up the stairs to my room. My unchanged room, the same as it had been when I turned eighteen. The same as when I'd lain my head down on the pillow sometime after eleven that night and fallen asleep, exhausted from a day of work, and woke in another world. Two days ago had been my nineteenth birthday, or my hundred-and-nineteenth birthday. Perspective made it both things.

I lay my head on my pillow and listened to her weeping. Heard my father speaking as he tried to comfort her.

"He'll be fine," father said.

"He's not fine," she'd said, and the words were sharp enough to cut your heart out. "No more than you were." She went to their bedroom after that, slamming the door shut, and I suppose she cried herself to sleep. Coming home is every bit as hard as leaving.

They come for you when you're asleep. They never take someone who is awake. Their world lies beyond dreams and nightmares, and so they come when you are dreaming, and they pull you through the rainbow doorway when you can't resist. Why would you resist? They offer you your heart's desires. Friendship. Love. Lust. Vengeance. Pain. Death. Life. It's a dream, you think, and it's such a pretty doorway. Nothing can happen to you there.

You are wrong of course. Everything can happen to you there, because it is not a dream. Dreams are the doorway, not the ending, and there is no waking up to laugh at the strange visions created by your mind when you're asleep. This is the real you, brought here along with the dreaming you, and whatever dream you were having becomes the nightmare you hoped to avoid.

But this nightmare is truth.

The lure came out of the water and I cast again, a little further this time. Beyond the wall of branches, the sizzle of rain began, but under the sycamore it was dry, still.

"Caught some good pike here last summer," Father said.

I nodded. I forgot to turn the reel, so the lure dropped down and brushed against the bones of the dragon's wings, coming to rest on one vestigial fingertip. We sat there like that for what felt like a year and a day. I stared at the bleached bones below, and he watched his bobber, sometimes giving his pole a jerk if he felt a nibble.

"Was it her?" he said, when I'd begun to think we'd never speak again, not for a lifetime of fishing trips.

"Who?" I asked. But I knew the 'her' he meant without him having to explain. It struck my core that he knew her, too.

He sat quietly for a while, as though I hadn't asked a question. I turned away from my examination of the dragon's bones and studied his back. He wore a worn wool shirt, the same he always wore when fishing, the red color faded from years of washings. His brown cap slouched forward on his head so I could see the close-cropped hairs in back. I didn't recall his hair being speckled with gray; it had always been dark black, like coal.

When he spoke again, his voice rumbled through his chest, pitched low, the words soft. "The woman with the green eyes."

Her court is full of people, each beautiful in their own way. Sometimes a pure beauty that brings instant love and devotion; sometimes the beauty of ugliness, and feelings of compassion and sympathy; sometimes the beauty of fear, full of repulsion and the trembling of your body as though it wishes to flee but cannot.

But she is the most beautiful of all, beautiful and ugly and terrifying. She sits upon her basalt throne, on a dais overlooking the ballroom, waited on by her many and varied attendants. Her hair is the color of your blood, and her eyes emeralds, the pure green of spring, visible even this far away from her throne. And when those eyes meet yours, your body comes alive. It's as though she strips you naked, sees beyond the clothing that covers you, the goosebumps that prickle your flesh, the warmth of your blood surging through your body. Sees inside you, for what you really are.

Sees your beauty. And she craves it.

Something nibbled and he yanked the line. "Small one," he said, pulling it in, the line moving in circling jerks. He lifted a small, silver fish out of the water, and it wriggled on the end of the hook, maybe five inches in length. Its belly scales flashed yellow as he took it behind the gills and gently worked the iron hook from its mouth.

"Back you go," he said. He leaned over the side of the boat and held it at below the surface of the water, letting it catch its breath. It lay there for a few seconds, then jerked. With a slash of its tail, it shot towards the bottom. I watched it move beneath the collar bone of the dragon and disappear.

My father reached for his jar and fished out another worm. "Was it her?" he asked again, as he slid the wriggling, dirty thing onto the empty hook.

I didn't want to answer, so I looked away. There could be only one reason he knew about her, and I didn't want to think about that. No one talked about it, not openly. You could only know if you'd been there. It was as if to talk about it was to curse the person who heard and they would be taken next, so everyone locked it up and kept it buried deep inside. Maybe there was some enchantment that kept you from talking about it to those who'd never been. I'd never thought that two who had been taken could discuss it, and it felt wrong to me, the way a snowfall felt wrong in the middle of June. A violation of the natural order.

A warm flush crept up my body, churning through my stomach and chest. My cheeks would be red soon. I let silence be my answer as I reeled in my line, and I suppose that was enough of a reply for him. We never were men of many words.

"I remember her," he said. Then he turned away and cast his line again, the bobber hitting the water with a soft plop.

At first it doesn't seem so bad. There are balls and dancing every night, food and drinks that never stop flowing, yet you're never full, never tired. You dance with the perfect people, some of whom you know are like you, taken from their beds and brought here for a time. No one says they are from the waking world, but you feel them in the crowd, the presence of those who Do Not Belong. It is a comfort to not be alone, enough to know they are there. It helps quell the ache of being separated from your family, those for whom love is a blessing, not a craving.

When the hours grow late, you find yourself alone in the crowd with her, the red-haired queen whose green eyes strip you bare. She takes your hand and guides you to the middle of the floor, and in front of everyone you dance. Your feet are light as you move in an open circle made by the audience as they pull back, the light only upon the two of you, everyone else in shadow. Faster and faster, her laughter slipping inside you head, intoxicating you. Your clothing slips off, as does hers, and soon you find yourself in a tumult of bodies, flesh surrounding you. You've lost track of the queen, but it doesn't matter, there's more than enough other lovers to go around. Other women to explore, soft and warm; other men who kiss you urgently, pressing their erections against you. You open yourself to all of them and let them take what they may from you, and for a time—days, weeks, months—you revel in the newness of it all. You are full with living in this dreamland, in ways you never were when you lived in the real world. You fall asleep each night sweaty, tangled with their bodies, surrounded by lust, thinking that this, at last, is what it means to be loved.

Then you wake, and you're bathed by attendants of the queen, and you're dressed, and you're taken to a festival, or a ceremony, or a carnival, or a parade, or on a great hunt for a white stag in the dark woods. And the days wear on, and the nights are infinite, and you repeat this again, and again, and again. Until the food no longer tastes like sweetness upon your tongue, but like ashes from the burnt remnants of a forest. The drink no longer slips down your throat like cool, clear water, but chokes you like the warm blood of slaughtered lamb. The sighs of your lovers no longer arouse you, but disgust you.

And you do this every day, over and over, for a hundred years.

I wanted to say something, but I didn't. I couldn't. My father and

I never talked about feelings, or school, or work, or emotions. He came home from the lumber mill late every day and ate his supper quietly. Every night he fell asleep in front of the fire with a book in his lap. The novels were always comedic, always something that made him laugh in that deep, throaty way that rumbled through the living room. He'd never been abusive, or mean, or scolding, or sad, or anything at all to me. He was the big, quiet man who lived in our house and left me to find my own way. I didn't know how to talk to him now.

I cast again, reeling the line in slowly. He watched his bobber and reached inside the basket he'd brought for a sandwich. Egg on coarse, brown bread, fried up this morning in a skillet full of butter. He'd made one for me as well if I was hungry.

He caught another perch, bigger than the first, and released it. They were going for the worms instead of the lure, but I couldn't bring myself to switch. I didn't want to kill one thing to lure another to its death, didn't care if I caught nothing today. I cast harder this time, the line singing as the lure traveled almost to the shroud of sycamore branches where they brushed against the water.

You've lost track of time when you witness your first death. A man brought forth in chains during a ball, dirty and naked but for the cold iron on his wrists and ankles. His hair hangs in limp tangles over his face, and he seems diminished somehow. He is forced to his knees before the queen. She leans over him, smiling, and tilts his chin up to give him one last, lingering kiss that leaves him breathless. Then a flick of her finger and one of the many beautiful people steps behind him and takes off his head.

You never knew a body had that much blood in it. It repulses you, so that you take a step back, turned your face away. But you assumed he must be guilty of some great crime or sin, and this was their way. You'd grow used to it, you decided.

Similar scenes play out from time to time so that you do, indeed, grow used to them. There were challenges that led to duels. Arguments that led to stabbings. Once, a woman made jealous when another slept with her favorite lover slays her rival while on a hunt, with a bow made from a yew sapling. You stand near the woman when the willowy green arrow appeared as if by magic in her chest. She slumps into your arms and coughs blood onto your clean, white shirt as you hold her, staining it red for the rest of the day. You only get fresh clothing in the mornings, so you are forced to wear the scent of her death until you retire to your bed.

The queen arranges spectacles where armies of men and woman fight with spears and swords and bows and all manner of weapons and even their bare hands until one last blood-stained participant remains. When she tires of hunting stags, she organizes hunts for people she has decided will play the role of prey. After a few years, you realize everyone is her prey. And she makes everyone hunt them. Even you have to kill to amuse her. So, you do, because what choice do you have? Because this is only a dream.

But the deaths aren't the worst part, nor having to kill. You can't die in a dream; you can only wake up from it and shiver in terror in your bed, wipe the sweat from your forehead. No, here the worst part is that they return the next night to dance and eat and drink and fuck. They don't wake from the dream but keep living it. And they remember what was done to them. Every second of pain is etched on the false smiles they press into their cheeks, in the hollows of their empty eyes.

And you, too, die to amuse her. She cuts off your head, tortures you, drowns you, burns you. And every time you die, you wake again in her world and start another day remembering your death, or your many deaths.

One day, you wake and realize the only thing left of you is despair.

The rain stopped. At the edge of the sycamore, water dripped off the leaves into the lake, an irregular patter that diminished with time. I felt the air warm as the clouds moved on and the sun came out again, though under the bower it remained cooler and darker than out on the lake.

"One last cast," father said. "Your mother will worry."

I nodded and sent the lure zinging over the glassy surface of the water. It fell into the lake with a single ripple. When I turned the reel, it flashed beneath the surface, twisting to shatter the twilight below the branches.

"I'm sorry," father said, unexpectedly.

He wasn't looking at me, but I felt him nonetheless. The space between us grew empty and huge, and there came a need for me to fill it with words. To say something, anything, to take away the guilt. I wanted to resist. This was my pain, not his, he had no right to assume it. It was my place to find a way to move forward, as I had every day for a hundred years. But his guilt drove mine, made me feel as though I'd let him down in some way. That by not responding, I would hurt him.

"It wasn't your fault," I said.

The tension eased a little. He nodded. Then his great shoulders heaved with a sigh and he settled, slumping like a piece of paper folding down onto itself. "I should have told you what happened to me. I let it define me for so long, kept it hidden away. Maybe I could have helped you somehow. Be more ready for it, maybe. If it happened." He shrugged.

"It wasn't your fault," I repeated. "Who they take, it's no one's fault."

Now he turned to me. No expression at all beyond the sad eyes. "Remember that," he said. "It'll keep you going when you can't stop remembering what she did."

My line jerked. His eyes shifted to the water and now his grin came, slow, like dawn breaking. "Wake up, boy, I think you've got one."

"I'm not a boy," I said, reflexively. I winced at the harshness. A century of living in a nightmare makes you less good-natured.

He laughed, though, unoffended by my comment. "True," he agreed. "But I'm still older than you."

The pole jerked in my hand and the line hissed as it ran out. I jerked the pole hard, setting the hook. Whatever I'd caught, it was fast and heavy, surging right and left as I pressed the thimble on my thumb against the unspooling line of catgut to slow down its attempt to break free.

"Don't let it bottom," father said. "If it gets under her bones, you'll lose it." He turned to face me, but stayed in his seat. Long ago he would have come over and helped me with the pole, guided me. Now he rested big hands on his knees, leaned forward, and watched me work for the catch. He'd let me decide if I needed his help. But his eyes sparkled with excitement.

People come and go. A hundred years goes by in a flicker of a candle, and a hundred years feels like forever. But when their century is up, the queen returns them to their bed chambers and new ones come to take their places. New faces, beautiful and terrible and scared and excited. Every day you meet new ones and feel the loss of the old ones.

You go through the motions day after infinite day. You eat, you sleep, you fight, you love, you fuck, you die. You lose track of time, years passing by before you've realized it. Every second of those years is an eon of pain and fear.

Then one day the queen takes you aside. In the center of a circle of her attendants, all the beautiful and terrible people, she strips you, straddles you, uses you. By now you are adjusted to her whims, no longer feel violated by the dispassionate way she treats her subjects, the stolen people. Merely disconnected, outside yourself, as though your consciousness floats on a nebulous thread that dangles far above the world, unreachable, safe.

You hear a voice. Not from below, where the queen kneels over you, smiling down at the lover who lays on the ground at her feet. From above. A deep voice, but soft. It rumbles through the cloud, stirring it. Calling your name, saying it's time to go home. You know that voice. You should return to your body before she does something else to it, but you climb the thread instead, following the murmur. Following it back up through darkness and dream and nothingness until your eyes open and you are in your bedroom, and you are nineteen now, and nothing has changed, and nothing is the same.

It leapt from the water, a monster of a fish. Black scales across its back blended into bright red ones below, with spots along its side. Almost as long as I was tall, with a torpedo-shaped body that flew through the water.

"Big damned pike," father said. He kept his voice low, but I could hear the excitement he tried to contain. "Never seen one that color."

I let it run, giving drag on the line to keep it from going too far. When it tried to dive, I pulled hard on the pole which doubled over under the strain. Enough of a jerk to pull its head around and convince it to move towards the surface again without breaking the willow wood rod.

And so, it went. Five minutes became fifteen before the fish began to tire. I'd grown tired, too, my arms aching as I kept it from tangling the line around the dragon's bones, or running so far that I ran out of line. Its movements began to settle, grow sluggish, and I nodded in relief. The fight dissolved into the slow spooling of the line as I worked it towards the boat.

Father lifted our net by the handle, chuckled, and tossed it back into the bottom of the boat. "No way that bastard will fit." He moved to the center, close to me, and reached out to place a hand on the line. He pulled when I turned the reel, helping me get it close to the boat.

Finally, we had it snug up against the hull. It lay on its side at the surface, gills fluttering as it sucked in water, trying to catch its breath. The fish looked almost as long as the boat, and the black eye on this side stared up at us as father held the line. The hook had barely caught in its lower lip. I'd been lucky it hadn't torn free.

Father reached down carefully toward the mouth full of tiny, sharp teeth. He slipped a couple of fingers under the gills, but I reached out and touched his arm.

He looked at me, and I looked at him. Two old men who'd spent a century dying at the hands of the queen of dreams. He didn't have to ask what I wanted. He nodded once in agreement, then took the fish by the hook. He gently twisted and pulled on the iron barb until he'd worked it loose from the mouth.

The fish lay next to us, resting. Long enough that I could slide over and place my hand on her side. She had white scars on her flanks from old battles she had fought, and her mouth was ragged, as though torn many times by hooks. An old soul of a fish. Maybe as old as myself. I wondered what dreams she had.

We touched it like that for at least a minute, my father kneeling next to me, watching her fins move in lazy spasms. Then she flicked her tail, slapping the boat so hard it rocked over and we took on some water before we righted. For a moment we could see her clearly, the huge shape moving down through the water towards the dragon below. It slipped beneath the skeletal ribs and, with a final flash of red scales, raced towards the Sycamore branches and out into open water.

Father sighed and rocked back. "Time to go home," he said. He moved to the center seat and took up the oars. We slid through the glassy surface of the lake towards the edge of the sycamore bower and out into bright, midmorning sun.

"You did help," I said, as I watched him row.

He nodded but said nothing in reply. Only stared woodenly forward as we headed toward the far shore and home, where mother waited for us, his eyes looking a century into the past.

ASTERIA III

BY MARJORIE KING

"All systems go," the launch director said over the communications link.

"Including my lunch," Elanor said.

Dr. Elanor Johnston was strapped down inside a metal tank (aka spaceship) that was attached to a controlled bomb (aka rocket). Her suit was hot as August in Houston, and sweat poured down every nook of her body. Every nook.

7... 6... 5... 4...

And her nose itched.

3... 2... 1... *PUKE!*

The mouthpiece in Elanor's helmet sucked the burger and fries combo meal down a tube away from her face. The filtered air blew hard to cleanse the smell.

"I told you to go light on the French fries, Supergirl," her Dad's voice said.

"That might have been my last Earth meal."

Earth had decided to remodel. She had pushed some tectonic plates here, relieved some pressure through volcanoes there. From the planet's point of view, all the changes were cosmetic. From the perspective of the minuscule lifeforms scuttling along its surface, they were named "The Next Extinction."

Humanity needed a new home. A whole galaxy lay at their doorstep if only they could cross the threshold, lightspeed.

"Well, looks like you got to enjoy the combo meal a second time," Dad said, interrupting her thoughts.

Of course, it wasn't really Elanor's Dad. He was living in a nursing home after Alzheimer's had hit him hard two years ago. She hadn't heard his baritone voice whisper "Supergirl" since. With *Asteria III* labeled a suicide mission, the launch team had graciously programmed her Dad's personality into the ship's computer.

Her friend, Quan Lee, and his AI development department had really stepped up. He ate through twenty-six bags of cheese puffs and pulled all-nighters to program the ship's computer with Dad's voice. Using Mom's old family videos, he and the team didn't just duplicate the sounds, Quan nailed Dad's pet phrases and personality too. Elanor was speechless.

"Honestly, Supergirl," Dad said, snapping Elanor back to the current time. "With your anti-grav installed, this isn't a bad ride. Astronauts a century ago had it so worse."

"Remember the hovercup ride?" Elanor said.

Yeah, she was the teenage girl who'd barfed on the hovercup ride. It was the ride safe for five-year-olds, and she splattered the attendant as they whipped past.

"Remember you stuffed yourself with funnel cake before it?" Dad asked. "You really should learn what not to eat before a festival ride."

"Being launched into space is a festival ride?"

"Eh, with anti-gravity technology, inertial dampeners, and tons more propulsion, but they're basically the same."

Dad could always make her laugh.

"Houston to *Asteria III*, Houston to *Asteria III*," the comm said. "First phase of launch successful. Jettisoning Stage I rockets."

Wow. Dad had managed to distract her through the first part of the launch. Maybe she could do this after all.

Until she died.

"*Asteria III* to Houston," Elanor said. "Copy that."

She touched the glowing comm link symbol hovering above the

control projector. Her message traveled back to Earth at speeds she hoped to exceed.

Asteria III.

Even the name forebode her future. Two Asteria missions had gone before Elanor. Two ships had attempted the Jump beyond the speed of light. Astronauts had manned both those ships. But neither had returned.

Those men hadn't just been numbers either. José and Damien had been friends. Their families were without them now, and Elanor was probably next. She kept her face calm, but her stomach churned.

"Stage II rockets jettisoned," the engineer said over the comm. "*Asteria III* is leaving the atmosphere."

"You know we won't survive this," Elanor said to her Dad.

"Fix that attitude, Supergirl. You've never admitted defeat."

I'm not Supergirl anymore.

Elanor's anti-grav system might be killing her friends and blocking humanity's escape to freedom. How could she be Supergirl? She was helpless against the invisible force hurting her Dad. How could she be Supergirl?

Elanor didn't say any of this out loud. Her Dad's personality was programmed into a super computer. She couldn't win.

"Houston to *Asteria III*," the comm crackled. "Launch successful. Godspeed and good luck, Dr. Johnston. The fate of humanity rests on your shoulders."

The comm fell quiet. The air in the tiny room charged. The tension built and built like a balloon filling.

"No pressure," Dad said.

"It's true." Elanor popped the latches on her helmet and lifted it off her head. "It won't be long before volcanic ash covers the sky. A summer with no sun."

"Don't stare at the problem. Focus on the next step of solving it."

The next step was getting comfortable.

Elanor put her helmet in the perfectly sized niche to her right and strapped it in place. She unlocked the five different buckles strapping her to her chair and stretched. Or tried to. Her hands hit the ceiling before she could extend her arms. Then came the ever so enjoyable process of removing the skintight suit.

"I always wondered what it would be like to skin a seal," her Dad said.

"Shut." Elanor pulled on the leg until it spit her foot out with a slurp. "Up."

She stuffed the suit into its compartment with her elbow and pushed the door closed on it. Finally, her skin could breathe. Her cotton t-shirt and sweatpants lay nestled in the cabinet to the back of the cabin. All Elanor had to do was turn and take a step to reach it.

Those clothes slipped on with ease. Her grandmother's favorite fabric softener wafted off the shirt and filled the room. Normally Elanor hated that smell. Today, it made the cramped cabin feel like home.

She lounged in the pilot's chair and pulled up the diagnostics from the launch. The holograph projector lit up 3-D graphs floating around her in the air. They looked like mountains with rivers and waterfalls and cliffs. Her eyes went straight to the anti-grav system, her baby.

"How'd your anti-grav do?" Dad asked.

"Strong and steady."

"I expected no less."

"Then why are two Asteria ships strewn across the stars?" Elanor threw her hands up.

"If the JumpShot probes can do it, so can we."

Nine probes had been shot off at faster-than-light speeds and successfully returned to tell the tale. The program had been dubbed "JumpShot" because the probes resembled metallic basketballs. But when that technology was strapped to a ship?

No ship returned. Families were called. Funerals arranged.

What was the main difference between the JumpShot probes and the manned spaceships? Elanor's anti-gravity system. Blame for the Jumps failure had landed on her and her creation.

Some NASA administration had tried to block Elanor from this mission because of the anti-gravity suspicions. But the other engineers had fought for her. She was the expert on the anti-grav system, and therefore the best person to diagnose any issues.

"We'll prove it wasn't your anti-grav's fault," Dad said.

"We don't have much choice."

Without anti-grav and inertial dampeners, human bodies were too fragile to survive space travel. So very fragile.

Her gaze climbed up one of the holographic mountains to a cliff.

"OK, I have to ask," Dad interrupted, "and you have nothing better to do right now."

"I have to jump to FTL in two months," she said.

"And until then?"

"Go ahead."

"Wanna play chess?"

It had been over four years since they'd duked it out over a good game.

"The team programmed you with chess?" Elanor sat up, her head passing right through one of her graphs, its contour lines traced along her left cheek.

"Would I be your Dad without it?" he asked.

"Definitely not. And you're on!"

The charts dissolved, and a chessboard materialized, holographic queens and pawns sparkling in the air. Elanor touched her fingertip to the white king's pawn's top and slid the image up two spaces. The king's pawn from the black side floated to meet hers. The game was on.

Elanor opened with patience, setting up her pawns, knights, and bishops first. Her Dad strategically matched move for move. They castled. Then out came the big guns, rooks. Last, but not least, the queen made her grand entrance.

Elanor licked her lips. She reached for her bishop, tucked over in the corner of the board.

"Oh nuts!" Dad burst out.

Elanor smiled, the smile of a general who's tricked her opponent into a trap. She slid her bishop across the board.

"Check."

"But not checkmate."

"Yet."

"I can get out of this. Hold on. I could move… Oh, nuts, no not that. But maybe." There was a pregnant pause.

"Well, shoot," he said. "Wanna play again?"

Elanor laughed. "Sure."

"Your brothers never did play chess with me much."

"Fred didn't have the patience, and Caidyn got tired of losing."

Elanor moved the back row of pieces into place with her fingertips.

"But you pushed through until you beat me. Occasionally."

"I didn't play to beat you, Dad." Elanor set the last pawn into position. "I played because you gave me your undivided attention for three hours straight."

"So, it was never about the puzzle? Never about the win?"

"Sure, Dad. It was the win too."

At least it was once. Not anymore.

It should've been a long two months, but between chess and their old favorite movies, time flew. Dad played every classic space holovid he could download, from *2001: A Space Odyssey* to *Firefly* to the newly released *Asimov Foundation* trilogy. Soon they were passing Pluto. Communications back to Earth took an hour and required precise calculations to hit the planet. It was time for the Jump, and Elanor was alone. Almost.

"We're far enough away from the gravity pulls of Jupiter and Sol," Dad reported. It wasn't something he would've normally said, making the voice sound more like a computer. "The ship can now perform the Jump."

It was time. Time to end this. Time to join her friends, José and Damien. Then she could wait for her father on the other side.

"OK, start the Jump sequence," Elanor said.

"No." That was her Dad's voice and a slap to her face.

"Excuse me?"

"There were times you played chess because you wanted to spend time with me, and there were times you played chess to win. Supergirl, I can tell from your face, you're not playing to win."

"What do you know! You're not my real Dad! Dad's back on Earth dying, and there's nothing this space Jump will do about it!"

Elanor sucked her breath down her throat. Had she just yelled that? Out loud?

"Can you delete that from the ship's records?"

Her voice was tiny. The voice of a little girl who had just made her Daddy cry.

"I don't know what you're talking about, Supergirl," Dad answered. "The last thing I have on record is me saying 'you need to play to win.'"

"Thank you."

"For what?"

But in her mind, Elanor saw Dad touch his finger to the side of his nose. That was his version of a wink; his way of saying, *this is just between us.*

"You know FTL is possible," Dad said. "You don't have to solve the whole puzzle, just the next move."

"And live to tell the tale."

But her voice had grit in it. Her love of the puzzle was rising. Elanor could envision the problem as a chessboard.

But it was bigger than any game she'd ever played with her dad. It was like the chess games from the old *Star Trek* series they'd watched together. Three levels of chess boards with pieces above and below. Elanor couldn't win the entire game alone.

But maybe she didn't have to. Maybe she just had to figure out the next step. After all, she had an entire army of brilliant friends back home ready and able to win this together. They just needed the next move.

Elanor could figure out one move. She could win that small battle.

"I've got an abort sequence all lined up," Dad said. "If you figure anything out, just say the word."

Her face hardened into her chess face. Elanor couldn't save her Dad, but she could save his family. She couldn't bring back her friends, but she could save their families.

Elanor had trained for this. No, Dad had trained her for it, to solve puzzles, one step at a time. That's all life was after all, one exciting puzzle after another. Somewhere along the way, Elanor had forgotten that. Maybe it was because Alzheimer's was a puzzle she couldn't solve.

But this anti-grav problem was one that she could.

"OK. I'm ready," Elanor said.

"Starting the nozzles."

She pressed the comm button. "Houston, starting the Jump sequence."

On the previously launched JumpShot probes, six nozzles surrounded the vessel: one on top, one on bottom, and four around the equator. On *Asteria III*, there were fifty.

As the nozzles started up, the ship stayed perfectly still, like the eye of a hurricane. But the air tingled. The hair on the back of Elanor's neck lifted like an electrical charge was building. The magic began.

The fifty nozzles, powerful magnets, stretched and altered the space within them. A stream of hydrogen shot into the center of each nozzle, where the particles ripped apart. From the viewscreen, Elanor could see the five nozzles attached around the ship's nose. Tiny fireworks sparked within. Sometimes the process looked like a pinprick of light, but other times? A hole in space itself. Light and a black hole, matter and anti-matter waging war.

How could Elanor describe the feeling inside the cabin? It felt like time and light were shifting, like the floor had changed to quicksand.

"Houston, Jump sequence progressing—"

But the comm suddenly hissed with static. The ship's screens flickered and buzzed angrily. The nozzles blocked all communications back to Earth, leaving her the only witness to the Jump process. Elanor was an island in the void of space.

"Well, NASA guessed the Jump cut-off communications," Dad said. "Now we know."

"If José and Damien could have sent back what they were seeing, then my mission may not have been necessary."

"But then we wouldn't have had watched Captain Reynolds together," Dad said.

That was true. The time together had been nice. Hearing his voice and laughing at inside jokes, again. But it had ached too, pressing into Elanor's sternum so hard, she'd almost cried.

Not now, I need to focus!

Elanor returned to the data on the nozzles, searching for something, anything, grasping. The diagnostics of the Jump process floated in the air before her.

She checked the nozzles: *Functioning properly*

She checked the G-load: *Progressing as planned*

She checked the Anti-Grav: *Operating within limits*

She checked the course: *Perfect*

Maybe the problem was her anti-grav. Maybe the problem was the size of the ship. Maybe the problem was unsolvable.

"There's nothing here..." The little voice in her head cleared her throat. "But..."

Elanor gave the anti-grav a second glance. It wasn't the strain that itched her mind. The system could handle that.

"It's the pattern." Her pulse quickened and more of the hair on her head lifted.

The graph of the Jump-field surrounding the ship looked like a football. At the two tips of the football, the anti-grav was operating fine. But just an inch in, where the white stripe would be painted on the football, bubbles appeared. As her gaze moved towards what would have been the laces, the bubbles stretched to empty pockets. Gaping holes ran around the midsection of the football.

Each strained bubble in the anti-grav system matched the location of an FTL nozzle.

But the nozzles should be exerting identical force.

Then the pieces fell together:

The *shape* of the JumpShot probes.

The *spacing* of their nozzles.

The *pattern* of strain on the anti-grav.

The *spacing* of the ship's nozzles.

"Holy crap! That's it!"

Elanor knew the next move. It was so simple too. Just a pawn's move. So many times the power of the pawn is overlooked.

"Abort! Abort! Abort! ABORT!"

"Starting the abort sequence," the computer said.

Pause.

"So, what did you figure out?" The voice had returned to her Dad's baritone.

Elanor's stomach jolted at the change in voice. Quan's program wasn't perfect after all. Or maybe the nozzles had interfered with the computer's function too? Elanor blinked and returned her focus to the graphs.

As the Jump sequence wound down, the holes in the anti-grav graph closed like wounds miraculously healing.

"Spherical," Elanor said to herself.

Pause. "Yeah, I'm gonna need more than that," Dad said.

"The nozzles were in a spherical arrangement on the JumpShot probes."

"And you think they need to be spherical on the larger ships too?"

"Check the anti-grav strain during the Jump. When the nozzles get too close to each other."

She rewound the graph, and the holes reopened.

"The fifty nozzles need to be perfectly spaced apart," Dad said.

"Exactly. And that can only happen on a ball."

Her Dad went silent for a few seconds.

"So you solved it? The next step, that is?" he asked.

"Yeah," she said.

"And the entire planet now owes its life to you?"

"I hadn't thought about it that way, but—"

"My Supergirl is the most amazing woman ever!" her Dad yelled in Surround Sound, turning the volume up on all the speakers in the cabin.

Elanor smiled so big, her cheeks almost split. Her head fell back as she belted out the loudest laugh she'd laughed in years. She laughed until the tears came. She slid down the chair until she almost fell off.

Then Elanor breathed it in for several minutes. It wasn't her anti-grav's fault. In fact, her anti-grav had helped her find the real problem.

"So, shall we send the good news back home?" Dad asked.

"Bring up the comm controls." Elanor reached for the comm button but didn't touch it. "Hope this helps, or I'm gonna look like an idiot and a coward."

"You have to risk looking like an idiot to solve the impossible problems, Supergirl."

Elanor touched the comm button, and it glowed green.

"Houston, this is Asteria III. Jump Sequence aborted. I may have found something. Check the anti-grav strain during the Jump start-up. The nozzles need to be arranged spherically."

Elanor ended the communication to Earth.

"So it wasn't your anti-grav," Dad said.

Now Elanor smiled, her checkmate smile. "True."

The pressure of the Jump had passed, and Elanor was light-headed. It felt like the elephant that had been sitting on her shoulders for years had just evaporated.

My friends' deaths weren't my fault.

Her ears buzzed, and stars twinkled before her eyes, and the glowing buttons and switches swam in her vision. She blinked and calculated the maneuvers to point the ship back towards Earth.

"Supergirl?" Dad asked.

"Yeah?"

"I know you've been beating yourself up because you couldn't save me, but you saved my wife. You saved my favorite daughter—"

"Your only daughter."

"My two sons, all my grandkids. Shoot, you even saved that ex-daughter-in-law we don't talk about anymore."

Elanor raised her right shoulder to wipe her wet cheek off on her old Astros shirt. Yeah, her Dad had been an Astros fan. Even though Elanor had never really understood sports, she'd packed this old shirt. At the time, the irony of wearing an Astros shirt while in space had made her smirk. Now it felt perfect.

"I'm proud of you, Supergirl," Dad said. "You know that, right?"

"I know, Dad. I've always known."

My Dad's illness isn't my fault either.

Two years and four months later, Earth launched the next manned spaceship, Dragon V. This one from China. NASA hadn't been the only organization trying to achieve the Jump. They also hadn't been the only organization to lose lives. All of Earth was invested together in this problem.

Instead of celebrating with her colleagues in Houston, Elanor had chosen to sit on a blanket in a graveyard at 3:42 a.m. In the dark, she checked the news glowing above the crystal marble of her personal holoprojector. Any minute the reports would come in.

Had humans survived the Jump? Could we colonize a new home?

Terraforming science had advanced by leaps and bounds. Space engineers had designed ARCHs, Advanced Residence and Containment Habitats, to transport tens of thousands of plants, animals, and humans in a single Jump. The perfect planet had been ID'ed. But was it reachable? Could it be a reality?

Elanor checked the tablet again. Still nothing. She shivered, rubbed her arms to warm up, and moved her iced bucket of champagne away as if it was stealing her warmth. She should have packed hot cocoa in a thermos instead of cold champagne. But if humanity succeeded, Elanor wanted something that popped like that industrial strength bubble gum her Dad had bought once.

They'd made a contest out of who could blow the biggest bubble. Bigger and bigger their bubbles had grown until... pow! Both their faces were covered in pink masks of gum. It took days to clean the moldy pink bits out of their eyebrows, her bangs, and his prickly beard. The bubbles in champagne always reminded Elanor of that moment.

The cold ground grumbled underneath her, vibrating up her rear and legs into her chest. The earthquakes felt so much like the vibration of her ship when it had launched those years ago. Her Dad's voice lingered in her memory.

Looks like you got to enjoy the meal a second time.

Elanor chuckled. She wasn't in danger of throwing up this time. The ground rumbled again, and she grimaced. Earthquakes had become a part of everyday life now. Humanity had to leave soon.

Her tablet buzzed. Elanor jumped.

Dragon V has survived the Jump! Repeat: Dragon V has Jumped and returned successfully!

In the distant darkness, shouts of joy erupted like a far-off football stadium cheering their team. One of her brothers had asked Elanor if she was jealous that she wasn't on this mission.

"After all," Fred had said, "you were the one who figured out the problem with the Jump."

"And Quan and his team programmed the computers," Elanor said, "and others calculated exactly how the ship should be designed. Others fabricated every piece for the ship and nozzles." She'd paused and swallowed a lump down her throat. "And others sacrificed their lives. We all get the credit."

"I still think you should, I don't know, get an award or something," he'd said.

163

Elanor shrugged. "They gave me a really nice plaque with my name on it."

Fred had looked at her like she'd grown green antennae, but Elanor didn't need anyone's applause. The only person she needed to impress had his name etched on the stone before her.

And her Dad had been always been proud of her.

In the quiet graveyard, Elanor sank her bottle opener into the cork and twisted down until it was buried deep. Then Elanor tugged.

Pull… pull… pull… POP!

The cork and opener went sailing across the graveyard and decorated the grass atop some bygone soul. But they weren't offended. All of humanity celebrated tonight, so why not the ghosts too? José and Damien weren't buried in this graveyard with her Dad, and yet, Elanor could almost feel their presence and joy hovering over her.

She poured the fizzing sunshine into a flute glass and toasted the gravestone by her side. Elanor took a sip, and as the bubbles tickled down her throat, she bent down to the hard earth and whispered.

"Hey, Dad, guess what? The configuration of the nozzles on that spaceship, guess how they were oriented. That's right, you guessed it!"

Her breath chilled to a soft white fog floating above his grave.

"Spherical."

There was no audible answer. No computer with her Dad's voice said a word. The silence hurt so deeply, but Elanor embraced the ache now. Some chess games must be won. The Jump sequence was that kind of game for her.

But maybe other games could be played simply for the memories, win or lose. Elanor couldn't explain it, but her Dad and his loss were that kind of game.

A FULL DECK

BY AVI SILVER

"Shit." The lights on the computer monitor flashed even brighter. "Câlisse de tabarnak de fucking *shit*."

Mads d'Arc slammed down her empty coffee mug, rubbing her face. She'd been staring at the leaderboard for hours now, trying to pull together any sort of viable plan. As the self-proclaimed leader of the Lucky Aces, it was her job, wasn't it? But without Bartok around to help, everything she came up with fell short—she just didn't have the same sick creativity as the little brat.

She grimaced into her palms. They would get Bartok back. They had to.

She reached for the coffee pot, hoping a top-up would clear her head, and glared back at the leaderboard. There were over five hundred Registered Demon Hunters in Toronto alone, filling every niche a nerd could possibly dream up. The paintballers-turned-gunslingers, the Battle of the Bands rejects who used their instruments as binding tools, the religious types who opted for good old-fashioned holy water—there were a million ways to hunt demons in this city. There had to be *someone* who could help them. Anyone but—

"You're going to have to call the Bastard, you know."

Mads had flung the coffee pot before she even registered who the voice belonged to, but the sleek *shnng!* of metal through glass and the click of high heels made it all too clear.

"If that had been full, you'd be *dead* right now, Mads," said Dani Brightstar, sheathing her sword and tossing her long black hair over her shoulder. She was posed like a murderous cake-topper, a vision in layers of lilac that complimented her copper skin. Mads had no idea how Dani fought in a petticoat; if she tried to replicate her style, she'd look like a haunted Victorian doll. "I just got this dress."

"You'd get a new one," muttered Mads. "With even more ruffles."

"Please, the shipping costs alone—"

"Would be refunded if we were back on the hunt!" Mads shouted, throwing her hands in the air. As if on cue, the leaderboard updated on-screen, announcing with a happy *ding* that the Bloody Vegans just brought in another four hundred points. Unbelievable.

Dani stepped daintily over the broken glass, daring to get closer to Mads' bat cave; according to legend, it had been a second bedroom once. Now it could generously be described as a "home office," if home offices had blackout curtains, an alarming number of newspaper clippings tacked to the walls, and several dubiously stacked computer screens. Today, it was darker than usual, mostly on account of Mads not replacing any of the dead lightbulbs. She was still banned from the local Canadian Tire after an incident with a nosy store manager and a fistful of salt.

"The Lucky Aces need Bartok," said Dani plainly. "Fine if you don't want to say it out loud, I'd hate to spoil your brooding, but we need to get them back. It's been days." She smoothed the bows on her skirt worriedly. "I don't like the thought of them being stuck in that place. Especially at the height of tourist season."

"At least they didn't have to pay for a ticket. Thirty-two dollars. Fucking highway robbery."

"Mads."

Mads grimaced. She could hear the concern in Dani's voice, and there wasn't much point in pretending that she felt any different. Bartok was the Ace of freaking Hearts. Where Mads brought the team's competitive spirit and Dani had the deadliest blade in the GTA, Bartok knew how to *talk*. Their easygoing nature made them a team mediator, and their popularity on the fan forums gave the Aces incredible PR. But beyond that, they were a damn good hunter. No one could negotiate with hellish denizens quite like them; it was unthinkable to leave them in the clutches of some abnormality. But to be forced to call her old nemesis, to consort with —

"Criss de viarge de *sacrament.*" She slammed her head down on the keyboard. An error code flashed on the leaderboard screen.

"You're absolutely right," said Dani Brightstar, tapping her jeweled nails on her phone case. "We have to call the Bastard."

It was a good day for Cat the Bastard.

Granted, most of his days were pretty good lately, what with the rate hunting was going. In the past two weeks, the Hell Hole had been crackling with all sorts of nastiness, spitting out ruthless demons at an unprecedented rate. Shops were being pillaged, possessions were at an all-time high, and the Green Line had been essentially abandoned between Yonge and Broadview. In other words: business was booming, and he was climbing the leaderboard like a particularly smug raccoon in a flood.

And now Mads d'Arc had called him, needing a favour. He was still deciding whether or not to bite — being a hero kept him in pretty high demand.

Behind him, an 8-bit version of "Smooth Criminal" began to play from his phone, the *'get up for real this time'* alarm. Cat stretched out on his bed, knocking off the clean laundry he'd piled onto it last week. Ah, well. He was going to have to put it away eventually. Especially if he wanted to bring over any partners this week. Human partners, that is—demons weren't particularly picky about the state of the bed, but he needed a bit of time off from that particular vice. It took a surprising amount of energy to summon incubi and succubi for a good time.

See, Cat was a negotiator. A good one. He knew how to strike a deal, and how to hold others to their end of the bargain. End of the day, a little bite of his soul for the lay of his life didn't seem too bad.

Was it morally reprehensible? Maybe. Did it work for him? Absolutely.

He hopped off the bed and wiggled into his binder, which was tighter than his leather pants by only a very slim margin. Over in a pile of dirty laundry, Bastard the Cat was working to get his belly directly in the ray of light that struggled through the basement apartment's tiny, filthy window.

"That's right, Bastard," Cat crooned, pulling on his studded gloves. "Show 'em what you've got."

It was almost a shame to work alone. Some hunted in teams, but not Cat. He was a lone wolf, a one-man-job, too capable and yet too roguishly vulnerable to really—

"CAT," yelled his roommate, who might have been named Jessica. "There are some weird girls here to see you!"

Shit. They must have taken an Uber. Cat scrambled to tastefully rearrange the piles of detritus, stuffing takeout containers under the bed, forcing his closet door shut. As he pushed aside a pile of books, he realized that the summoning runes were still on the floor. He scraped at them with his foot to no avail. Landlord was going to love that one.

"Cat?" called Jessica—Jennifer?—again, banging on his door. "Are you seriously still asleep? I need to get to class and you still have my keys!"

"Give a man a moment to get his face on!" With an apology to Bastard, he yanked the cat's bed over the incriminating symbols—the last thing he needed was to get slapped with a fine for improper summoning. Not to mention what it would do to his reputation. He wiped off the previous night's smeared eyeliner, grabbed his black cowboy hat from the bedpost, and opened the door.

"Mads," he said, leaning casually against the doorframe. "Brightstar." He tossed the keys to his roommate. *Smooth criminal.* "Would you like to come in?"

Mads d'Arc grimaced at him. "Absolutely n—" Dani thwacked her in the leg with her sheathed sword. "Oh, câlisse de—sure, fine, sure. Thank you."

"My pleasure." Cat strutted over to his vanity, sitting on the stool and gesturing for them to cram onto the small loveseat in the corner. Dani perched on the arm, smoothing her dress and looking to Mads expectantly.

A long silence passed.

"So," Cat said slowly, looking between the two of them. They were quite a sight, Dani Brightstar every bit the magical girl and Mads d'Arc looking like a modern dance instructor turned assassin. The only thing their getups had in common were the card-shaped enamel pins, with Dani sporting the Ace of Spades and Mads, the Ace of Diamonds. "You need my help."

Mads grunted, dropping into the loveseat.

"At least, that's what I gathered from your voicemail?"

Mads made a sound not unlike the revving of an old Buick.

Dani Brightstar took the opportunity to step in, rolling her eyes at her teammate. "Bartok's been taken by an incubus."

"An incubus?" Cat frowned, reaching down to pet Bastard the Cat. "How does that work? I thought being asexual made you immune to incubi and succubi. Lucky Aces and all that."

"That's a misconception," Dani said, crossing her arms with dainty annoyance. "We're much better hunters, for sure, but we're not all entirely resistant. I'm as close to immune as people come, and I can still sense when attraction magic is being cast near me. And grey-aces don't always have an easy time of—" Mads cut her off with another loud car noise. Dani pursed her lips, taking a deep breath before continuing. "*Anyway*, that's not how it got Bartok. It's some kind of abnormality. From what we've gathered, the demon's still using sex as a lure for some allosexuals, but it's evolved its magic to manipulate romantic attraction."

Cat paused, suddenly thinking back to a private summoning from about a month back. A good night: waxplay by way of ritual candles, handcuffs, a certain incubus who stuck around for some pillow talk until the binding wore off.

"You're strong," the demon had purred in its many-toned voice. "Not many humans have the willpower to end a night with me."

"What can I say?" Cat had laughed, reaching for his fallen cowboy hat. "I'm well-practiced, desensitized to the usual lures—got 'strong boundaries,' as the kids say. Can't let you bleed me dry in one go; I have to save some for later."

"Is that what humans call 'falling for' someone?"

"Hardly. I'm aro as ever, pal." Cat had shrugged. "Sex is more of a hobby than anything. I just know not to waste it when I have something good." He'd winked at the incubus before straddling its hips, considering how much more he could take before the fatigue started testing his binding spell. "Though that would be something."

"What would?" The incubus had scratched its obsidian claws along Cat's waist, making him shiver. What was that about willpower?

"Romance. If you could drain a soul through romantic attraction—" Cat had shook his head, amused. "From what I've heard, love is one hell of a drug. A nice date and a 'powerful connection,' and people lose all sense of reason. First incubus to harness that would be a *real* nightmare."

Ah. Shit. He hadn't thought it would *listen* to him.

"Cat?" Cat looked up with a strained smile. Dani crossed her arms, tapping her fingernails in annoyance. "Are you even paying attention?"

"Oh, yeah, sure—the, the incubus. It, ah, it feeds off of romantic desire that it triggers through…?"

"Forming a connection, sexual or otherwise. We learned that the hard way when it seduced Bartok." Dani put a hand to her chin. "I think it must have known we were coming, researched us. All it needed to do was pull out some rare Magic the Gathering card… Black Lily? Lotus? And that was it for Bartok. They've been stuck with the incubus ever since, under the illusion that they're in love."

"In Casa Loma, of all places," Mads sneered. "Tourist trap."

"And since Bartok's demi," Dani continued, "it's even riskier the longer they're trapped. It's bad enough that they're ensnared romantically—we don't need the demon draining them through sexual attraction, too."

"Right," Cat said, mouth gone dry. Bastard the Cat swatted at his hand, demanding more attention. He cleared his throat, trying to compose himself before the remaining Lucky Aces realized something was up. Maybe this was his incubus, maybe it wasn't. Either way, the two hunters in front of him didn't need to know what he'd been up to.

"So, what does this have to do with me?"

Dani Brightstar hesitated. Beside her, Mads sunk further into the loveseat, not meeting Cat's eye. "You... are a very capable hunter."

"Fourth best independent contractor in the city, actually." He smirked. That was a well-earned title. His proficiency in both binding and negotiating had landed him a high charisma score on the fan forums, which almost made up for his slanderously low intelligence score. The public was cruel. "But if you're asking to collaborate... we've been over this, d'Arc. I'm a lone wolf. I—"

"You egotistical shit!" Mads leapt up from the couch like an irate Jack-in-the box. "I was the one who fired you!"

"It's not a matter of ego, Mads." Cat rolled out his neck, sighing. "It's just my nature. I'm too *intense* for most people. Too good at what I do. Feelings get hurt."

"No, *no*, you work alone because you're insufferable! You lie, you cheat, you pull *barely* legal moves in combat with no regard for your teammates! Remember our hunt in Trinity Bellwoods?"

Cat did not.

"Oh you got to be—" Mads snarled, sticking her finger in his face like she was ready to curse him for ten thousand years. "Let me refresh your memory. Seven hours of trailing that spirit. You followed along with my plan as long as it suited you, *thanked* me for all I had taught you, just to throw it back in my face and steal my killshot! You compromised our safety, took credit for my work, and never so much as apologized!"

Cat frowned, feeling terribly misjudged. "That was one—"

"The hellbeast in the Eaton Center. The minotaur on the Danforth. That *thing* in Midtown! This is not a *one time* mistake, you're a pathological piece of shit!"

"All that anger can't be good for you, Mads."

"Neither can my foot up your ass but—"

Dani Brightstar's sword suddenly appeared between them, the ribbons on the hilt fluttering as the blade glinted threateningly in the light. Cat raised his hands, unruffled, and while Mads glared holes into him, she moved no further. "We need your help," said Dani, "because Mads isn't aro and I can't do this job by myself."

"Your weapon suggests otherwise."

"We're *not* cutting down an abnormality," hissed Mads. "We need to bind the incubus, learn what triggered this evolution. More demons like this could be disastrous for the Aces—"

"And the city," Dani added, giving Mads a reproachful look as she sheathed her weapon. Cat had always appreciated how competitive d'Arc was, even if it was what had put a wedge in their friendship. A very one-sided wedge. Even now she was making a face at him like he'd stuffed a cigarette butt into her Twinkie—and yes, maybe sometimes he played dirty, but so did every hunter worth their salt. He hadn't done anything worse than anyone else on the leaderboards.

Except maybe influence a fuck-demon to change its career path and become Casa Loma's most eligible bachelor.

"Please, Bastard," Dani said, ignoring Mads' hissing in the background. "Cat. Bartok needs us, and you're our best way to them."

Cat took a deep breath, rubbing his face. His conscience was a real buzzkill. Working with others had never gone well for him in the past, but he wasn't likely to get this mess cleaned up without help. And if he could pull it off without anyone knowing the incubus was his fault in the first place, that would be all the better. "How are we splitting the pay?"

By the time the Lucky Aces (feat. Cat the Bastard) reached the castle's grounds, the sun was well on its way to setting. This was mostly the fault of a streetcar catching fire. The first responders had been unable to determine whether it had resulted from mechanical failure or demonic interference, but it certainly set up a dramatic scene for the team of hunters. Warning signs had been put up all around Casa Loma's grounds, complete with listed rewards for the demon's removal and requests to *'keep an eye on our socials for updates on our grand re-opening!'*

"Repeat the plan back to me," Mads snapped, hoisting her backpack over her shoulder. She wasn't about to let the Bastard claim ignorance should he spoil their plan. She'd been fooled by his nonsense before, and she wasn't having any more of it. Not with Bartok on the line. If it had been her or Dani in trouble, they would have finished the job days ago.

"Again? Gee, I'd love to," Cat said dryly. "So, for the hundredth time, I go in and look for the demon while you and Brightstar secure the perimeter with runes to keep it contained. Once I find it, I send you a pulse through the handy linking spell you slapped on my arm, which is still super itchy by the way, and then you both head in my direction. I approach the demon and use my fine self as a distraction—"

"And you don't—"

"And I *don't* bind it, not even a little, because I'm not a good-for-nothing points stealer with some kind of complex. Then Brightstar charges in with her sword so you and I can co-bind the thing and break its hold on Bartok. We turn it in to the authorities, collect our winnings for the leaderboard, and never speak to each other again. Sound about right?" He scratched at the linking spell's mark, looking far too bored for Mads to be comfortable with.

"No texting either," Mads added, pulling out her binding materials. "Or, or *instabook* or anything."

"Instagram," corrected Dani.

"Whatever. No contact."

"Fine by me," Cat muttered, straightening his idiotic cowboy hat sharply. That was strange—if Mads didn't know better, she'd think the Bastard looked stung.

"You're sure you're comfortable with this?" Dani interjected, giving her sword a few practice swings. It was soundless in the air, save for the soft *swish* of her ribbons. "I've heard incubi and succubi are really hard for allosexuals to resist. Even experienced Registered Demon Hunters struggle. We might not be on the best of terms, but Mads and I aren't trying to get you ensnared."

"Your concern is appreciated, but I'm not too worried." He flashed a smile that was probably supposed to be charming. Or clever, at the very least, but he wasn't pulling it off. Mads squinted at him, wondering if it was possible for a person to be any less trustworthy. As if reading her thoughts, he waved a hand at her. "I have some experience with these demons. With—with fighting them. I'll manage."

Mads opened her mouth to protest, to ask what he was hiding, but then they broke through the gardens, meeting the sounds of merrily bubbling fountains. Cat thumped a statue with his fist, turning away from the two Lucky Aces.

"See you on the other side," he said, strutting up the walkway in his studded boots. Mads glared, feeling suddenly underdressed compared to the costume party she was traveling with. Absurd.

"Just—just stick to the plan!" she called back, clenching her fists. "Find the demon and then wait! We're a *team*, Bastard—the points belong to all of us!"

"Yeah, yeah, d'Arc. Don't get all burnt up about it."

Dani Brightstar stifled a laugh.

"Traîtresse," Mads muttered.

"It was kind of funny," Dani said, reaching up to fluff the bow in her hair. "Try to relax, Mads. This is an easy job. The Bastard's kind of a loser, but I don't think he's malicious. It's not like he's going to go rogue the second he's left alone."

The Bastard was going rogue.

He scrambled into the Great Hall with all the cool he could muster, doing his best to appreciate the free, if rushed, tour. It had been a while since the castle had been open to the public—a number of demons had claimed it since the Hell Hole opened. More often than not, they took each other down before the hunters even got a shot at them. Which was a shame—taking a demon out of a tourist zone made for killer points on the leaderboard. That is, unless one went and got themselves captured like good old Bartok.

Cat tore through the library, trying to figure out how he was going to bind this demon before the Aces showed up. Contrary to Mads' belief, he wasn't actually looking to steal anyone's points—he just couldn't risk anyone finding out that this demon might be connected to him. A hunter being a bastard was acceptable. A hunter being ethically dubious was tolerable. A hunter using his skills to not only summon a demon but to *empower* it was as good as banished from the leaderboards. And that was a fate worse than death; it was an insult to his personal brand. Christ, he'd have to get a real job.

I'm Cat the Bastard! he thought, trying to stifle the oncoming panic as he ran out of Sir Henry's study. *I'm an antihero, not a complete scoundrel!*

The linking spell felt tight on his arm; it wouldn't be long before Mads expected his message to come in. As he made his way up to the second floor, his ear caught on the sounds of laughter. What had the brochure said that was? The Windsor Room? No, the name didn't matter—he just had to get there and finish this.

Cat kept his footfalls quiet as he approached the door, listening to the low, sensual sound of the demon speaking. That was his incubus, all right. Cat closed his eyes, bracing himself against the shiver of pleasure that rushed through his body; he had almost forgotten the disorientation that came with unbound attraction magic. He took a deep breath and pressed his back to the wall, listening closely to the voices in the Windsor Room.

"Alright, for my turn I'm just going to cast Sphynx's Revelation for six," said Bartok, sounding oddly chipper for someone whose soul was being drained from their body. "I'll draw six cards and gain six life."

"For my turn I'll... tap five?" The words clashed absurdly with the hypnotic stacked vibrations in the demon's voice.

"Yup! So you've got five black mana to work with now."

Cat made a face. If this was what passed for romantic love, he was more confused by the concept than ever. He reached for his binding pouch, steadying his hands—

"And what little morsel do we have lurking by the door?"

Cat froze, shoulders tight with fear, knees weak with something else. He grasped at the linking spell on his arm; this was his last chance to call Mads and Brightstar, to fess up to his mistake and ask for help fixing it. He could be a team player.

But would they still be on his team if he told them the truth?

He didn't know. He didn't really want to find out. So Cat straightened his vest, took a deep breath, and stepped over the threshold.

"Just a humble gentleman caller," he said, tipping his hat for good measure. The Windsor Room was a bedroom meant for royalty, its ornate cream and blue walls accented in gold. The furniture looked too ostentatious to touch; Cat was half convinced the perfectly made bed was some kind of mirage. Bartok and the incubus sat together on the floor, a deck of cards spread out on a decorative rug.

"Cat the Bastard," the demon purred, its body adjusting into something decidedly more Cat's taste. Spectacularly dangerous, unreasonably sculpted. Horns and claws intact, curling with tempting menace—there was probably something Cat ought to unpack there. "I thought you smelled familiar."

Bartok looked up impatiently, their short silver hair falling into their eyes. Their small stature and slight frame was usually a hunting advantage; many demons had made the mistake of underestimating their power. But here, under the control of the incubus's imposing presence, they just seemed frighteningly small. "It's your turn, my love. How do you spend your mana?"

"My apologies, dear thing. Let's see..." The demon reached out, smoothing the worry from the ensnared hunter's brow. The performed affection was eerie, especially when Cat got a closer look at the state

Bartok was in. As always, they were stylish as an idol on their world tour, but their face was gaunt, and their normally glowing skin had taken on an ashen tone. Even their Ace of Hearts pin looked like it had lost some of its shine. Cat had never seen someone whose soul had been so quickly and dramatically stolen from them. How much longer could they possibly last like this?

When Cat summoned his own incubi and succubi, he used a light binding spell to keep himself in control. The demons didn't argue, and the thrill always felt worth the risk. After a couple hours, Cat would feel the soul-fatigue setting in, along with the general body fatigue that came with a rigorous fuck, and that was the cue to wrap it up and order some pizza. But as it turned out, love had no refractory period. The demons could gorge themselves, and all the while the humans would never realize just how far things had gone.

All the heat in Cat's belly froze into dread. What had his careless comment brought into the world?

"I spend my five black mana on Bloodgift Demon, and I attack." The demon's smooth voice broke through Cat's sudden, sobering realization.

"Okay, nice one! But you can't attack yet, he still has summoning sickness."

"Summoning sickness, hm?"

"Incubus," Cat said firmly, trying to garner as much authority as possible in the face of his own hubris and a ridiculous card game. He was running out of time before Mads and Dani came looking for him, with or without his coordinates; he needed to fix his mistake, and fast. He reached for his binding pouch—there was no time to draw a proper circle, but he could try some raw spellwork. He had to try something.

"Listen to me—"

"I'm afraid I'm a bit busy right now," the demon drawled, stretching out on the rug. "Call on me later, once I'm sated and can be rid of this tedious game. I'd be glad for some celebratory company."

Bartok didn't even seem to hear the demon's words, so busy they were with their cards. They stopped on one, stroking its softly glowing edges—that was it, the Black Lotus! Cat grabbed his pocket knife, flicking it open and throwing it at the card. But the incubus was faster. It knocked the blade away, moving up on Cat and grabbing him by the shirt.

"No," it murmured. "I don't think that will do at all."

Cat grit his teeth, trying to ignore the dizzying waves of lust that pummeled him. He was out of luck, and there was no way he could use the linking spell without making things worse. Bartok slumped against the chair, weaker by the moment as the demon became stronger. If he tried to use any magic, the demon would only drain them more quickly.

"Incubus, stop!" Cat gasped. He looked back to the demon, anxiety rising in his chest. "Is this seriously what you want? To waste away playing full-contact Uno with this nerd?"

"I'm sorry," Bartok slurred, "but those two games are not even remotely similar—"

"Their adoration feeds me well."

"Not as well as I could!" The words came out like a punch. Cat wasn't sure if he was bluffing or not, but all he could do was roll with it. He should have called the Aces, he shouldn't have tried to do this alone, but there was no turning back now, and he couldn't let Bartok suffer for his mistakes. The demon loosened its claws from his shirt, curious. "If you let Bartok go, you and I can work out a contract. Our meetings—I'll bind you less tightly, offer up more of my soul in exchange. You could call on me, even. As often as you'd like—as long as you keep me alive when you're done. Think of it as a... a renewable resource."

It wasn't an awful fate, really. The demon was the lay of the century, and funny, too. Cat had called on it multiple times in the past; sometimes they even watched movies together. But seeing Bartok was a bleak reminder to Cat that, above all, it was a *demon*. And it seemed his overconfidence had gotten him well and truly in over his head.

"You would offer this?" The incubus' voice was sultry, hungry. Cat could feel its interest squirming under his skin, and he bit back a groan. This was good—if the demon was latching onto him, it would have to ease its grasp on Bartok. "You would bind your freedom to my whims? You would shame yourself, lose all your precious ranking, for my own pleasure?"

It wasn't a good plan. But it was all he had. Not what he wanted, but what was right. "I guess I would, yeah."

"Well—"

"NOW, BRIGHTSTAR."

Before Cat could so much as barf or shout a *hallelujah!*, Dani Brightstar came flying through the air, blade drawn. The demon dropped him with a roar, stumbling back as she rained down blow upon blow, too fast for it to deflect. Cat looked into the furious eyes of Mads d'Arc, and thought he had never been happier to hear her voice.

"Mads!" he choked out, laughing hysterically. "Mads, perfect Mads! How long have you—"

"Bastard!" she barked. "Help Brightstar while I deal with Bartok!"

"Right, right—" Cat dove into the fight, crouching down and quickly drawing a binding circle on the floor, murmuring the spell so fast he thought he'd bite off his own tongue. Behind him, he could hear Mads shouting at Bartok in French, trying to pull them away from the cards that tied them to the incubus.

"I'm in the middle of a game!" Bartok whined, shoving at her weakly. "And I met the nicest guy, Mads, so if you could just give him a shot for once instead of biting his head off—" With a handful of salt and the right incantation, the circle lit up. The incubus let out a terrible sound, struggling against its bonds. Cat could feel his spell straining, a deep ache in his bones and a heaviness behind his eyes. He couldn't hold the binding circle alone, not for much longer.

"The card, Mads!" he cried over the sound of Dani fighting back the demon. "Destroy the card! I need your help, I can't do this by myself!"

With a particularly loud *tabarnak*, Mads saw to the task, and the cards went up in a burst of flame, breaking the demon's enchantment over the hunter.

"No!" Bartok wailed. "My Black Lotus!"

"Finish it!" Dani shouted over the chaos. Mads rushed to Cat, slamming her palms down on the binding circle and echoing his spell. Their voices were strong together; it made Cat wonder why he had been so insistent on doing things alone in the first place. With one last flash of purple flame the incubus collapsed in on itself, folding and folding until it flew into a small crystal bottle Mads held out to capture it.

All was quiet in the Windsor Room, save for the soft whimpering of Bartok, who was cradling the ashes of their cards like a dead lover. Dani sat down beside them, out of breath, and patted their back sympathetically. In theory, all was well.

"Well... final shot was yours, d'Arc," Cat croaked, wiping the chalk from his shaking hands. Was he shaking? It had been a long time since he'd truly been scared like that. "Two hundred point bonus for the leaderboards."

She gripped the crystal bottle so hard he thought it might shatter. "You... you..."

"Gave you the highest points?" he offered meekly. "Finished the job? Saved your friend?"

"Are a bastard. A demon-fucking bastard."

Cat flopped back on the floor, laughing in spite of himself. She wasn't wrong.

Mads d'Arc sat on the stairs to Casa Loma, looking over the leaderboard where she and the Lucky Aces had shot up in rank. The Bastard's rank had lifted too, but she supposed there was no helping that. The bound incubus had been passed to the paranormal authorities, and now all they could do was rest and collect the reward. If Casa Loma re-opened for long enough, they might even get year-long passes. Maybe she could trade them for new lights in her bat cave.

From behind her came the sound of gaudy boots thudding against the ground. Mads swiped away from the leaderboard, rubbing her temples.

"Did Bartok and Brightstar already head out?" Cat the Bastard asked, picking at his teeth.

Mads nodded. "Bartok needs rest. They look like hell." She paused, frowning as Cat sat down beside her. "Though I couldn't say if it's because of the incubus or the cards I wrecked."

"From what I caught of the screaming, it sounds like you just torched the equivalent of a new car."

"Câlisse."

"Mm."

For a moment they were both quiet, looking out on the abandoned grounds of Casa Loma: tourist trap, movie set, a castle out of place in the heart of a busy metropolis. In the low evening light, it could have been seen as romantic, if Mads didn't regularly fantasize about strangling the Bastard, whose brand of aromanticism didn't care much for anything fleur-bleue.

An uncomfortable feeling struck her then—the particular twist in the gut that meant she might have done something wrong. It wasn't a feeling she experienced often, but try as she might, she couldn't force it back.

"I'm going to say something," she began cautiously, not looking at Cat.

"All right."

"It's going to be nice."

"... All right?"

"And if you laugh, it will end there."

Cat let out a little noise of amusement, but quickly covered his mouth when she fixed him with another one of her signature glares. "I'm not laughing!" he insisted.

Mads opened her mouth, closed it, sighed, groaned. Why did this have to be so difficult? She tried to think of what the other Aces would do, tried to summon Bartok's patience and Dani's dedication. "You kept your end of the bargain today. Maybe you didn't stick to the plan, and you lied to us, and also this was pretty much entirely your fault—"

"Didn't you say this was going to be nice—"

"—but you saved Bartok. You saved my friend, and the Lucky Aces. And from what I overheard, you were willing to make a pretty hefty trade to make that happen." Even now, the idea of it made her stomach turn. There was very little in this life that she could imagine selling her soul for—if Cat was willing to do it to right a wrong, he had to have some sort of moral compass, however poorly calibrated the needle. "So... I'm sorry. I apologize for having so little faith in you."

She tensed, waiting for him to tease her, to brush off her sincerity with the same old Bastard affect, but nothing came. He took off his hat, fidgeting with it in his lap. "Apology accepted," he said quietly. "Though I guess I can see why you were so wary. I made a really bad choice."

"Summoning a demon to get you off? Ben oui, colon."

"Hey!" Cat laughed, nudging her with his elbow, which she tolerated. "I don't criticize your hobbies."

"My hobbies don't include jeopardizing the safety of the entire city."

The Bastard's grin transformed into a cringe as he shrugged. "About that... you don't think it told other demons its plan, do you? I'd like to think it kept the secret for itself, wanted to monopolize the market. But I don't know." Something strange came over him then, something that looked nearly like shyness. Or shame. Mads didn't dare look at him long enough to confirm, not wanting to make this interaction any weirder than it already was. She wasn't supposed to have heart-to-hearts with her nemesis.

Former nemesis, perhaps.

"I guess we'll just have to see," she said, imagining the numbers rising on the leaderboard already.

"Maybe…" Cat began, "maybe it would be smart for us to keep in contact. To work together again. I show some integrity, you show some faith. A full deck needs four aces, and from what I heard you're in the market for some Clubs."

"You hardly qualify as an ace," Mads said with a snort. From the corner of her eye, she watched Cat's shoulders fall. She shook her head a little, hardly believing what she was about to do. Shit. Câlisse de tabarnak de fucking shit. "…but we could use a Jack. At least until this thing's dealt with."

Cat's head shot up, hope flickering on his face before he quickly tried to mask it with something cool. It didn't work. It made her like him more, reminded her of the awkward, charming kid that she had hunted with back in the early days. "A Jack, huh? Jack of Clubs?"

"He also wears a hideous hat. And your presence is often like being beaten over the head."

"Well, as long as the hat's involved, I'm in." The Bastard offered his hand, grinning. "Until my mess is cleaned up."

"That could be a very long time," Mads said, shaking on it. She felt a strange tug on her cheeks—seven hells come up from Union, the Bastard had her *smiling* at him. Before she knew it, she might end up trusting the guy, and then she'd have to go through the trouble of finding herself a new nemesis.

"In the meantime, what should I do with this?" Cat rolled up his sleeve, jabbing at the linking spell she had cast on them earlier that day.

"Keep it for now," she said, feeling the gentle hum of her own mark. "Never know when it might come in handy."

All things considered, there were worse things to be bound to than Cat the Bastard.

HALF A HEART

BY REN OLIVEIRA

You come in the dawning of my three hundredth year alone.

Your presence in my kingdom is but a reverberation in my mind, an echo of movement and energy that sinks into the flow of the forest easily, mixing with the hundreds of souls linked to me as if you have always been here. But you have not, and the newness of you jolts me from my slumber, my eyes opening to the sunlight filtering through the trees to reveal a mess of green and yellow and deep, reddish brown. It's summer again and the birds' songs flow through my veins as the forest grows and dies, rejoicing under the reigning star. I can feel them all: the worms deep inside the Earth under my hands, the foxes hiding in the bushes, the whisper of the serpent in the grass. They are all mine and I'm theirs but you are not. You are new. You are an intruder.

It was winter when I let myself fall asleep; the vines on my arms now twist around the tree at my back and my bark-like skin blooms with flowers and leaves. When I stand up, the bird nest resting on my left shoulder slips off, and I carefully place it on one of the lowest branches. The three eggs in it are intact and I can feel the parents nearby, their minds calm before my constant presence, their chirps growing louder now that I'm awake. Awake because of you.

Your presence pulls my gaze north, to where you now lean against a tree in a glade, knees brought against your chest. The grass under your feet hums with curiosity; the forest around you sighs with expectation. Your fear tastes bitter to them, to me—and that is new, too. Fear here is primal, from prey to predator, but yours is poison, dripping with things far more complicated than the need to survive.

Hesitation burns inside my chest for a moment, the heart of the forest aching against my thorny ribcage. I should leave you be, but I find I cannot. My fingers touch the tree I slept against for so long as if from their own will and I sink into its trunk slowly, my limbs still stiff and awkward. The forest welcomes me into its bloodstream and I slip from branch to branch to you. My feet make no noise when I land on the grass before you, but you startle all the same, your big, gray eyes on me. The look on your face entertains me; I haven't seen an actual expression in so long, and yours is so much more intense than what I remember others' being—your mouth curved down, your eyebrows risen to meet your fair, messy hair, your nose crunched in disgust or surprise. I can't tell.

I tilt my head, for your sake. Mortals never liked my stillness.

"You're a child," I say, and you blink. Your ears are pointed too, and when you open your mouth, sharp teeth poke behind your lips. "An elf child," I continue when you don't say anything, the fear in your eyes finally becoming clear to me.

I step back, lowering myself to your eye level, more conscious than ever of my antlers and hard skin and thorny fingers. You still don't speak, and I don't know how to react. In the past, these meetings were scheduled, planned well in advance and mediated by proud, eager parents. It was never supposed to be like this.

I stay quiet because it doesn't occur to me to fill the silence.

At last, you take a deep breath and raise a trembling hand as if to touch me. I stare at it, curious, and pink floods your cheeks.

"You," you say, and I hum at the sound of your voice, the first I've heard in more years than I can count. "You," you repeat and I wait. I still remember how your people talk: full of pauses and lies and masked, hidden thoughts better left alone. "You're... the forest spirit?"

It barely sounds like a question. My hand moves to my chest, and my ribcage unravels, twisting away to reveal the forest heart beating lazily against my wooden bones. You gasp and lean forward as if tempted to grab it, but I don't move. The forest heart can't be taken, only given, and I would die before letting go of what was entrusted to me before the world was born.

My bones move, slowly returning to their initial position, hiding away the heart from your prying eyes. You turn them to me, and the fear in them is gone, replaced by something that, at first, I can't place. But hundreds of years of watching those like you grow and die like flowers in the winter were not in vain. I do know what it is.

Hope.

This is my secret: I did not see the end of the world.

As the world broke and wailed like a dying beast, I walked through my forest in peace, watching young apprentices learn how to manipulate the blood of the now agonized Earth, their guardians hovering over them. They bowed to me when I approached, hope shimmering in their eyes just like it did in yours. It was easier for me to recognize such things back then, as it was to laugh and frown and build expressions from nothing, to shape my voice into questions. I was, slowly, becoming like your people, years of teaching the ways of earth-blood manipulation carving away at my nature.

I didn't mind it then, and neither would I mind it now. Change is life; staying still is to fade away, to slip into the bloodstream of the world like so many spirits do. I welcomed your people, taught them my ways, learned how you and yours think and talk and live. My price was words, stories of the world I helped maintain but would never be able to see. It was a fair trade, and for many of your mortal years I was happy.

But your people stopped coming. News never arrived, their bearers lost to space and time, maybe their own selves swallowed by the hungry darkness. The silence of the outside world was poison to those still learning with me, and they grew restless, worried. We went to the border, then, and we saw it.

The void bleeding into the stars of the clear night, the shadows enveloping pockets of earth and sky like the sea embracing her islands, the nothingness of the beyond opening its maw to swallow a broken, barely tethered world.

At the edge a silvery barrier stood, keeping it at bay.

A barrier I would never be able to touch.

"You can teach me," you say when we arrive at the edge of my forest. You step outside, eyes staring into the distant darkness, but my attention shifts away from you and the ruin of the world at my doorstep. My eyes are glued to the faint footprint of your small shoes, carved against the earth a hair's breadth away from the shadows my trees cast. A simple, insignificant step for you, but one I can't, for all my strength and magic, take.

I raise my eyes only when you turn to me, all that hope still shimmering in your eyes. I can't stop looking now, memorizing the simple, small movements you make, the way your breathing changes, how emotion manifests in you like a flower blooming to the night. I missed this. I forgot this.

But I can learn again.

"You can teach me," you repeat and I blink, processing the words, the intonation, the thoughts hidden beneath. "How to get through the barrier, I mean. With magic. Can't you?"

I don't answer. The silence stretches, the forest sighing, watching. Your face falls, crumbles like leaves to the wind, but you summon back a smile, hands curling into fists at your side. Is this resignation? Determination? Hope, still?

I can't tell. Your people have always been so hard to read when I least expect them to be, and the ease with which I saw each emotion earlier disappears like smoke around my fingertips.

"This was one of the training forests, wasn't it?" you say, and I still. Was. You are right, of course, but it stings. The forest falls silent, but you do not notice. "You taught my people how to use magic, didn't you? That's why they were able to leave."

That's why they didn't come back. Even though they promised to.

It's been so long, and that gave me more than enough time to think. Were human and elven promises what I thought them to be? Had I understood your people's words and intentions wrong? Was it a gap in my knowledge, a bridge between both our natures that I couldn't— still can't—cross?

You could answer me now, but I don't ask. I'm not sure I want answers, I realize.

The forest shivers.

Spirits always want answers.

"Please," you say, voice low. Hope still stares back at me from your gray eyes, and for a moment the urge to shatter it consumes me. The wind blows, the trees shake, their leaves falling over us, and in the distance a lone, painful howl crosses the silence.

You don't move. Neither do I.

Change is life, and life itself is dangerous. You will change me, if I accept, and I will change you. That's how things are, in the end. But you are young, your nature malleable, more attuned to the endless churning of life than mine will ever be. You will adapt and survive once you leave; I will unravel and scatter until time builds me up to what I was before you, or maybe I will follow my own people and fade into the blood yours prize so much. I can't tell.

It happened before, when they left. It will happen again, when you do.

The hope in your eyes is so clear, so fragile. Was mine like this, back then?

It doesn't matter. I do want to learn again.

"There is a price," I say finally and you falter for a second before nodding, eyes wide, eager. I tilt my head, and for the first time in years a smile tugs at my lips. "Tell me a story."

You are a terrible storyteller.

You can't weave a story or craft images and emotions with your words. The forest distracts you; you pause constantly, losing the tales you are trying to bring to life before they reach your mouth, your fascination for my kingdom clear in your wide eyes. The forest longs for you just as much as you crave its strangeness, so I don't say anything.

"Once upon a time," you try again as we walk, but your eyes immediately go to the golden stag watching us through the trees. You stop, gaze on the stag's sharp teeth and bone antlers, and shiver under its intelligent, cutting stare. You take a deep breath, color blossoming in your cheeks once you realize you got distracted again.

The stag's amusement presses against my mind and I smile, the forest humming in answer. You don't notice me, but you do notice the trees and the wind and the birds and the creature still watching us—you don't know, but he came here only for you—and the story is once again forgotten. I don't find it in myself to mind.

You ask me for breaks and I give them, though it confuses me. You ask me for food and water, and while it doesn't surprise me, I'm still intrigued by your antics. At night, you tell me—vaguely annoyed, I suspect—to stop and you curl up against a tree, falling asleep almost instantly. I stare at you for a long time and the beasts of the forest do the same, curious but not confused as I am. On some level, they are more like you than me, though I do eventually realize you are not going to be up any time soon. When the sun bleeds through the trees hours later, you jolt awake and continues our journey as if nothing happened. I follow along, and you do the same thing when the night comes once again.

I don't voice my questions, my doubts, and you don't seem to notice them. As you sleep, I think back to the many elven and human children I once taught, but I was never supposed to stay with them as I stay with you now. They had their guardians and I had their stories and it was enough.

It isn't enough now.

"And they lived happily ever after," you conclude one night while trying to stifle what I've learned is a yawn.

My jaw fights me, stretching in a mirror of you until a yawn forms and I'm left reeling. I don't sleep. I shouldn't yawn, and I didn't know how to until a week ago.

"Master," you say, interrupting my thoughts. I look up to see you curled against a tree, gray eyes shimmering under the fire's warm light. The title feels strange to me, but you insisted. *Aren't you my teacher?* you'd said, but I don't think you wanted an answer. "Tell me a story now. I have told you so many already."

I tense. The forest falls silent. "I don't have any," I say quietly and you frown. Much of the awe that shone in your eyes upon seeing me is now gone, days of traveling rendering me common to you. I should mind, I think, but I can't bring myself to.

"Impossible," you say. "Everyone has stories."

That gives me pause. Does everyone? I cannot think of one that is mine, acquired through my own adventures or listened to around a campfire. All the stories I know came from someone else, coins used for my knowledge and services. I stay quiet, but the look on your face makes my throat ache with words I hadn't planned on saying. "I never left the forest."

I watch your expression, memorizing, analyzing, saving it up for later. If I am to live with you for the years to come, I want to relearn how your people express themselves. It's far too different from how mine once did, back when I was but one of the dozens in this forest, but it works for me. I do not wish to unsettle you.

I watch your expression and I commit it to memory.

"You never left?" you ask. I remember to nod. "Why?"

I touch my chest. "The heart cannot leave the forest, and I am its host."

You bring your knees to your chest, resting your chin over them. You watch me in silence and I can't quite grasp what emotion hides behind your eyes. The forest sighs around us and I close my eyes, trying to mimic the way you sleep. I have noticed my being always awake is strange to you, and I do not wish that. I do not wish to be strange any longer.

There is a moment of silence and then, "When will you teach me?"

Manipulating magic itself is easy. Learning how to be ready for it is not.

The Earth's blood comes to me like breathing, deeply rooted in my essence since I came into existence more than a few thousand years ago, but it is not so simple for you and yours, whose link to our broken world's heart is not as strong as mine. That was what I discovered hundreds of years ago, when the first elf and the first human entered this forest in hopes of convincing me to teach them. The idea had me reeling, back then—how can one be taught to care?

Because that is what it is, as you slowly learn. To touch the Earth's blood, to survive it, you need to care for it first.

It is not as simple as caring for a forest or protecting an animal, like many of you seem to think. Caring about the Earth's blood, about the Earth itself, goes beyond refusing to kill a beast or cut down a tree. Hunger is natural, as is the need for a home, but not acknowledging the loss of life when you act upon these needs is not. It wasn't, at least, in the beginning, when I watched your people be born into this world. It shouldn't be, especially now.

There are easier ways to use what you and yours call magic. The blood of the Earth is not the only source of power. It might not even be the strongest in the sense of what mortals consider strong. It wasn't created for fighting, though it can be used for destruction, and if you aren't ready for it, it can be volatile, unpredictable. Learning, as you do here with me, is not accessible or simple, it doesn't make kingdoms more powerful, and it doesn't bring anyone money or even fame. Not by itself, at least. But many chose it in the past and you have no options.

So I teach you.

We lie down on the grass, listening to the forest growing and dying around us. I tell you to pay attention, to track down the sounds and songs, to understand what is happening around us, and let the silence reign afterward. The forest is a pulsing heart in my mind—I'm never not listening to it, but letting myself relax makes the life I'm responsible for shine brighter, like stars in a dark, moonless night. Birds sing nearby and a half-owl, half-tiger creature stares at us between the branches to our right, curious. The trees in this part of the forest are mischievous, hungry for new things; they lean towards you, their roots sliding under the earth to where we are.

"Master," you say, startling me from my thoughts. I open one eye to see you sitting, face contorted into a frown. "This is boring."

You are courting a tantrum. I've seen it enough times in the weeks we've been together to know what to expect from it, so I just tug your shirt until you are lying down again and whisper, "Shut up."

You gasp, flustered, but obey. Seconds pass in silence, but it doesn't last long. It never does, with you.

"Master," you say again, voice almost a whine. The owl-tiger finds you funny. The trees are delighted. I sigh and prop myself up on my elbows, staring you down. You go quiet, expression now one of embarrassed guilt, with just a tiny bit of mischief lurking underneath it. I'm satisfied—weeks ago, I wouldn't have been able to read so much, to understand this much.

"Do you want me to show you what I feel?"

That piques your interest. "Can you do that?"

"There isn't much I can't do here," I say simply, because it is the truth, but you only send me an annoyed glare. I raise my hand and you eye it for a second—my skin rough like bark, my wrist covered by vines, flowers blooming between my fingertips, nothing, nothing like yours— and take it. I close my eyes, for your sake, and you do the same.

I pull you in, opening the linked minds of my forest to you. I hear you gasp, feel your wonder and awe through the bridge now between us, and guide you through what I think will interest you more. The owl-tiger amazes you, as do the birds, but it pleases me—though I don't quite understand why—that the trees are ones that hold your attention for longer. They are happy with it, too, and I can almost feel your smile.

We stay like this for hours and the days after pass easily, and you put in the effort, eager to learn what I've shown you. I quickly learn, too, that this is how you work—with clear goals, a concrete, visible result you can fight for in your mind. You are what I never was: relentless.

You have been here for three years when you get angry at me for the first time.

Our progress through the forest is slow but constant, and you grow stronger, my teachings coming to you easily now that we are past the struggles of starting. Time has taken the childishness from your face and body, pushing you mercilessly toward adulthood. You are not there yet and won't be for a few more years, but you reach my shoulders now and the forest doesn't scare you any longer. You are still fascinated by it, which makes me gladder than I ever thought it would. I do not wish to lose the admiration you have for me.

It happens because you find a fox pup in the bushes, lost and dehydrated and hungry, death already calling for it. Its parents are gone or dead. You don't ask and I don't search for answers, though I could easily find out if I wanted to. The pup is tiny, disgruntled, dirty, but you are immediately enamored with it. You nurse it back to health, give it a name, play with it. It amuses me and it makes you happy, and that makes me happy, too.

But one day we leave the pup in a glade for a lesson. All goes well until we are already heading back, you talking, I listening. A bolt of alarm crosses the forest, and I see it too quickly: the fox pup, a bird of prey, blood on the green grass. I turn to you, but your eyes are already widening with horror—you know enough to feel it too, the forest, though not nearly as much as I do—and you sprint past me to the glade. It's too late, of course.

I've seen you cry before, but not like this. It tugs at something in my chest, makes my fingers tingle with the need to do something, but I stay still, watching you mourn the little pup with vines blossoming in my lungs, flowers pushing against my throat. The forest is quiet, quieter than it has been in years, and in the silence your agony reverberates, echoing through my bones. It's the worst, most painful thing I've ever heard.

But then you turn to me.

"Master," you say, tears falling down your cheek, cheeks flushed red. For the first time, the title is not said in admiration or even in teasing, but as an accusation, a blade too sharp for me to grasp. "You could have saved him, couldn't you?"

I go still, your words throwing me off. Could I?

There is no need to question myself. Of course I could have. A single warning down the forest would have kept the bird away. It would have been easy.

I hesitate, but my silence is enough for you. Your expression turns furious, your hands balled into fists, and even your posture changes, becoming hard, taut, poised to defend or attack. It would have fascinated me at any other time, but it breaks the heart I don't really own here, now.

"How could you?"

I have nothing but the truth to tell you. "I didn't think," I say. "I'm not supposed to intervene. I'm not supposed to use my power to stop nature."

You scoff. "What do you think you are?" *A spirit*, I almost say, but something tells me that is not what you want to hear, so I don't. "You can't just choose to do nothing." You sneer at me. "I hate you."

These are childish words, but they cut deep. I watch you go in silence, the forest murmuring in your wake. I stay still, vaguely noticing the way my heart beats angrily in my ribcage. I don't follow you, nor do I try to watch where you go—I sit against a tree and wait, fingers mindlessly playing with the grass.

"What did I do wrong?" I ask, and can almost hear the tree scoff, insulted. I close my eyes.

It takes you three days to return. I feel more than hear you coming, footsteps almost silent, like I taught you. I get up, a bolt of doubt and anxiety running through me. I don't know what to expect from you and I don't quite know what I should do or say either. It's a maddening, infuriating feeling.

But you give me no time to think. You are in the glade and on me before I can quite comprehend what is going on, your arms around me, face on my shoulder. My first thought before hugging you back awkwardly is that it can't be comfortable for you, with my rough skin and pointed bones, but you don't seem to mind.

You sniffle against my collarbone, voice low but teasing, "You are so bad at this, Master."

I don't say anything. You're right, after all.

You lean back, pulling away from me. "I'm sorry," you say, not quite looking at me. "I shouldn't have said any of that." The words come off like you are pulling teeth. I can't help but smile. "I don't hate you, and I understand now that you have your role to fulfill to the forest. I mean," you sniffle again. "I knew that before, but I was angry."

Your hair is too long. It falls stubbornly over your eyes. I push it away. "You were sad. It's all right."

I reach for what I've been working on in the past three days and your gaze follows my hand, frowning when the tree spits out a pendant onto my palm. I close my fingers around the stone, a bright green emerald that is still warm to the touch.

"It's for you," I say, and you frown, leaning in for me to put it around your neck. "I was given this when this world was new, to remind me of my duty." I gesture to my throat, where the emerald used to be, and your eyes widen. I smile. "I took it too seriously, I think. It made me not act when I should have. I'm sorry." You say nothing, gaze going from my throat to my face. I can't quite place your expression. "This is my promise to you: I will guard what you hold dear as if it were so to me as well. More, even. I'm sorry."

You blink away tears, clutching the pendant so strongly your knuckles turn white, but I still can't quite understand the expression on your face. It's too complex for me, for whom all of this feels foreign, different.

After a moment you sigh, resting your forehead on my shoulder. "Stop that, Master."

I'm confused. "Stop what?"

"Your thing," you say, voice muffled. "Trying to figure out what my expression means. You know."

My confusion turns to bafflement. I didn't know you knew. "I'm only trying to learn them," I say, and you let out a long suffering, fake sigh that would bring a smile to my lips if I wasn't so startled.

"You don't need to do that."

"My lack of expression bothers your kind though," I say. "You are not used to it."

"My kind might not be," you say. "But I am. I can understand you well enough."

That makes me pause. "Can you?"

You lean back, smiling now. The mischief in your eyes is impossible to miss. "Of course," you say, as if it's obvious, as if generations of mortals just like you hadn't spent their lives here with me, trying to figure out how to act around someone so different, so strange. "The forest," you say and I freeze, so surprised the trees around us fall in complete, absolute silence. Your smile widens. "See? It always reacts to you. It's easy to understand you if I pay attention to it, too."

Your expression turns satisfied, proud. "You're not that hard to read."

There is a long moment of silence and then the forest comes to life, trees murmuring to the wind, birds singing, the sound of life filling my home to bursting. I don't need to anymore, but I smile.

The end comes too soon, even if more than seven years have passed since I found you in that glade, afraid but hopeful, daring since the first moment. I don't tell you, but I grow uneasily quiet, and I think you understand or at least suspect what is to come. We are almost at where we started, having journeyed through the whole forest with no real pattern or plan to arrive here, where my existence began.

Every spirit has an origin and mine is the lone tree standing in the middle of the glade, not far away from the edge of the forest. The tree is nothing much, as I was nothing much when the world began. But it is special to me, and I want it to be special to you too, even if any other tree would work just as well.

When we enter the glade, the sun is just beginning to rise. The forest is deadly silent and the heart inside my ribcage flutters wildly, stealing away my breath. For a strange, reality-shattering moment I think about leaving, about telling you I won't give you anything anymore, but the thought goes just as fast as it came, leaving nothing but guilt in its wake. I have no right to imprison you here with me. I want you to be happy, and for that you must leave.

"Come," I say, offering you my hand. You take it without hesitation, eyes on the tree. "It will be fast now. It's almost over."

We kneel by the tree and I touch its trunk in greeting, humming quietly when its presence bumps playfully against my mind. If I were to have any family, my guess is that this tree would be the closest thing to one; its roots built my body, its sap my blood. It's an honor to make you part of my family, too, in the end.

Your hand touches the tree's trunk beside mine and my throat closes. The forest is still silent. It hurts to breathe. "I'll bring it to you," I say. "The Earth-blood you need to be linked to the world. It will hurt a little, but—"

"Master," you interrupt me, and I turn to you. I don't need to analyze your expression anymore, but it still amazes me, how much emotion you can put in it, how worried and eager and hesitant you can appear, all at once. "I have been thinking." I arch an eyebrow and you roll your eyes, though your voice trembles a little. "You never asked me how I ended up here."

I don't say anything. I don't think you want me to.

"I got separated from my family when the world ended," you continue. "But that was ten years ago."

There is a surge of movement and sound in the forest. Ten years ago?

"I know," you say. "It didn't make much sense to me at first. You talk as if you've been alone for a long time." *Three hundred years*, I almost say. "I crossed into this land with the help of someone else a few weeks before I ended up here in your forest. They weren't going the way I wanted so I was left alone." A pause. "And it left me thinking, this difference, you know? Maybe time broke as well. Maybe it was ruined when the world shattered. Maybe it passes differently for people in different lands." Your voice almost breaks, but you go on, not looking at me now. "Maybe a thousand years have passed for my family. Maybe none at all. Maybe they are gone, and I've been fighting to get to them for nothing."

Something bursts inside my chest. Hope. It feels ironic, inappropriate, and I swallow it down.

"But I still want to check, you know? I need to be sure." Ice fills my veins. I can't speak, so I just nod. "But," you say, and your voice turns to steel, your fingers closing around mine with so much force it hurts. I don't push you away. "I want you go with me, Master."

I freeze. The forest erupts in chaos, a cacophony of sounds and feelings, of movement I can't quite control. Again, you don't seem to notice anything but me and my origin tree, and for a moment it feels like nothing else exists beyond us three. I force myself to swallow past the lump in my throat, because I know that isn't the truth. My forest exists. The heart that doesn't belong to me beats inside my chest. I shake my head.

"I can't," I say. "You know that."

But you lean forward, your other hand going to my chest, where my false heart beats. "The heart can't leave," you say. "But you can, Master. You can come with me. I can show you everything I talked about in my stories. The mountains, the sea, my kingdom, if it still exists." You smile. "If it doesn't, we can explore. Find new places. New people."

I open my mouth, words to refute you making their way to my lips, but you are relentless. You have always been. You touch my origin tree again, reach down with your mind and pull. Shock floods me, and I watch in silence as you pull the Earth-blood to you through my origin tree. You sigh, biting down a grunt of pain, but you don't stop. The Earth's blood shines under your skin when you let go of my tree and you move quickly, as if you have thought about this too many times to hesitate. And you must have, I realize. You have been planning this for a while.

You touch your own chest, eyes closed, sweat running down your face. Your whole body trembles but I do not interrupt you. You have come too far for me to treat you like the child you aren't anymore. You are strong. But I already knew that, didn't I?

When you bring your hand to me, something shimmers above it in a bright shade of red. It hurts, looking at it, but I do anyway, barely listening to the forest roaring in my ears, to the wind howling and howling in my mind. When you speak, though, everything fades away—your voice is clear like water and you smile, pointed teeth poking your own lips. You are proud. I am too.

On your hand, your heart burns bright.

Half of it.

"Leave the forest's heart, Master," you say, your other hand still holding mine. "My heart is enough for both of us."

I lean forward, resting my head against yours. The warmth of your heart presses against my throat, against my chest, seeping into my rough skin.

"It is, Master," you say quietly. "That is my promise to you. Come with me."

I smile, and for the first time in my life I let go of the forest and its trees and animals, pulling away from my eternal, unwavering watch. I relax and I laugh, pressing my lips to your forehead.

"Yes," I say. "Yes."

You are the one guiding me now, as we make our way to the border of what has been my home for my whole life. You step outside, smiling under the sun, and turn to me, offering me a hand. Your heart— my heart now—beats comfortably inside my chest and I can still feel the other one, the heart we left in my origin tree. It's still mine too, in a way—I will never abandon this place.

"Master," you say, mischief in your voice. "It's your turn."

"My turn?"

Your smile widens.

"Tell me a story."

SHIFT

BY MIKA STANARD

Sometimes, Olivia wondered when she was going to tell her best friend that she knew she was a werewolf.

It wasn't that hard to tell, really. Every so often, Alexandra would spend a whole night away, only to come stumbling in around six in the morning, dead tired (though she always made it to class—even if she had class at eight thirty). At first, Olivia had thought it was some sort of party scene she didn't know about, but Alex never smelled like alcohol when she came in that late. And Olivia knew she wasn't hooking up— when Alex did that, she was back by two A.M. sharp.

It hadn't taken Olivia more than three go-rounds to notice that this only happened at the full moon.

She'd been sitting on that information for just over a year. Since Olivia and Alexandra had been assigned to be roommates at Lewis & Clark College their freshman year, they'd gotten closer than Olivia had to maybe anyone she'd previously known.

The world knew that shifters existed, of course. There were all kinds—selkies, kitsune, swan people, werewolves, and others about whom fewer legends had been crafted. Just because the world knew, however, didn't mean it was happy to accept the fact. Some people expressed their displeasure only with their voices and their votes, but others were more violent—up to and including murder. Plenty of shifters stayed in the closet for their own safety. Clearly, Alex was one of those. But Olivia couldn't keep pretending she didn't know. That felt like a lie. And, the closer they got, the less Olivia liked lying to Alex, even by omission.

So, she made a plan.

It was a Friday night, nowhere near the full moon. Olivia and Alexandra were sitting in their room after a long week of classes.

Alexandra sat on her bed with its blue geometric-patterned comforter, under her Florence + The Machine posters, women in science calendar, and pictures of her family. Olivia sat at her tidy desk, under walls that were bare except for a drawing of a chameleon Alexandra had done for her, pretending to work on her Spanish homework.

Out of nowhere, Olivia spoke up.

She couldn't just ask Alex if she was a werewolf directly. That seemed likely to scare her—and, if Olivia was being honest, she was too nervous. If she did this wrong, Alex might think she was being overly intrusive and take offense. Olivia doubted it, but years of her mother's taking offense at the slightest thing had left her uneasy about rocking the boat in any way. Worse, Alex might get hurt. Olivia knew the idea she had instead probably wasn't the best way to go about it, but she couldn't think of any better way.

She just had to set the right context, and it would be fine. Olivia hadn't been to many sleepovers as a kid, but she knew the theory.

"Hey," she said, having judged it late enough at night that her idea had a chance of being accepted. "Do you want to play a game?"

"What sort of game?" asked Alexandra, looking up.

"I ask you a question, and you have to answer honestly—and then you do the same with me," said Olivia, moving to sit on her bed across from Alexandra. "We keep going until one of us isn't willing to answer a question, or until we run out of questions, or until we want to go to bed."

A flicker of nervousness crossed Alexandra's face, but then she smiled. "Sounds good to me."

Olivia decided to start off conventional. "What's the most embarrassing thing that's ever happened to you?"

Alexandra thought for a moment. "Probably the time I threw up on stage in my middle school play," she said. "I'd been feeling sick all day, but I'd wanted that role so bad, and I was so determined to go on... I knew what was gonna happen pretty soon after I went on, but I couldn't just run offstage mid-scene—kid logic, you know? One of my moms and my little brother were in the audience, and I just—I just puked mid-sentence. And then I kept trying to go on with the scene, and one of the teachers had to come out and take me offstage, and I honestly don't know if they went on with the play or not, because I went home after that."

Olivia smiled. "Oof."

"Yeah," said Alexandra, smiling back. "My turn. Who was your first kiss?"

Olivia froze. She'd been afraid of this question, or questions along these lines. But she was probably going to make Alex very uncomfortable later in this conversation. It was only fair she experienced a little discomfort herself. "No one," she said. "I've never kissed anyone, and I never plan to. I'm aroace."

Alexandra suddenly smiled wide, and her body seemed to expand. "Oh, cool!" she said. "I might be aromantic. I'm not sure yet."

Now it was Olivia's turn to smile. "Awesome," she said. "I was worried you'd think I was weird."

"What? No way!" Alexandra vehemently replied. "I try not to be a shitty person. I'm not going to judge you for your orientation."

"So, what's your thinking on the might-be-aromantic thing?" asked Olivia. "That's not my question—you don't have to answer if you don't want to—I'm just curious."

"You'd better make it your question," said Alexandra with a quirk to her mouth, "because I'll tell you, but I'll need some incentive."

"Okay," said Olivia. "If you're sure you're okay with that. Why do you think you might be aromantic?"

"First, I have a question for you—this isn't part of the game. Are you comfortable with me talking about sex around you?"

"Yes, as long as you don't get too explicit, or make jokes or anything that put me in a sexual situation," said Olivia. "Like—don't imply that I like someone in that way, or stuff like that."

"Gotcha," said Alexandra. "This is a long story, so buckle up."

"I have all night," Olivia replied.

"All right," said Alexandra, settling herself. "Well. I was sixteen, a junior in high school, and I had this friend named Nathan Middleton. He was cute, and I knew he had a crush on me, and one day we were eating lunch in our little corner of school grounds, under a fire escape, and... he kissed me."

"What happened then?" asked Olivia.

"I kissed him back. And from then on... things were different. At first, it felt great. He was paying all this attention to me, he liked me. And we kissed, and eventually we started sleeping together, but other than that, nothing really changed. But then... he wanted me to spend more time with him than I spent with any of my other friends. When I talked to him about it, he said, 'I thought we were more than just friends,' and I realized... I had no idea what he was talking about. Because what's just about friends?" Alexandra asked.

"Ugh, I hate that expression," Olivia groaned.

"Yeah, me too," said Alexandra, twirling a shiny strand of long, dark hair around her finger. "Friends are the most important thing there is to me, after my family. And... I had a whole social circle, and he was one part of it, but he wanted to be the most important thing in my life. And he never could be. I thought something was wrong with me, that I didn't want the same thing he did. I tried to fix it, I tried to want what he wanted, because you hear all these stories about people falling in love and it being the best thing ever, you know? But I wasn't feeling anything for Nathan that I hadn't felt all along, and I didn't think I'd loved him for as long as I'd known him—not like that, anyway. I did some Googling, and I found the word aromantic. And I realized that I've totally thought people were hot—I'm not asexual by any stretch of the imagination—but I've never really had a crush, the way other people seem to. I don't want to—I don't know, what do people even want when they have crushes?"

"You're asking the wrong person," said Olivia wryly.

Alexandra laughed. "Yeah, I guess I am." She leaned forward. "Okay, now it's my turn to ask a question." She looked down. "What's the biggest secret you've ever kept?"

Olivia looked up, thinking. She knew why Alex had asked that question, and the way she answered might influence how comfortable Alex was in telling her secret. She knew it wasn't the same thing at all, but at the very least an honest answer might help demonstrate that she trusted Alex, and thus was more likely to be okay with whoever she was.

There was one answer that immediately came to mind.

"I didn't tell my parents I was applying to out-of-state schools until I got the scholarship," she said. "I knew they wouldn't pay for me to leave. I bought my own plane ticket. My mom was so mad…"

Alexandra winced. "I'm sorry."

"Yeah, I'm used to it," Olivia replied with a shrug. "And now I'm here."

"Now you're here." Alexandra smiled faintly.

"Okay, my turn." This was it. Olivia swallowed the knot in her throat and looked Alexandra square in the eye. If this went wrong, she could lose the only best friend she'd ever had—and, more importantly, hurt Alex. "Are you a werewolf?"

Alexandra looked like she was stuck in the path of a speeding train.

Olivia looked down. "I'm sorry," she said. "I probably shouldn't've asked like that, I just... I wasn't sure how to tell you."

Alexandra took a deep breath. She fiddled with the corner of her comforter, where a bit of thread was coming loose. She bit her nails, already gnawed down. She twirled her long, dark hair around one finger—a frequent habit, but she was tugging on it in the way she mostly did when she was nervous.

"Mom Lina made me promise not to tell you." Alexandra's voice was quiet. "She says it's dangerous for anyone to know. I wanted to tell you, but—"

"I'm sorry," said Olivia. "I'm not upset that you didn't tell me or anything. And I'm sorry if I put you in an awkward position with your mom. I just—I couldn't keep pretending I didn't know."

Alexandra gave Olivia a long, curious look. "Is that what this game was about?"

"Maybe," Olivia said. "I didn't want to just bring it up—I wanted to give you the chance to find out some stuff about me, as well. And this doesn't have to change anything—Alex, you're still Alex—but if you want it to change some things? I can totally adapt."

"I'm glad you're not freaking out about this," said Alexandra. "I was worried that if you ever found out you would."

"You didn't need to worry, but I get why you were nervous," said

Olivia. "I don't blame you for being cautious, not at all. But I just want you to know you'll always be safe with me."

Alexandra smiled. "Thanks," she said quietly. "It goes without saying that you won't tell anyone, right?"

"Of course," said Olivia. "I would never." She took a breath. "Is there anything you want me to know about you—like, things I can do differently?"

Alexandra nodded. "Yeah. You may have noticed, my mood and energy levels vary on a fairly regular schedule. The first bit's called transformation sickness. It happens right after you change back to a human from being in wolf form, and it sucks. Normally around humans I can pass it off as a cycle thing—my other cycle, I mean—but yes, I get depressed and irritable. Then my mood and energy build up until I shift again. That sounds like a good thing, but in the last few days before a shift, it can actually be a problem—you're bouncing off the walls, super jittery, sometimes snappy and irritable again. If you could just... be patient with me in the days right before and after a full moon, and understand that if I seem a little snappy, it's not personal."

Olivia remembered the days immediately following one of Alex's long nights out. She took long naps, struggled to complete her homework, and barely ate (complaining that "everything tastes like nothing," which Olivia had decided was either a profound philosophical statement or a reason to accompany Alex to the dining hall to make sure she was eating something). In the days leading up to a full moon, Alex would come back to the room around midnight, even more jazzed up than usual, and alternate between trying to get homework done, shouting at said homework for being difficult, apologizing for shouting at her homework, and wanting to talk about anything and everything. Once, she'd suggested karaoke, only for Olivia to point out that it was past midnight and they should probably let the rest of the dorm sleep. Alex had suggested going outside, and Olivia hadn't had the heart to argue with the look Alex gave her, so they'd wound up loudly singing Adele under the nearly full moon.

Olivia nodded. "Anything else?"

"We have altered senses—even when we're not shifted, though it's stronger when we are. So if you could avoid bringing stuff that smells really strong into the room, that would be great."

"What do you mean, altered?"

"I mean senses closer to the animal you shift into. Like me—I have a much better sense of smell than most humans, because I shift into a canine. Bat shifters, back when they existed, would have better hearing. And so on."

"You have a better sense of smell... so, does the orange stuff I put in the washer to get rid of smells bother you?"

"No. I'll admit it did at first, but I'm used to it by now. It just smells like you."

"You could've told me."

"I know, but I didn't know you well yet, and besides, I didn't want to make up some lie." She paused, face falling. "Oh... my moms need to know you know."

"Why?" asked Olivia. "Won't they get mad at you for telling me? Wouldn't it be better to just keep it a secret?"

"You don't understand," said Alexandra, frustration flashing in her eyes for a moment before quickly fading out again. "When you have a secret like my family does... you have to trust each other, or you'll have nothing."

"Okay," said Olivia, raising her hands in a placating gesture. "We can tell them. I'll come with you, if it helps—or I can stay out of it. Whichever is easier."

"It'll probably be better if you come along," said Alexandra. "I want them to be looking at you while I tell them. It might make them more sympathetic. And besides, if all goes well, they might decide to adopt you."

"What?"

"Not literally. Just, what better way to make sure you don't betray us than to make you part of the family?" Alexandra explained, as though it was the most obvious thing in the world. "And besides," she said, voice dropping into a sympathetic mutter, "based on what I know of your birth family, it sure seems to me like you could use another."

Olivia gave a slight nervous laugh. The idea of Alexandra's family taking her in sounded like the sort of thing that only happened in stories. Then again, over the past couple years, she'd gotten a full-ride scholarship to college, gotten out of her house, and met Alexandra. Who knew what else was possible?

Olivia sat in the car outside Alexandra's house, while Alexandra, sitting next to her, took a deep breath.

"It's gonna be fine," Alexandra told herself.

"Whenever you're ready," said Olivia.

In a single quick motion, Alexandra got out of the car and made her way to the house. Olivia followed.

Cynthia—a white woman with a blonde pixie cut and blue eyes, who Olivia had seen in the pictures of Alex's family that hung on her walls—opened the door. "Hello," she said, holding out her hand for Olivia to shake, "You must be Olivia. I'm Cynthia. I've heard so much about you!"

"It's nice to meet you," said Olivia, shaking Cynthia's hand and walking into the house as Alexandra and Cynthia hugged.

As soon as Olivia was through the entryway, she found herself in a living room with Alex's brother Chase—a sandy-haired, young teenage boy—sitting on the couch, playing on his phone. He looked up when Olivia entered the room. Then, he looked back at his phone.

"Chase!" said Cynthia, exasperated. "Introduce yourself."

"Hey," said the boy, glancing at his screen periodically, even as he mostly looked at Olivia. "I'm Chase. What's your name?"

"I'm Olivia. It's nice to meet you."

"Oh, you're Olivia," said Chase. "Alex talks about you all the time."

"Yeah," said Alexandra from directly behind Olivia, "I kinda do."

Olivia jumped.

"Oh, sorry," said Alexandra. "Didn't mean to scare you."

Just then, Lina—a white woman with shoulder-length dark hair, whom Olivia recognized from when she'd helped Alex move into the dorm—walked in, carrying a plate of cookies.

"I made your favorite," she said to Alexandra. "Peanut butter chocolate chip. I trust you'd have told me if Olivia was allergic to peanuts?" She turned to Olivia. "Are you?"

"I'm not," Olivia replied. "Those smell delicious."

"Thank you," said Lina, smiling. "Go ahead and have one. They're still warm."

Alexandra, Olivia and Chase each took a cookie.

Olivia broke off a piece of the cookie and put it in her mouth. The edge was chewy, softening towards an almost gooey center, with pockets of molten chocolate. It was sweet and salty and tasted like the cookies Olivia had read about in books.

"Did Pippa get one?" Alexandra asked.

"Yes, I brought her hers first," Lina assured her.

"You said Pippa's not always comfortable around strangers, right?" Olivia said. "Tell her I said hi."

"Will do." Alexandra paused mid-bite of her cookie and swallowed uncomfortably. "Mom Lina, Mom Cynthia, uh... there's something I need to tell you."

Chase promptly stood up and left the room, practically tripping over his own feet in his haste.

"What is it?" asked Lina.

Alexandra looked down. "Well..." She took a deep breath. "Olivia knows... about us."

Lina's face went cloudy, and Cynthia looked shocked.

"I didn't tell her! She figured it out on her own! I just... answered her questions."

"How much did you tell her?" asked Cynthia, eyeing Olivia nervously.

Olivia took a deep breath. No matter what happens here, I'll be fine. She'd gotten this far essentially on her own. If she had to go back to that... well, it would hurt, but she would manage.

She looked over at Alex, who was looking up again. She seemed more confident now.

"Nothing important, I swear," said Alexandra. "She knows we

shift, she doesn't know how."

"Okay," said Cynthia, "this could be worse." She turned to Olivia. "What do you think of all this?"

Olivia looked at Cynthia. "I think Alex is Alex, and I'd be a lousy friend if I didn't accept her for who she was."

Alexandra smiled. "Mom Lina, what's for dinner tonight?"

"I was thinking mac n' cheese," said Lina. "Do you like mac n' cheese, Olivia?"

"YES!" shouted Alexandra. "Mom Lina's mac n' cheese is the best you've ever tasted, I promise."

"I mean, I've never had homemade before," said Olivia, who was more accustomed to the contents of a blue box, "but I'd love to try."

"You're gonna love it!" Alexandra enthused.

"This is delicious," Olivia exclaimed when she finally came up for air between bites of very hot mac n' cheese.

Lina and Cynthia were seated at opposite ends of the table, Chase was sitting across from Alexandra, Alexandra was sitting next to Olivia, and even Pippa, Alex's ten-year-old sister with sandy hair like her brother's, had come out at the promise of mac n' cheese. She wasn't looking at Olivia, but she didn't seem overly bothered by her presence as she dug into her mac n' cheese with a spoon.

"Told you so," said Alexandra smugly.

"Thank you so much for having me."

"Of course," Cynthia replied. "It's been lovely having you over."

"Alex told us you want to be an interpreter," said Cynthia.

"That's right," said Olivia. "I love people, and I love languages, and it just seemed like a good mix."

"That's wonderful," said Cynthia. "I wish you the best of luck."

"Thank you," said Olivia.

"I think they're well on their way to adopting you," said Alexandra to Olivia in the car on the way back to their dorm.

Olivia scoffed. "Really? They were just being nice." She knew it was ridiculous, but some part of her was worried that, if she dared to say out loud that Alexandra's family was genuine in their efforts to include her, it would turn out not to be true.

"Yeah, give it a few more dinners and you'll be family. To all of them, not just me," said Alexandra.

"I…" said Olivia. "Thanks."

"Don't be silly, of course you're my family. Which is why, if you hadn't figured out the whole deal with me being a werewolf—I was going to tell you. Family is incredibly important to me—but I'm at the age where I'm starting to expand my family. And I want you to be part of that."

"Wow," said Olivia. "I… I'm honored."

Alexandra smiled. "Welcome to the pack."

Olivia grinned.

"So, if you ever need us to rip someone limb from limb for you, let me know," said Alexandra with a glint in her eye.

Olivia looked alarmed.

"I'm joking," Alexandra reassured her. "...Mostly."

Olivia laughed.

"But seriously," said Alexandra. "You need anything, you ask. My family—we take pack seriously. And you're part of that now, or you will be soon. So, don't even think about pretending you don't have problems anymore, okay? We're here. We've got you."

Olivia stared out the window.

No one had ever said anything like that to her before. Back home, she'd been admired by her Model UN team for her ability to stay cool in any situation, for the way she never missed a meeting—essentially, for pretending not to have problems. At home, complaining wasn't an option—her mother expected perfection, and her father never argued. Olivia's entire life had been spent learning how to manage on her own, because she knew no one would help her. The idea of having people she could go to if she needed help—of not having to work everything out on her own—was such a monumental shift that she wasn't sure how to process it.

"Sorry if I'm overwhelming you," said Alexandra.

"No, it's okay."

It was a lot to take in. But Olivia knew she had time.

Alex was her best friend, and she wasn't going anywhere.

Through the dark, in quiet, they drove on.

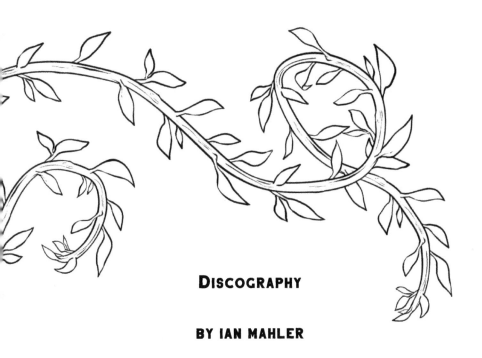

DISCOGRAPHY

BY IAN MAHLER

it must've been a fortune cookie, or maybe the
radio, *falling in love is the human condition,*
meaning humanity doesn't come in odd numbers,
meaning I'm something other than human,
meaning I might not be real, *listen,* I'm
getting tired of this music, I'll never know what all
your favorite songs are about

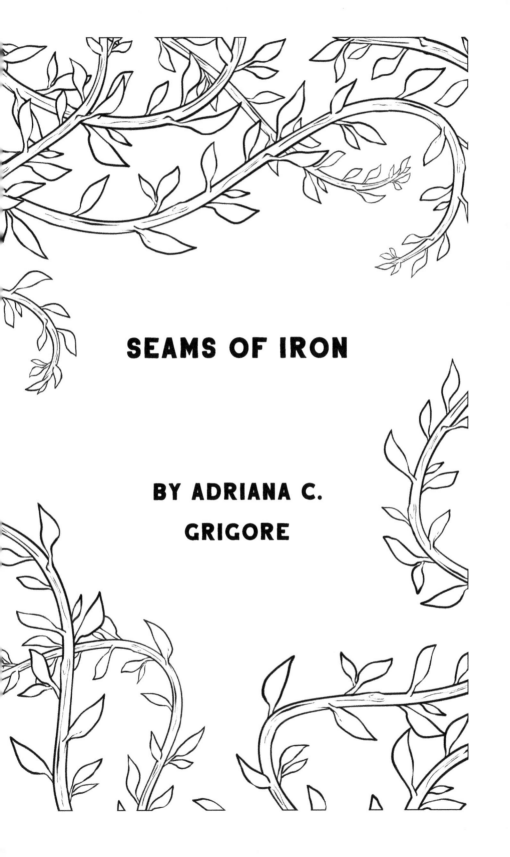

SEAMS OF IRON

BY ADRIANA C. GRIGORE

When Erin first found the witch's hut, it was past dusk, and birds were slicing the last spill of sunlight from the horizon, letting it fall like ribbons into the wild, rippling sea. The wind was so strong that the wood of the walls creaked, as if the hut was of half a mind to just let itself be taken away, broken and splashed into the air, like a dry image of a shipwreck. The thistle and chamomile and hyssop that lay around the garden fence were blown back from the cliffside, nearly doubled down to the earth, then shaken around, when the wind turned.

It was cold, but wonderfully so. Erin rushed to get out of the feeble shelter of the hut's shadow and turned to face the sea, letting the gale splash into her like the waves down below. She could barely hear them at the bottom of that grey cliff, so loud was the call of the world, the winds that pulled the night from over the horizon.

It made her feel clean.

It made her feel *light*, as if she could have let go and flown away at once with the house. Yet she didn't, and the house held its ground too, in quiet solidarity. Instead, Erin swept her ruffled hair out of her face, took a deep breath of sharp, brackish air, and pushed the gate of the witch's fence inward, dragging the frayed edges of her dress up the short, pebbled path, to the door.

The witch didn't answer her knocks for a good long while, so long that Erin thought of seating herself and her stuffed wicker basket down by the door and waiting for the morning, when maybe she would come out. Yet, on her fifth round of knocks, something was knocked over in turn on the other side, and she heard a string of curses muttered far within, before the door finally opened, forcefully enough to make the wood of its frame groan.

The witch looked at her as if Erin was someone come to beg the

231

last piece of bread off her—tired, irritated and drained of patience. She was tall, and younger than Erin had expected someone like her to be, with only a few untimely strips of grey in her long, dark hair. Her eyes were like the sea at night, her face like a wraith's lost in the forest. She stared at Erin loudly enough that she didn't need words.

Erin made herself smile, and held her basket up between them. "Do you need a cloak?"

Her father used to have the most wonderful cloaks, when she was younger. Not few were the days when Erin would take one of them, wrap it around her body, and run to the edge of the woods, imagining she was a huntress, or maybe a woodsman, or a groundskeeper like her father. She was so short then that she would come back home with the hems all muddy and scratched by briars, and she'd do her best to put them all to rights again before anyone saw.

She mostly learned stitching through that alone. The rest she learned from the castle maids, who were only too happy to see her busying herself every once in a while with something more sensible than play-fighting with her brothers, wearing her father's clothes, or following him around the castle grounds.

They weren't a wealthy family—that was what they said, when someone saw the brooches holding their robes, and wondered at their frayed clothes.

When their great-grandfather had been offered the chance of living in the castle, their father told them once, he'd already been groundskeeper for half his life. At the time, he'd refused the king, politely, meekly, saying that their home was already close enough. Yet, afterwards, the walls of the castle grounds had started shifting, year after year, until they had stretched far enough to encase their home too. As if it had been the land itself that wanted to hold its keeper close; and nobody had ever realised when it had happened, least of all the groundskeeper, or the royalty.

They hadn't been born into richness. Rather, it had gathered at their seams anyway, like dirt in the wrinkles of their clothes, like dust lingering in the corners of a hastily swept room. Royalty was always something next-door, something that was always there, with all its funny ways of being, familiar and unfamiliar, like all people one only saw through slanted windows.

They *weren't* a wealthy family, yet sometimes dregs of wealth slipped in under the door. At wintertide, Erin and her siblings were gifted golden brooches on one side of the garden wall, and straw dolls on the other, and rejoiced equally over both. At summertide, their father served them venison on wooden plates and plum pie in silver bowls. It was a strange dance they did around fortune, blending it in their life while hanging on to an idea of humility.

A peculiarity, that was all it was. While others had neighbours that liked to sleep in bed with their chickens, they had neighbours that liked to sleep on sheets of silk, kings and queens and eleven princes with golden birds hanging over their beds.

The witch went deeper into the darkened hut and sat heavily in a chair. There were a great number of pots and cups gathered on a long table beside her, and before turning to Erin again, she busied herself by adding another spoonful of dark honey in a steaming mug and stirring it too little for it to actually melt.

When she faced Erin again, her sour expression had not changed.

"I can't stay outside in all that wind, I'm gonna catch my death," the witch said, a bit hoarsely. "What did you want from me again?"

Erin held her basket tight. "To give you a cloak," she said.

"Why?"

It was a dry word, and colder than the wind outside. The witch raised the mug to her mouth and took a deep gulp, and yet her eyes did not leave Erin, as if she expected her to try to steal something from right under her nose, or maybe take a poisonous snake out of her basket and throw it at her. Others had thought the same.

"I thought you might need one," Erin said, nevertheless.

"I do?" the witch asked, and set the mug down. "How would you know that? What do you know of me?"

"Nothing," Erin admitted. "I just thought this cloak was meant for you."

Here, at last, the witch's gaze lowered to her basket, and Erin only wasted a moment of that sombre stare before pulling out the cloak and holding it up to the dim candlelight. It was a good size, almost as tall as her.

"What is that?" asked the witch, after a few moments. "Nettles?"

"Yes," Erin agreed, and lowered the cloak just enough so that they could look at each other again. "I finished it just yesterday."

It had taken her little longer than a month. She'd gotten fast, over the years.

This time, the witch, at last seeming overcome by a bit of curiosity, rose from the chair and took a couple steps closer. "How am I to wear this?" she asked.

"You won't," Erin said. "I mean, you will, but not like this. I need to give it to you first."

Then, instead of trying to explain herself further, she shook the cloak in the air once, and in place of the wilted, brownish green of before, it turned to a smooth grey, like the face of the cliff they were standing on. She held it out to the witch, only getting to feel the softness of the fabric for a moment before it was taken at last out of her hands.

Erin then stood there, with only nettles and other weeds left in her basket, and feeling both a bit relieved and a bit empty, as she always did after doing this. She watched the witch turn the cloak this way and that, as if to see if any trace of the nettle thread still remained. It didn't—there was Erin's needlework, her careful hemming, the very pattern she had chosen to knit into it, but the thread she'd used had disappeared completely. As it ought to. It was a rather pretty cloak, all in all.

The wind was roiling outside, as if goading her to come back, to come outside and let it press her on another path, another road. Already, Erin could almost feel her bruised fingers itching to begin again.

The witch raised her eyes to her again, suspicious, distrustful, but perhaps still a bit curious.

"You're not a witch," she said, but she didn't seem to doubt that, at least.

A welcome change.

Erin felt like smiling again. "No," she said. "Just cursed."

She remembered that day in bits and pieces, shards and glances. The important and unimportant alike took equal space in her mind, offering her only what was most vivid. It had been sunny, nearly summer, and Erin had been sixteen.

She was out at the edge of the woods, picking old cones she wanted to fashion into a sort of present for one of her brothers, when a cry from deeper into the trees made her look up. When she listened more closely, she recognised some of them as laughter, yelps of joy, but also something else, there, at the edge of hearing now. The cry of a stricken bird.

Leaving her basket on the ground, Erin started walking farther into the forest. The deeper she went, the more clearly she could hear the pained chirps hidden behind more laughter. She was almost afraid to step into the clearing when she found it, but once she did, she found the crown princes gathered together, boasting at one another.

They were clad in the brightest white, and their hems and seams were of golden thread, beautifully sewn, but in their hands they held crude slings, and around them were the bloodied bodies of several small birds already.

"What are you doing?" Erin called, but her voice was swallowed by another cry, impossibly loud, piercing the air.

And a raven fell into the grass. A great bird, larger than any that flew around there, longer than her arm, twitching like a twig in the wind. They all marvelled at it, but only for a moment.

Then the winds shifted and the woods cracked, almost as loudly as the cry of the bird, and into the meadow stepped an old woman, prim and tall, dressed in peasant's clothes. She looked at the raven for a long while, before raising her gaze to the princes, something in her pale blue eyes making them take a step back.

"Who did this?" she asked, but then she saw the slings they all held, the other birds lying around, and her expression soured. "Ah, so it's like that. You've hurt my dear…"

She went closer to the raven and gingerly picked it up in her arms.

The princes were silent as never before. Erin held her breath too, trembling. The sorceress looked back at them.

"Such black hearts in such fair faces," she said. "To be so wicked while so young, you must have been rotting from the cradle. I saw, however, that even bad seeds need a chance to grow. So let's see what can be done. May you spend half of every day as those that you so joyfully killed here, and may your eyes not see sunlight but through their eyes, and may it be so that, when seven years have passed, you will be all the wiser for it."

Then the sorceress shifted one hand, and mist started enveloping the helpless princes, and before they were even completely hidden by it, Erin saw them twist and turn to birds, great black ravens, which all gave a cry when the spell was done, loud enough to shake the woods. And took flight, disappearing into the trees, leaving all their fine clothes and slings behind.

The sorceress then looked at Erin, who still could not flee, terrified to her core. And she too must have only seen her brooch, glimmering in the light, and not her simple clothes and calloused hands, for when she spoke again, it was as if she thought Erin, too, was of royal blood. That was, at least, what she'd reasoned later.

"You have never given a thing away in your life," the sorceress spat, in the same tone. "Not because you wanted to, not because it gave you joy."

She couldn't say, *That is not me.* She couldn't even think it. The shriek of ravens was the only sound left in her lungs, echoing endlessly, hollowing her from the inside out. She'd left her basket at the edge of the woods. It hadn't been much, but it had been hers to give. And she couldn't say a thing.

"So I curse you to *give*, all your life, only what was sewn by your own hands," the sorceress went on mercilessly. "I curse you to give them to whoever is in need around you. And only weeds are to be your thread, and may thorns pierce your heart if you ever think of locking yourself away from this."

A *curse*. No way to break it. Erin stared at her, petrified, all her bones trembling within her. Then the old sorceress raised her chin, and pointed a finger at her.

"Seven years, and no sound. Do as I said, and speak no words, and when seven years are passed, your hands will be yours again."

The storm came soon after Erin left the witch's hut, and lasted for days, so that when she was finally able to go into the woods again, all the plants were soaked, feeble in her hands. It was a bit better in that the nettles didn't sting as much now, but it also meant she would have to be thrifty with her thread while the weeds dried enough for her to spin them into anything new.

The witch found her just as she was carefully gathering sprigs of burdock in her basket, one clear, early summer morning. She didn't move loudly, but neither softly enough to seem unnatural. In fact, in the light of day, she seemed like quite a common person, a tired woman not much older than her. She was wearing the cloak Erin had given her, though, and she didn't seem sick anymore, so it had worked well.

"I thought the rain had washed you out," she said, as a way of greeting.

Erin glanced up with a smile. "I have deeper roots than that," she said, then yanked a more stubborn stem right out of the wet soil, as a comparison.

The witch said nothing at that, choosing instead to look at the small sleeve poking out from under the weeds gathered in the basket. "Who is this for?"

"I don't know yet," Erin said, breaking off a couple more sprigs and then getting to her feet. "I only know when it's done."

"That's a strange curse," the witch said.

Erin shrugged. "It's the one I have."

Which made the witch smile, just a bit. It was nice, Erin realised, to talk about this freely for once, easily, where others would have either shrunk back or shown only pity. She hadn't met any other witches before. And so, she decided to chance it.

"What's your name?"

"Sigrun," the witch said, unexpectedly easily. "What's yours?"

"Erin," she said.

Sigrun pulled the cloak tighter around her, a thoughtful frown on her face. "My cough stopped when I put it on," she said.

Erin smiled again. "It was meant to."

Sigrun didn't seem to want to say anything more after that, but wandered off a bit as Erin peeled lichens off a tree. Yet, when her basket was full, Sigrun came near again, hands full of plants and a strange, conflicted look on her ashen face.

"Can I watch you?" she asked then. "While you're making it?"

Erin blinked in surprise, beyond words as she hadn't been in years. Yet—

"Of course," she found herself saying.

Seven years of her life had passed loudly enough to make her turn her head against the wind, if only to quiet everything else. That was why, in the end, she let herself be led to the sea. She'd thought the earth louder than the world.

After the crown princes had fled from the castle in the form of ravens, Erin came back crying to see the castle in utter chaos, the news having been passed to them without her help. And in all that shared turmoil, few other than her family observed her own distress, and none knew what she had to do. Not even herself.

The next morning, she found herself walking outside, barefoot, up to the wildest corner of their garden, gathering the newly-grown nettles there. She couldn't stop or move away. She just sat there, kneeling, until she'd gathered them all, and afterwards she took them, one by one, and started rubbing their needles in her palms, teeth gritted against the pain. That had been her first thread.

She'd started knitting it while hiding in the stables, making stitch after clumsy stitch, purls and knits intermingled badly. It took her two months to finish that first shirt, and then ten more followed. She spent her first year under the spell that way, rubbing blisters into her fingers and poking herself bloody with the knitting needles, but, in the end, finishing all eleven shirts.

She made them all from memory alone, adding a few inches, guessing and sometimes staring at her brothers long enough to make them even more wary than her silence had. For, unlike her, the princes did not return to the castle, neither by day, nor by night. Sometimes, Erin wondered if that hadn't been the wiser decision, sheltering them from any dubious stares as they nursed their curse in solitude. Sometimes, she thought she felt their dark, beady eyes following her from the trees.

The first shirt was the smallest, and the least well-made, and the seams around one sleeve kept coming undone, no matter what she tried. Yet, they were there. She hid them in the topmost tower of the castle while being watched from the window by a flock of dark birds with human eyes.

Then she left home for good. No words for her father, none for her brothers. She dressed, gathered all her remaining thread, and set off. Her fingers were burning from the nettles, but also itching to start another cloth, and then another. And these seemed to call her from far away.

She passed through villages and towns, sleeping in the open or in barns or in kindly-lent rooms. Every time she passed by a new place, her hands spurred her to start another shirt, another sweater, another cloak. She never knew what she was to do with them until she did, and it always helped. Something to soothe the bones of a weary miner, the eyes of a scribe, the sickness of a maid. They always helped, somehow. That was the good part.

For seven years, Erin didn't utter a word.

Then, on the seventh summer, the day for which she'd counted in her mind again and again reached her, when she'd just finished a woollen, burdock-spun coat, and given it to a lonely mother somewhere halfway between her home and the sea. Erin stood by a narrow road crowned by rustling trees and rose bushes, and fretted her blistered hands, wondering—was this it?

She expected someone to appear, a bird to come flying out of the sky and set her free, give her back the freedom she'd lost the feel of. And she thought she saw exactly that, too, a glimpse of wide, dark wings, floating somewhere far away, coming towards her, and her heart hammered, and her breath quickened, and she had to lean back on a rose-decked fence as she watched it come closer.

But then, her awe was shattered by the loud sound of a child coughing, a bit lower down the path. And, surprised, Erin turned towards them, and saw them stop their little cart of wares and raise a hand to their mouth. The sounds they made were wet and wracking, horrible to see coming out of such a small frame. Erin had heard their like enough times, along the years.

"You've kept your word," a voice said then, and Erin wheeled around in a panic and came face to face with the sorceress from seven years past, now standing across the path from her.

Farther away on the fence Erin had been leaning on, her raven preened, seemingly completely healthy and even larger than Erin remembered.

"And you've done good work," the sorceress continued. "The princes too, they're all back with their family. They appreciated the shirts you left them, even with a fallen sleeve. It's your turn now. I didn't expect you to go quite so far."

She raised her hand, and Erin widened her eyes, holding her breath. Then, once again, she heard the coughing of that child. One, two times, before it got even worse. She forcefully turned her head that way, and saw them doubled over, one hand over their chest. They couldn't last many more weeks, like that. She'd known some who hadn't. She'd known some who had been cured of it by her own work. Was she to chance it?

"What's the matter?" the sorceress asked.

When Erin looked back at her, her hand was still raised, no smoke or mist around her yet. Erin opened her mouth, then closed it again, and bit her lips. Her hands itched.

The child coughed. The sorceress stared. And Erin felt like crying. *It wasn't fair.*

She pushed away from the fence and ran to the child's side, helping them stand up. Their lips were a bit bluish already, their face wet with sweat and tears. Erin pushed their hair out of their eyes and ran her hand over their back.

"It's alright," Erin said, tears brimming in her eyes. Her first words, a possible lie. "It's alright. We'll do something, I'll make you something, and you'll be alright."

The child's breaths started evening in her arms, as Erin kept rubbing their back and shoulders with hands that almost burned with how much they wanted her to pick up the knitting needles once more. Which she would. She would go back to where she'd buried them when she'd thought this all done, and pick them up again.

Her life was a bitter thing, at the back of her throat. When she looked back, both sorceress and raven had disappeared from the path.

"How old were you then?"

"Twenty-three," Erin said.

Sigrun's hut was a less sombre thing in daylight. Erin had found this out maybe the third time she'd returned there, after taking another garment to another person in need of it. Dawn and dusk seemed both to avoid her shabby windows, and yet, so close to the cliff's edge as it was, there was nothing to keep it in shadow, and the sea and the pale blue horizon seemed to be enough to see by, on most clear days.

"How old are you now?" Sigrun asked after another moment.

Erin had given up counting after it became irrelevant. She counted now. "Twenty-seven."

Sigrun kept quiet and continued mixing seeds and powders in a salve someone in the nearest village had begged her for a day before. They were both helping in their trades, willingly or not.

"That's still young," Sigrun said, but without any easily perceived emotion, and without looking at her.

"It's enough," Erin said, and watched her instead.

She'd set her work aside for the day, wanting to focus on hers instead. Sigrun's hands were as calloused as hers, where they gripped the mortar and pestle. The grey hairs on her head might have been mirrored in Erin's, had her hair been darker. She spoke little, and yet she was not quiet, and didn't seem to mind Erin getting into her space every so often, to bring fresh flowers into the house or clean herself a little corner for knitting.

When Erin knit, Sigrun seemed to take it all in, watching her twist fresh leaves into thread and then cast it into neat stitches as if it was a nature of spell she had yet to learn. When Sigrun worked, though, it didn't seem look a spell. It reminded Erin more of watching the kitchen maids prepare bread and broths than of the witches people had to stay away from. She made it seem easy, but also complicated, and altogether very natural. It was everything Erin's strange thread-making wasn't.

Her gaze drifted back to her weeds and nettles, deep green and grey and purple, half-knit in her basket. Her blistered fingers urged her to get back to them immediately, but she'd wanted to move around, to ignore them for a while. It didn't do to spoil curses too much, lest they grew of their own volition. This, she'd learned only later.

"It's a wicked spell," Sigrun said.

"It's the one I have," Erin said again, and grinned when Sigrun scowled at her.

Yet, she was always swift with her looks, and so her face soon softened again, and she ran her pestle gently over Erin's hands. The salve it left in its trail was greenish against her reddened fingers and it soothed them almost instantly.

"I don't know how you can keep yourself so cheery," Sigrun said.

This time, Erin let her smile turn a bit wry. "It's the same either way, isn't it? My attitude won't change it. It's out of my hands."

She chuckled, and held her hands up.

"Actually, it's *in* my hands."

Sigrun let out what could almost be an amused huff then, and returned to pestling the last ingredients into the salve.

Maybe they were both a bit lonely, a bit alone, living there by the sea, or out in the open road. Maybe she'd grown used to it, Erin thought, in what she now realised had been ten year journey far from home. Yet, it was nice to feel her heart opening a bit more still, to receive friendship after being quietly starved of it for so long.

She was, like she'd said, resilient. Her life had deep roots in the earth, even if her feet didn't. Threadbare as she'd felt for years, her seams were iron.

A while ago, she'd started a new cloth, far more complicated than those before. She could only hope that, wherever she would have to go next, it would never be too far for her to come back, in the end.

When she was little, she'd wanted to know big things about the world. Now that she was a bit bigger, Erin found herself wanting to know little things.

She liked being taught how to prepare teas for different kinds of ailments, and how to make them taste better. She liked letting Sigrun test various ointments on her bruised fingers and being carefully listened to when she described the effects she was feeling. She liked watching the sea change colour outside the window, and listening to the ceaseless cries of birds, so different from those at home.

Most of all, she liked almost living with someone again. She liked getting to know someone more slowly, not over the course of one meal before she set off again, but day by day.

After living all her childhood with so many brothers and beside a castle that seemed always full, it was as if she'd lost part of herself once she had nobody to share it with anymore. There was that shade of her that wanted to be known, to be seen and understood, and to see and understand in kind. It was the simple happiness of having someone to share a thought only you could have had.

Crammed in a small window seat overlooking the sea, Sigrun watched the gulls soaring by. *Like flies, but peskier,* she called them.

She had been cursed with a heart of iron, was what she'd said. Or was it stone? Some cruel, age-old spell that had made her go far away from all that loved her, for fear of her heart stopping in her chest, or she stopping theirs. It was alright with Erin, though. The cursed didn't poison each other; it was thought they were already too full of their own venom.

"Was there anyone you missed?" Erin asked, carefully arranging their plates into order.

Sigrun frowned a bit at the sea, a grimace smothered in her palm. "Not quite," she said.

Erin missed her father and her brothers with a dull ache that seemed to coat her soul. She'd go back one day, she'd told herself. But had never been ready to see the pity in their eyes again.

"All my childhood," Sigrun began, almost tentatively, "I've longed to have someone close. I wanted a hand in mine, when needed, someone with whom to appreciate the warmth of a winter fire, the first taste of summer. I realised, when I was betrothed, that I wasn't going to get that with the one promised me, however. So, no, I guess I didn't miss a thing."

"You didn't like them?"

There was something more unsure than displeased about the downturn of Sigrun's mouth. "It wasn't that," she said. "It seemed like we got along, at first, and then our expectations suddenly split in two different directions. I didn't mind marrying, I liked the constancy of it, but I didn't understand the passion that came with it, the infatuation, the jealousy. I didn't like it and I didn't feel any of it back, nor did I wish to. When the curse set, I almost thought, *Good.*"

Erin looked at her, tried to see past the reflection of the sky in her eyes. She had a feeling she might have seen something she recognised there.

"It doesn't have to be selfish," she said.

"I know," Sigrun shook her head and sighed. "But I still felt like what I wanted was for others some sort of a middle ground, just a path that led from one place to another. And nobody wants to live their life on the side of the road."

The gulls cried outside, yet between the two of them it was quiet, quiet.

"My father never married," Erin said.

Sigrun looked up.

"All of us, we were just... children nobody cared for, that nobody had time and food for. If someone had a child they could not raise, they looked for him. He was such a lonely man, and he lived all alone, they used to say, he never refused a soul. But for all that, I don't think he ever felt lonely. He was constant and content by himself, yet I know he loved us all well enough. Was that a life spent on the side?"

"I don't know," Sigrun said, yet there was something petulant about her now.

She did know. Erin smiled.

Sigrun seemed to feel her smile, for she scowled and pushed herself off the window seat. "I'll make tea. Stop your smirking."

And Erin did, although only on the outside.

"What did *you* want to do, before all this?" Sigrun asked her, somewhat reproachfully. "Did *you* ever want to marry?"

After a beat, Erin burst into laughter. "No, no," she said, hands on her cheeks. "I wanted to be a candlemaker!"

"A candlemaker?" Sigrun asked, confused.

"Yes," Erin grinned. She'd forgotten. The memory was sweet as honey. "We kept bees at the castle, and sometimes we would carve patterns into the wax."

She didn't remember if she'd ever told that to anyone. At the time, it had just seemed like something she would get around to do one day. Back when her life had seemed to stretch endlessly and quietly before her.

"I make candles sometimes," Sigrun said, tentatively, as if she still didn't think Erin was completely serious. "I use tallow, but you can help me, if you like."

Erin beamed. She had around her a frayed sweater someone lower in the village had given her, months before, and she pulled it closer now, thinking—this was a nice place to live.

"You'll have to teach me," she said.

Sigrun raised an eyebrow at the mugs she was filling with hot water. "From what I gathered, you can teach yourself."

The new cloth seemed to take her longer than anything before, and she didn't know if it was because she was purposefully slower, or because she was constantly changing the pattern. Yet, it was not done. *Not yet, not yet.*

She would have gathered her seconds one by one, like grains on sand from the beach, if she could.

It was a cold, yet clean autumn day, maybe a year after she'd first reached the coast, when Erin climbed down the precarious rock-strewn path to the shore and let the wind and sea-drizzle envelop her like a low-ground storm. She drew her knees to her chest and pushed the hems of her dress under her bare feet to keep it in place, and let out a sigh, watching the ashen sea.

Earlier that morning, she'd finished the garment she'd been working on for nearly as long as she'd been there. It was a coat, long and heavy, a dozen patterns whirling like the wind over its wilted surface. She'd felt no pull, no knowledge of whom it belonged to, not yet. Perhaps she had come to the sea so that it would roar loudly enough in her ears that she would never hear it, that the gales would keep that part of the spell at bay.

She didn't want to go away. She'd left her home once before. This time, she just wanted to hold onto something for herself.

She didn't expect it, when she glanced to the side and saw the sorceress, but neither was she frightened. After eleven years living with someone's curse, you started to learn something about them. She'd never regretted a day's work, when she gave her garments away and saw the gloom over a person's head lift a bit.

Yet, a curse was a curse—it refused to let itself be cherished. At the end of the day, any compulsion tasted bitter on your tongue.

"You've been difficult to find," said the sorceress.

Erin raised a shoulder, looking back to the sea. "I've been here."

The sorceress came closer, her dark dress and cloak already gathering the pale dust of sand, making her look nearly statuesque. She watched the sea too, for a while. Her raven was a bit farther away, following and running away from waves in a rhythmic hopping-about.

"I wanted to give you this," she said. "It was wicked to see it cling to you, and do nothing."

From the sleeve of her cloak, she pulled out a single swan feather, lighter than the whitened sky. She held the feather out to Erin, and she took it, before the wind could tear it away.

"When you wish to, break it in two," the sorceress said. "The curse will go then."

Erin gazed at the feather, turning it between her fingers. So feeble, it seemed. She wouldn't have to do much to break it at all. Yet, it was strange. She almost wanted to put it safe, to be sure she didn't break it by mistake.

"You'll have to give something to yourself too. Can you do that?" the sorceress asked.

Erin gazed up at her, then took a breath of air and saltwater.

"Could you give me something for my friend too?" she asked, quietly.

The sorceress looked at her, then she wrapped her cloak more tightly around herself. "I already did, it seems."

When Erin reached the hut again, she found Sigrun tending to the last autumn plants in her garden. She looked back at Erin in surprise, for she had come panting past the garden gate, but any words she might have said were lost as Erin bounded into the house.

She came out with her basket of threads and needles on one arm and the coat on the other, and then she marched with them to where the fence was closest to the cliff side. Then, before she could hesitate at all, she tossed the basket over the side. It should have been impossible for it to reach the sea, and yet, when she leaned over, she saw it splash into the roiling waves.

"What are you doing?" Sigrun asked, having risen to her feet to watch her.

Yet, Erin did not say a word as she held out the weedy coat in front of her, and then gave it a forceful shake in the wind. It turned woolly and light grey in her hands, almost in an instant.

"This is mine!" she told Sigrun, voice a bit frantic, short of breath still. She twisted the coat around and wrapped it over her shoulders, and then she pulled the swan feather out of her pocket. "And this is me."

Then Erin broke the feather in two.

And somewhere, birds cried, but not in pain. Almost at once, it was as if a great weight was lifted from her soul, out of her bones, so that she was so light that only the heavy woollen cloak seemed to hold her feet to the ground. Before her, Sigrun raised a hand to her chest, and looked down, in wonder.

"Is your heart iron still?" Erin asked, voice catching, the wind almost stealing her words.

"No," Sigrun said, after a while.

Then she raised her eyes to Erin, and she smiled, at last.

"It's light as thread."

NOT TO DIE

BY ROSIEE THOR

Magic was laughing at me. I would have laughed back but for the thick, cold mud in my boots, the smell of impending sunrise, and coffee on the horizon. I'd walked all night to get there, carrying memories far heavier than the pounds of thread slung across my back. More than the coin I'd earn, it was the promise of a chair that lured me on toward the Perennial Market, a spectral shadow of tents in the night. My aching joints couldn't afford to stop now to indulge the otherworldly.

The otherworldly didn't much care for my schedule, though. It was almost as if magic didn't want me to go to Perennial, but we'd been everywhere else, and it was time to return. Ten years away didn't make it any easier. A mocking wind whipped through my grey hair, peals of laughter sticking to my skin like dewdrops.

"Very funny," I growled, casting my eyes up to the fading stars. Magic was all around, of course, but after a decade alone on the road, it helped to imagine it was stationary—or as stationary as the sky could be. We'd been all over this damnable earth together, magic and me, but still it felt like we'd gone nowhere, stuck in the mud like my too-large boots.

I bent to pull one shoe loose but lost my balance. I swore loudly, rewarded with a face-full of mud. Typical.

"Thanks for your help," I said, words dripping with sarcasm as I climbed out of the mud, one boot short.

"Sorry! Oh my, I didn't see you."

I looked up. Magic laughed and cried and swooned like the rest of us, but it had never talked back before. And still, it hadn't. At least it was consistent in that respect.

Someone stood a few paces away, reaching a hand out to help me too late. I couldn't see them through the mud in my eyes, but took the hand just the same.

"Are you all right?" they asked.

I grunted, trying to wipe the mud from my, well, everywhere. *All right* was a loaded phrase. I hadn't been *all right* since Altair and Cassia abandoned threadwork for war. I'd left *all right* back in the crowded market streets of Perennial ten years ago.

They'd promised to return someday, but the war was over and they weren't going anywhere. I'd promised I'd never come back, but promises didn't mean much to me anymore. Magic snickered at the irony, its thorny spines tickling the air around me. Magic lurked, as always, in the space between existence and not, close enough I could feel its movements, far enough we'd never touch.

"Long night," I said, ignoring the cold whip of wind and flickering stars fading into the peach and violet sunrise. Me and magic would have words later.

"Well at least it's over. Here, let me take that." The stranger gestured to my pack, which was full of thread waiting to become fate.

I clutched the strap. "Sorry. Nothing against you, but no one handles my wares but me."

"Fair enough." They shrugged. "Come on. Let's get you cleaned up, at least. Someone's started the coffee, so breakfast is only a few yards and a change of clothes away."

I followed, keenly aware of magic's silence as we crossed the boundary from the world into distinctly *not* the world. In daylight, the barrier protecting the Perennial Market looked like a bubble, transparent, but somehow still cloudy as though an invisible curtain rippled in the wind. At night, I barely noticed it but for the distinct shift in tension, in texture, in time. Magic must have felt it too. It almost always had something to say, but for once it had shut up. *Good.*

"I'm Prima, by the way. And you?" my rescuer asked.

"Huh?"

"Your name."

It had been days since I'd spoken to anyone but magic, which must have been apparent. "Oh, sorry. Ursa."

"It's okay. It's not every day a strange girl finds you in the mud — you sit here and I'll get you a towel."

She parked me on a low stool and disappeared into a small tent. "Strange girl, indeed."

Magic bristled, ruffling the grass as though shaking its big, cursed head.

When the sun rose, so too did the market. Brightly colored tents and tables were a rainbow against blue skies. Grocers, artists, musicians, and sages all peddled their services, a chorus all their own. It was a song I knew well, the words of the sale never quite forgotten during my travels, but long ago I'd lost the will to sing. Instead, I'd painted my melody to a wooden plaque:

Knots of Love

Simple. To the point. Altair had once suggested "What's Knot to Love?" and we'd all had a good chuckle over it, but laughter felt like a waste of time these days, too quiet to rise above the din.

I leaned the plaque against a basket on the makeshift table I'd fashioned out of an old tree stump—no use nailing it down. If I'd learned one thing over the last ten years, it was that permanency didn't exist. It was a lie carried on the back of hope, promised by the dusty figure eight of the Perennial Market. I didn't have it in me to make that promise anymore, no matter that the coin was better if I lied.

I did my best to arrange my features into something resembling a smile while I waited. I'd cleaned my face of mud as best I could by the early morning light with minimal help from Prima, though not for any lack of effort on her part. She was a sweet child, but I'd known too many sweet children in my lifetime. Sweet children grew up to ride off to war, leaving sour family behind. The muscles in my face were unaccustomed to an upturned shape, aching and straining to remain pleasant. I only hoped I could maintain it throughout the day.

My first set of customers were a young couple, no older than sixteen. They approached, a tangle of limbs and levity. A tall boy with sharp features pointed out the threads littering my work station. The other, shorter and fuller of frame, ran a thumb across his partner's wrist, a sly twinkle in his eye.

I was annoyed already, and they hadn't even spoken a word.

"Are you a real weaver?" said the tall one, a hint of skepticism in his voice.

"I'm a knotter." I tapped my sign, indicating the word *knots*.

"Right, but you are a *real* knotter?"

I knew what he meant, and why he asked it, but still the question stung. Peddlers in every market up and down the countryside made empty promises. They pretended to read the stars or palms or leaves, the futures they told too vague for fact. One in every dozen, perhaps, really heard the whispers of magic, and one in every dozen of every dozen shared what they heard. For magic rarely relayed good fortune, and that was all most customers wanted to hear.

"Does it matter?" I asked.

The boys glanced at one another and shrugged.

"Suppose not," the tall boy said.

The short boy doubled over, laughing at the wordplay.

I waited. Eventually, the pair recovered from their little joke, and I instructed them to each choose a spool of thread.

"Please hold it tightly in your hand and close your eyes." After a minute or so, I asked them to exchange threads and repeat the process. "Now give them to me." I held my palms open in wait.

I felt the magic before I felt the fibers. It collected their emotions like a harvest, spinning them into the threads in my hands. Magic spoke the only way it could, tying and twisting threads in a rapid pattern through my fingers. It was an odd thing, to converse with magic, where nothing was ever truly said. We wove a frenzied dance. Magic lead; I followed.

When my fingers slowed and I opened my eyes, the cord was complete. Green and mauve threads twined together, the story of their love and all the bumps and bruises along the way. I was glad to see their knots had little in the way of turbulence. As obnoxious as I found happy people, I much preferred to knot a future full of joy. It was harder to explain a cord with frayed edges and tangled loops. Harder to get paid for those too.

My smile was real as I presented the cord. "You are lucky to have found each other," I said.

As though magic called to them too, the boys simultaneously reached to touch the threads.

"What does it all mean?" asked one.

I gestured to the knots. "See for yourselves."

They squinted at the knots, pausing at the bulkier parts of the cord, running fingers round the threads until they found each other's hands again.

"So, will we be happy?"

I discarded the smile. "That is only for the threads to say. I'm not a fortune teller."

For a moment, the boys only stared. One began to twist his expression into disappointment, the other, frustration. But then, the taller boy cracked a grin. "*Knot* a fortune teller! I get it!"

And they were laughing again. Coin passed from hand to table, and thread from table to hand. Then, they were gone, swept along by the crowd.

"So, will they be happy?" a familiar voice came from across the walkway.

Prima stood by the florist's cart, a handful of roses in her fist. In the light of day, she looked altogether older and younger. She had dimples, broad shoulders, and eyes both dark and bright all at once. Her hair was tied back in an orange cloth, but small curls escaped the front, black coils against the russet skin of her brow.

I shrugged. "I don't speak for the threads." I bent my head toward my table as I waited for my next customer.

"Why not?" Prima's shadow fell over the threads. "You know what they mean, don't you?"

"Yes," I said, straightening the threads into even rows. "And no."

Prima leaned forward, chin in her hands, elbows resting on the table. "What's that mean?"

I hesitated. The bond I had with magic was unlike any other, sacred it in its quiet, constant presence. Our communication was a covenant shared only through knots. To give it voice felt like a betrayal of a promise I never made. But magic wound its way between, slinking around our legs in a figure eight. Maybe magic wanted to be shared, but I wasn't ready to share it again—not yet.

"You ask a lot of questions," I said.

"There's a lot I want to know."

I looked up. Honest eyes looked back. "How old are you?"

"Seventeen."

"And how old are you *really*?"

Prima screwed up her face. "Twenty, I think."

I nodded. "It's easy to lose track of time at the Perennial Market."

"You've been here before?"

"A long time ago."

"So how old are you, then?"

It had been a long time since I'd looked in a mirror, but I knew dark freckles and worry lines marred the pink skin of my cheeks and brow. Years of travel, of wind and sun and rain, had hardened my appearance. Still, my outsides did not reflect the weathered soul within.

"Older than I look."

Prima smiled, dimples burrowing into rosy cheeks. "Sorry. Didn't mean to pry."

"'I don't know' is the honest truth." I wove my fingers together, knotting them in my lap as though magic itself had instructed me to. Prima echoed the questions I'd asked myself along the way, but time had lost its meaning after Altair and Cassia died.

Prima nodded, a somber tilt to her chin. "I came here looking for family," she said. "They told me at the orphanage that I'd come from the Perennial Market, that my parents had left me with the priestesses to grow up."

I wanted to look away. Something about Prima's tone felt private, like she'd torn a piece of herself off to give me. It was the kind of closeness I tried to avoid these days, the kind of closeness a part of me still craved.

"I spent all my life waiting to leave, to come here and find my family. Maybe I should have known that was only a story, the kind of fable you tell children because the truth is too hard." She stared down the path, eyes unfocused, rolling her lip between her teeth. "I should have left a long time ago, but still I look for myself in every stranger who passes. Just in case."

"It's hard to leave a place like this, where the young stay young, the old stay old, and nobody dies." I stood, busying myself with straightening the threads on the table. I'd said too much already. Magic nipped at my heels, herding me forward anyway. "Nobody truly lives here, though. Nothing changes, no one grows. We're all trapped in an endless cycle, the same day over and over again."

"So why'd you come back?" Prima asked.

I slipped my hand into my pocket absently, my fingers wrapping around the cord I'd made for Altair and Cassia when they married. It was all I had left of them, a love they shared, cut short by war. They were together in the end, just as the cord had shown, but magic had only told me they would be happy together; it hadn't told me I would be alone. I'd lost a brother and an apprentice. I'd lost more than I'd known I'd had in the first place.

"Because I don't want to live anymore, but I'm too afraid to die."

The next day, Prima watched me again from the flower cart as I knotted the fortune for newlyweds, young lovers, and old lovers alike. She followed my hands with her eyes for hours. It had been a long time since anyone had watched me work like that—like they cared about the process as much as the result. Finally, as afternoon arrived, the sun moving through the motions of a day I'd lived a thousand times and then some, Prima crossed the path looking like the sun itself in bright cotton, a lunch of grilled red and purple fruit in hand.

"Have you ever been in love?" Prima asked without preamble, handing me a skewer.

My stomach rumbled as the familiar aroma of apricot, fig, and strawberry hit my senses. I pulled the first berry loose with my teeth. It tasted of a time left behind, and I wondered if I hadn't once eaten the same exact berry on the same exact spot many years ago. "Why do you ask?"

Prima dropped her gaze to the threads on my table. "No reason, really. You just spend all day knotting futures for couples. I wondered if you ever knotted one for yourself."

"I haven't—been in love, I mean." I swallowed and set down my plate. "And I won't."

"Did magic tell you that?" She gestured to my hands.

"No. I don't need magic to tell me my romantic future when I already know I don't want one. That kind of love isn't for me."

Prima bit into her skewer, sucking the end of the wood, deep in thought. "What about me?" she asked, so quietly I could barely hear her. "Will I fall in love?"

"I don't know." I shrugged.

"But the threads—"

"Only tell me the fate of a relationship—whether romantic, platonic, or something else entirely—not the fate of one girl."

Prima chewed the skewer and brushed her fingers over the threads on my tree stump with a delicate touch. "I don't think I want to fall in love. There's just too much heartbreak in it."

"Lots of different kinds of love out there, Prima," I said, fingering Cassia and Altair's cord in my pocket. "All of them can break your heart."

It was near closing when they came, four men with blades worn at their hips.

"How can I help you?" I said, careful not to let my voice wobble. Weapons, I knew, were commonly worn by travelers, but still I could not shake the feeling of dread filling me as their hilts glinted in the sunlight. Magic lay uncharacteristically still around me, its silence a warning bell inside my mind.

"Weave us something," said the leader of the group, a tall man built like armor.

"All of you are together?" I asked, readying my hands to knot a polyamory cord.

The Tall Man leaned over my table, his shadow spilling like murky water over me. "Just me," he said.

Cold capped my fingertips like the barest hint of frost in the morning, but I shook the feeling away. "I'm afraid I only do connectivity knots, reading the relationship between two or more people."

"Me and the kid, then," he said pulling forward one of his men—a youth no older than Prima with adolescent limbs too long for his body.

The Kid eyed me and then the big man with hesitant eyes, but the Tall Man held him tight.

"Both parties must be consenting for the magic to work," I said quietly, eyes averted. I couldn't bring myself to look such men in the eye, such men who carried such weapons.

"Do I look like I care?" said the Tall Man.

I sat straighter, my eyes flicking to their swords and back up. Weapons of war, weapons of death—like the kind that killed Cassia and Altair. Like the kind that might kill me too.

Still, magic remained silent, and I couldn't tell if the tension in the air was real or of my own imagining. I took a breath. These were only ordinary market-goers, nothing more. It wasn't worth getting upset over. I was overreacting, that was all. If I did as they asked, they'd be on their way in no time and I'd be alone again.

"Select a thread, please," I said through a forced smile.

The Kid selected dark blue, and the Tall Man grabbed a light yellow without looking.

"Get on with it."

The moment the threads touched my hands, magic swept my fingers into action. I closed my eyes, letting it fill me up. Jagged edges and tight knots sprang from my fingertips. Turmoil and pain, riches and ruin… the magic tore out of me and into the fibers like a storm. I wanted it to end.

And when it did, I opened my eyes on a rough future. The blue threads were eclipsed by the yellow, buried inside an overwhelming sun. They disappeared completely near the bottom, and I could only hope it meant he chose to leave these people rather than the alternative.

I ran my fingers over the threads once before looking up to pass along a more palatable interpretation. But there was no sign of the big man or The Kid. They and their friends were gone, leaving me with an ugly cord, weighing far more than its combined threads ought.

"Ursa!" Prima's body slammed into my table, her momentum a heavy thing. She must have dashed across the path at alarming speed. Her eyes were a wild tangle of amber threads. "Ursa, are you all right? Did they hurt you?"

"I'm fine." I pushed myself up, peering around the corner at their retreating backs. "They didn't want their cord, I guess."

"Well, of course not," Prima said. "They wanted to rob you."

"Rob me?" I laughed, but the sound slackened and died as I reached into my pocket and found it empty. I didn't have much of anything these days, and those scoundrels had taken it from me.

I pushed Prima out of the way and took off, my boots pounding against packed earth as I pursued them, but they were too far gone. The only thing I'd catch was my breath when I stopped.

"Ursa, you—" Prima began when I returned, sweaty and tired.

I didn't listen, brushing past the translucent blue cloth I used as a door. I needed to be alone.

I was always alone, had been for all ten years since I left Perennial in the first place. Now I'd be alone forever, living out eternity in this hellish place with empty pockets. I'd no coin to spend, but more than that, the cord I'd knotted for Cassia and Altair was gone. I'd come back to Perennial to both live and die at once, to walk this earth as a husk, a shade passing through the world, feeling nothing, doing nothing, being nothing. I was a corpse still moving, and they'd plucked the last piece of life from my still warm carcass.

"Ursa, please. Are you all right?" Prima's concern echoed from far away.

Magic raised its head, a question, a suggestion.

I ignored it, tucking myself away, under the blankets, and curling into the patch of earth I'd claimed for myself. It was all I had left.

"What do the little knots that look like roses mean?" Prima asked. She was waiting for me in my stall the next morning, perched on my stool, legs criss-crossed beneath her.

I just shook my head and shooed her out of the way. Magic hummed a disapproving note, but I pushed it away too.

"I think I have most of them figured out, but that one has me perplexed. The texture suggests a cyclical element. Is it about a pattern of some kind? An argument that repeats throughout a relationship?"

"No."

"Some other kind of repetition then? A tradition or an anniversary?"

"I really don't feel like teaching today, Prima."

Prima stopped then, lowering herself to her knees and leaning her head against my table. "That's okay. Maybe tomorrow?"

"I don't take on apprentices."

"But I'd be no trouble, I promise. And I want to learn more than anything!" She looked up at me with bright, hopeful eyes.

I could feel magic's eyes on me too.

"I don't take apprentices," I said again, more firmly this time.

Prima backed away, the smile gone from her face, shoulders low and cautious. A dark look crossed her eyes, as though I'd stolen something from her like the brutes had stolen from me, and she said, "You used to."

Before I could reply, she crossed the path and turned away.

She did not look back at me all day as I knotted threads and communed with magic, disgruntled though it was. I worked as though in a haze, like I'd drunk too much and the world spun me dizzy. We were out of sync, magic and me, dancing to different rhythms. By the time the market closed, all I wanted was to lie down and fall into the blissful pit of slumber, but magic had other plans. Nudging me forward, it goaded me to my feet and pushed me across the empty path.

I found Prima tucked into a corner of her cart, plucking petals from her leftover flowers. They would all grow back overnight, but still it felt violent, their parts strewn across Prima's lap like a battlefield.

"I don't take apprentices."

"So you said." Prima did not look up.

"Not anymore." I sighed and sank to the ground beside her. "You were right—I used to. I did, once."

Prima began destroying another flower, discarding the stem of the last at her feet.

"She was a good apprentice, focused and hungry to learn. She was my first, and my last, full of passion for magic and hope for the future. She'd learned at my side for two years, first as my pupil, then as my sister-in-law."

"She married your brother," Prima said. "A happy marriage."

I cast her a glance. She couldn't have known—but perhaps someone else at the Perennial Market had told her, someone who recognized me somehow after my ten years away. "Yes, a happy marriage. It was a joy to watch her fall, first in love with magic, then in love with my brother. Love is a splendid thing, and we'd had more than enough of it for our little family. And that was all I wanted, not marriage or children, but to have a family. With them I was content."

"What happened?" Prima asked, her fingers slowing to a stop, half the petals still intact. "What was the little rose knot?"

"The little—" I peered at her, and there it was: guilt etched into her gaze, a gentle kind, like she suspected rather than knew she'd done wrong. "The little rose knot."

"I found it on the ground near your table." From her pocket, Prima withdrew a dusty cord, pale blue and violet threads knotted together by my own hand. Cassia and Altair called to me from within those threads, the only piece left of our happy family.

I snatched it from her, tucking it beneath my chin, embracing it like I might a small animal. A tear ran down my cheek, seeping through the knots. "You should not have taken this," I said. "It was not yours to take."

"I know." She sniffled, and I realized with a pang that she was crying, too. "I didn't think it was important at first—just a cord you hadn't sold. I wanted to practice, to understand what the knots meant so I could learn to be like you."

"Like me?" I whispered.

It had been a long time since anyone had wanted to be like me. All the others who'd come and asked to learn had wanted to be better than me. They wanted to take what I knew and exploit it for their own gain. They didn't care about the threads. They didn't care about magic. Cassia had understood the weight of being a knotter. She cared what magic had to say and held it in high regard, always. Perhaps I'd lost some of that along the way, treating knotting more like a transaction than a sacred practice.

"When you knot the threads, it's like—it's like someone is singing very far away, and if I could only understand the threads I might be able to hear them." Prima set the flower down, half-plucked. "But as I studied that cord, I realized it wasn't meaningless. It was yours as much as theirs, the couple you made it for, your apprentice and your brother."

My chest tightened, as though magic's hands thought me a thread to knot. But I was alone. I had no one with whom to be knotted. The threads told only of connections, and I had none left.

"The little rose knot," I said through a heavy breath. "It's the Perennial Market. It represents a break in the cycle of life and death, a period of time where nothing changes." I pulled the cord from beneath my chin and laid it flat on the ground between us. I pointed to the first rose knot. "Here, they entered the market. They lived a happy life, protected by the invisible sphere separating us from time." I let my finger trace the knots and landed on the second rose knot. "And here, they left."

"They died, didn't they," Prima said, her finger brushing my own as it touched the knot. "They left you behind and didn't return."

I couldn't even nod, the pain of it lancing through me like a blade so sharp I was certain that had I stood outside the Perennial Market, I would have bled out and died.

I waited for magic to curl around me. The sheer comfort of its presence would get me through this moment and the next, one moment at a time. But it didn't come. Instead, Prima scooted toward me, closing the distance between us, and placed her arms around my shoulders. It was as awkward as a hug could be, but I sank into it, the comfort of another human heart beside me almost more than I could bear.

"It hurts to be left behind," she said quietly into my hair. "But you don't have to be alone."

When dawn broke over the Perennial Market that morning, I'd packed my things into my satchel. My blankets, my threads, and my worn, wooden sign. All my belongings fit neatly into one bag, and I'd no need for more. I'd begun to understand, though, that what I needed wasn't all there was to life. Sometimes it was good to want something too.

"You're leaving." Prima stood before me across the narrow path carrying an armful of red, white, and pale orange roses.

I nodded, slow and somber. "I can't stay."

"Will you come back?" A sad smile cracked across her face. "Or is that something only magic can tell?"

I shook my head, ignoring the smug rumble of magic in the air. "No. I won't be coming back. It's like I said, this place is just a waystop to put your life on hold for a while. I won't work through anything here, by myself. I need to go so I can grieve, and then so I can heal."

Prima nodded, a tightness in her face.

"Come here." I gestured for her to join me and bent to open my pack. "Pick one."

Prima stared down at the collection of threads, eyes wide. "Really?"

"Really."

She plucked a tangle of dark red cotton thread from my pack and held it out it to me.

I didn't take it and instead and passed her a spool of leaf-green silk.

"For—for us?" she asked, a hesitant note of hope in her tone. "You're going to make us a cord?"

"No," I said, closing her fingers over the threads. "You are. And I'll teach you, if you care to go with me—as my apprentice."

Prima dropped the roses, letting them bounce and roll along the path. "I'll get my things."

It took her less than ten minutes to collect her belongings, leaving behind the flower cart as though it were nothing more than scenery. She practically skipped as we made our way through the market toward the exit, her steps as happy as my heart.

At the market border, a speckling of round, polished stones the size of fists lining the edge, I stopped, placing a hand on her shoulder to calm her movements. "Are you ready?" I asked.

Prima glanced out at the world beyond, eyes round and resolute, and then back at me. "To grow old and die?"

I shook my head, eyes sliding over green pastures, snow-capped mountains, and glinting silver cities in the distance: a whole world lying in wait. The last time I'd crossed over from the market to the world, it had been only magic and me. For ten years, we'd wandered, and I thought I'd seen everything I cared to see. I'd left the world behind, a ragged and wanting thing. It was as old as old could be, a silent witness to our wars, our deaths, our lives, and loves. But standing beside Prima on the brink of the rest of time, it didn't look so worn.

"No, my dear." I laughed, and magic laughed with me, a short but soulful quake. "Not to die. To live."

BUSY LITTLE BEES

BY POLENTH BLAKE

I was the first bee. I wasn't born first, but I was a bit chubbier than the other babies, like my mother had been as a newborn. That's why she kept me and not the others. She imagined I'd grow up to be just like her. I was already managing not to live up to that as a teenager. I'd taken up knitting instead of card making. I enjoyed singing instead of playing the clarinet.

"I'd want to go to the school party," she declared, after discovering I'd declined a date.

I paused from my knitting, as I didn't want to drop a stitch. "It's not my thing."

"It all started when you dyed your hair." She wiped away a tear. "I shouldn't have let you."

Not that she'd had a choice, as I'd done it by the time she knew. She'd never dyed her hair blue. Never considered it. She made it clear that I obviously didn't love her when I did something like that. She'd used all her savings to get an identical copy and this was how I repaid her.

It bothered me when I was younger. The tears would start anytime a sun spot developed in a different place or I tanned to a different shade, because it reminded her that I hadn't lived an identical life. I'd started to realise that this wasn't actually my problem.

"You'll want a family one day," she continued.

I rolled my eyes and went back to knitting. I already had a family. The one she left behind when I was born.

We stood outside the hive. It was a sleek building with white curved walls and plenty of glass. There were large grounds around the building, filled with trees and lush green grass. It all seemed rather idyllic on the surface, but the details gave it away. The glass was reflective, so the open feel was an illusion. There was no way to see what was going on inside. The grounds were to block the view of the rather less idyllic town that had grown up around the hive. It was a carefully crafted lie for the company brochures.

X asked, "Are you ready?"

"Are you going to puke again?" I replied.

They smiled, which didn't mean no, but at least they didn't feel like death anymore. X got motion sick on boats, which wasn't the best when travelling to an island.

I took the first step down the path to the place where we were born.

X was the second bee. We met through the most boring route possible. I gave my details to the Honey Network, a non-profit that tried to reunite bees. X had done the same thing. We shared our genes and our birthday.

Our first meeting was in a tearoom. I didn't think any bees had tried to murder all their siblings, but we were still conscious that we were strangers. We sat looking at our drinks and pretending they were a bit too hot to drink yet.

X turned out to be a coder and still lived with their family. That was pretty unusual for unwanted bees. The classic family who adopted was wealthy and wanted to get in on the clone baby fashion, but also wanted to be able to take the moral high ground. After all, they hadn't commissioned a clone. They'd just adopted an unwanted one from someone else, out of the goodness of their hearts. But X's family sounded like they might be genuinely kind.

I took a sip of my tea as I struggled to come up with small talk. "What sort of coding do you do?"

"I wanted to get into game design, but there's more work in finance."

"That's still cool," I said.

I'd never really had a dream job. My dream had always been getting out and finding my siblings, so I took the first job I could find. It wasn't the best thing to say to continue the conversation, so I was back to not being sure what to say.

"Do you stay in touch with her?" X asked.

I knew who they meant. My mother had no interest in talking to the other bees. I didn't even know how many had tried to contact her. As far as she was concerned, it had been a failure and a waste of money. She wasn't going to live forever through any of us.

"No. She never liked that I was so different."

"I'm sorry to hear that."

It was a nice thing to say, though X had been rejected by her far earlier. They looked different enough that we'd pass as siblings who weren't identical at all. They were slimmer and shorter than me. The line of their jaw was smoother. However, they did share my mother's lighter skin tone. I got unexpectedly dark after my first year, which wasn't odd for my mother's family. She was the oddly light one. It didn't stop it being the source of endless angst. She thought she must have gotten the environmental variables wrong and tried to stop me going outside.

"What games do you like?" I asked.

"Puzzles are my favourite."

"I love puzzle games. There's one on my phone with the purple jellybean, and I've still got some of the secret areas to find. And that probably sounds silly."

X grinned and got out their phone. A bouncing purple jellybean graced the screen. That was the third thing we shared.

The waiting room was smothered in pictures of smiling babies in bee costumes surrounded by cartoon DNA strands. I'd probably have found it cuter if I hadn't grown up with bee t-shirts, lunch boxes, and birthday cards. Everything designed to remind me that I was a clone and wasn't supposed to be my own person.

A receptionist looked us up and down. We were dressed too nicely to be from around here. "Can I help you?"

X handed over the paperwork. "We're here for a surrogate reunion."

The receptionist glanced at the papers. "Take a seat."

We sat in silence. Too awkward and too watched to feel like we could say anything at all.

Meeting our surrogates hadn't been part of the original plan, but we'd hit an issue: the eighth bee hadn't made it off the island. We couldn't get onto the island without an excuse. So we all filed requests to meet our surrogates. After months of nothing, X's surrogate agreed.

That was more of a surprise than anything else. Most requests were denied. The few that were approved were tightly controlled meetings with hive representatives present. I didn't expect to find anything in this meeting, but once we knew who we were looking for, it'd be a start. The surrogates had all given birth on the same day, so it was the best lead we had.

After an age, a person in a suit came to get us and guided us through a maze of corridors. I tried to keep calm, but I could hear my heart pounding. I had no idea what we'd find.

We were led into a room with a circular table. Three people in suits were undoubtedly the company representatives. The one remaining was most likely Martha, the woman who'd given birth to X. I admit, I'd had expectations, and Martha didn't really fit them. All the stories of poverty on the island made me think she'd look ragged, but she was clean and tidy. Her clothes had a few repairs and the colour was faded, but they were in generally good condition. In hindsight, I was expecting what my mother would have expected. That was something I needed to work on.

One of the people in suits said, "This is Martha. Ask anything you want."

I wanted to ask a lot of things, but I wouldn't. We'd been advised by the Honey Network not to ask any questions that could get surrogates in trouble. We'd get to leave once this was done. The surrogates wouldn't. It was easy to imagine riding in and solving all the problems, but the hive wasn't something that could be dismantled by a couple of tourists.

"I'm Chrysanthemum, but call me Zanty." I offered my hand for Martha to shake and she took it tentatively.

X also held out their hand to shake. "I'm X."

Martha looked a little surprised by the name, but I suppose the paperwork had legal names rather than actual names.

We settled down at the table and tried to pretend that everything was fine.

"I don't expect you remember me," said X.

Martha smiled. "I remember all the babies."

"Do you like it here?" X asked.

I was pretty sure X's question fell into something that could cause trouble, but Martha responded smoothly, "Life is good here."

The discussion continued for our allotted twenty minutes. Martha had two daughters, who worked at the fishery. Most people ate fish, because they couldn't grow many crops on the island. It was artificial and the salt tended to seep through the base into the soil. This was fine as fish was very good for babies, with all those vitamins. Martha liked rainy days best, because it reminded her of home.

"Well, we're at our deadline," said one of the company people. "Always warming to see everyone getting along."

They were either not noticing the awkwardness or had come to imagine that regimented interviews were normal.

We shuffled to our feet and everyone headed out of the room. Martha brushed past me and I felt something being pushed into my hand. I quickly put my hands in my pockets until we were out of the building.

"What now?" asked X.

I pulled out my hand and opened it. The item was a slip of paper with a time and a place.

X and I met the third bee together. All we knew is she was called

Deeny. What we hadn't known is she was six months pregnant with a baby for a nice couple that lived in the same town as her. Which explained why she wanted to meet in that particular restaurant where the run to the loos wasn't too far.

There was a lot about Deeny that I didn't really understand. She was different from me in many ways. Constantly smiling. Hair cut short and dyed blue, but not the dark tint I had going on. She'd bleached it first, so it was a more neon blue. Deeny was someone who stood out, whereas I faded into the woodwork.

The pregnancy was just one more thing. I'd never liked the idea, but being a surrogate sounded even worse. We'd all been born that way, and I hadn't been comfortable with the stories about the way our surrogates were treated. Deeny appeared in good spirits about it though.

"How do you get into that?" I asked.

"Oh, there are groups, you know? It's really exciting! You meet up and see if you hit it off. Dev and John are just so cute, they'll be great dads."

X had been considering it quietly. "Will you miss the baby, do you think?"

Deeny laughed. "I'm only going to miss all the crying. I'll be Auntie Deeny and there for the fun bits like birthdays."

"I'm starting to see how this could be a good thing," I said.

Our order arrived at that moment. Deeny had ordered dessert first, which went with her personality. She was the most bubbly person I'd ever met, which is quite something coming from a family of introverts.

None of this should have been a problem. I didn't expect my

siblings to be identical, but I had expected them to be broadly similar. Deeny didn't really share anything at all, from hobbies, to life, to personality. This wasn't her problem. It was mine. As much as I liked to think I'd left my mother behind, those attitudes about perfect copies still lingered.

It did make me wonder how different the rest of the bees would be.

The town consisted of rows of identical houses, which was probably because it was cheap rather than a subtle reinforcement of the cloning theme. Visiting clients and bees were not encouraged to wander out here. We found the right number and knocked on the door.

Martha opened it and motioned for us to come in. Inside was a dining room with a plastic rectangular table and seven people sitting around it. Martha joined them to make eight. A little convenient on the numbers given the circumstances. I'd expected the surrogates to know each other, but not to find them all here.

Martha fixed us with a steely gaze. "Sit down."

Neither of us argued. Martha was no longer the shy and quietly spoken woman from the hive who loved rain and eating fish every day.

"Why are you here?" she asked.

"I, er… came to see you," said X.

Martha simply stared for a moment. "Six requests to meet us came in on the same day, all from the same birth."

This wasn't how we'd planned it, but there didn't seem any reason to hide why we were here. "We've been trying to find each other. We think the eighth is still here."

There was silence in the room as all of the surrogates glared at us. Had we been lying, I think we would have fallen apart at that point.

"It's okay, I think they're telling the truth." The voice came from the doorway into the rest of the house.

Martha sighed. "This is Tay, Julie's son."

Tay stepped into the room. He looked the same age as us and had the family's distinctive hooked nose. His hair was long and dark, the slightly off-black colour mine had been before I dyed it. He was somewhat between X and me in build. He reminded me of Deeny in that respect. The oddest thing is he was wearing a single glove.

"Very well," said Martha. "Lunch first, and then we have something else to discuss."

We had to go through a security check to meet the fourth bee. Jessica had ended up in prison after a string of crimes. They mostly involved stealing things, so she wasn't considered dangerous, but the law never cared about that.

The visiting room wasn't quite what I thought. There was no screen between us. Just a series of tables, each with a prisoner on one side, and visitors on the other.

We sat opposite Jessica and I tried not to stare too much. She was the perfect copy my mother had always wanted. Everything from build, to hair, to skin.

"Hi, I'm Jessica, and you're looking at me funny."

"Sorry, you just look so much like my mother."

"I thought you'd look more like me," she admitted.

I was getting used to awkward silences after meeting several bees. The best thing was just to roll on through them until someone came up with something to say.

X put a paper bag on the table. "I brought you a book. They've already checked it doesn't have a nail file in it."

Jessica picked up the gift. "I didn't think there were so many of us, you know what I mean? It's like, I thought there were only two of us. Now there are four."

It took a moment to figure out what she'd just said. We hadn't mentioned Deeny in the original messages and Deeny would have told us if she'd made contact first.

"Wait, who is the fourth?" I asked.

"Oh, you didn't know? Callie's my lawyer."

The meal was more comfortable than I'd expected. Everyone talked about things they were doing, their children, and a football game that was coming up soon. Martha's answers in the interview hadn't been a lie in the sense that there were good things on the island. It was just more complicated than that. People making the best of a bad situation didn't mean it was okay.

Afterwards, most drifted away, until it was us, Martha, Julie and Tay. The comfortable part was over.

I shifted in my seat. "There was something you wanted to talk about."

Martha had softened a little during the meal. I guess it was clear we weren't up to anything bad. "We want you to take some information back."

"There have been news stories about this place. It's not stopped it."

Julie placed a folder on the table. It was marked with the company logo. "They gave me a job in the offices, cleaning up. Thought I couldn't read."

"What's it about?" asked X.

"All sorts of things." Julie flipped it open to reveal photocopies. "It's not just how they treat us. They've been sabotaging research into artificial wombs. It'd cost more to maintain them, so they'd rather keep things as they are."

"Couldn't they just charge more?" I asked.

"The focus groups say people value surrogate births over artificial wombs. They see it as more natural."

It was so natural that clones were all born on the same day as their parent, but people didn't like to think about that. I wondered if there was any proof of that interference in the folder.

"What's the eventual aim?" I asked. "Ending the surrogacy programme?"

Martha and Julie answered at once. Yes and no.

"I'm sensing disagreement," said X.

"Julie wants to see better regulations," Martha began, "but I want them to end it. I think people will still be coerced."

"That's why we need social changes at the same time," said Julie. "More jobs and systems to support people who can't work."

They both had a point, but Julie's version was more likely to happen. The cloning company had already made their own island to avoid laws against what they were doing. It might be possible for public pressure to force them to improve conditions, but closing down was something else. I could also see where Julie was going with the artificial wombs. It wasn't just something to reduce the need for surrogates, but something that would provide alternative jobs. Whether those jobs would go to former surrogates was more debatable.

It all sounded reasonable, but there was a problem. "I'm not convinced people will listen. It's dismissed as outsiders not understanding what's going on. That people here don't expect anything better. People have tried."

"We could record statements," said Tay.

"No," said Martha. "They'll come after us."

Martha was good at seeing the problems before they started, but she didn't have all the information. Tay looked so much like Deeny apart from the long hair and different clothes. Things that wouldn't be that hard to change.

"What if we could get someone out to tell the story? Not just the files."

Martha looked from Tay to us. The implication must be obvious, but we didn't look enough like him.

"I don't see how," said Tay.

"I know someone who looks a lot like you."

Callie was the fifth bee we contacted, but not the fifth bee we met. Her work as a lawyer had her busy most of the time. Plus, she'd married a man and had three children, volunteered for several charities, and probably a few things I'd forgotten. We'd ended up chatting in email instead.

It was an odd feeling, opening the pictures of her family. The thing my mother had always said I'd want. I didn't mind children, but the whole process of getting there didn't appeal.

"Cute kids," said X, looking over my shoulder.

I typed: X says your kids are cute.

X frowned. "You don't think they're cute?"

"It's not them. It just makes me uncomfortable sometimes. I don't feel that way about people. The husband thing, not the kids. But everyone expects it."

"I don't expect it."

"My mother expected it. She had a point in a way. If everyone leaves to start families, they'll all be like Callie, and I'll be alone."

"I'm not going anywhere."

"I thought you wanted kids."

"I love kids, but you're my sister. I'm not leaving you behind."

It wasn't entirely rational to worry about it. Deeny had her little family and there was no reason why I couldn't be an auntie as well. I knew families came in many different shapes. It was still hard to shake though, because my mother hadn't wanted me. It's harder to believe that people won't leave when they've done it before.

X wasn't my mother. I needed to make myself believe that. "I can knit them hats."

"I'd like that."

Deeny's surrogate had a startling change of heart about meeting her. When the request went out, I also contacted Deeny to tell her about the island. Obviously, the company would read everything, but I cautioned that it was cold here and there were no hair dye shops. She'd need to bring warm clothing and all the supplies she needed. I added a last bit about my roots showing, so she'd bring some sort of blue dye for me, even if she didn't get the hint about the rest.

"Are you sure she'll agree?" Tay asked.

"Pretty sure. She's very outgoing."

We'd been working on Tay's accent and behaviour. Trying to make him a bit more like Deeny. It wasn't going to be perfect, but no one had done this before. We had to hope that security wouldn't be looking for it.

Julie came in with a white piece of cloth. "It's an old sling. We can make it look like you broke your arm."

The puzzlement must have shown on my face.

Tay raised the gloved hand slightly. "I was born with one hand. The original had two, apparently."

"She did," I agreed.

My mother would have hated that. It was one of those things that wouldn't usually be an issue, but when a baby is expected to be identical, there's no room for missing limbs. That would have been an uncomfortable reminder that we were different people from the moment we started growing. No two pregnancies would be the same. People caught up in bee marketing didn't like to think about that.

"There's metal in your hand?" said X.

"Some," said Tay.

"Martha's working on a replacement," Julie added, "but the

fingers won't move, so we need the sling."

"It's making sense," I said.

In more ways than one. The company hadn't wanted Julie as a surrogate after Tay, because they couldn't sell a baby that looked so different to the original. So they'd shifted her into a new job and given her the baby. They might come to regret both of those things.

The eighth bee wasn't one when we met him, which we only realised the night before Deeny's arrival. Everything was ready. Tay had a temporary hand made of newspaper and glue. Julie had gathered up some tools for cutting Tay's hair, which we'd leave until the last minute. There wasn't anything else we could do, so we sat around the table playing a card game with rules I barely understood.

I tried to put down my pair of aces.

Tay waved me away. "No, two threes is better than two aces."

"I'm completely lost," I said.

"Put down the five in the second pile," said X. "Hearts get a bonus."

"You're making this up as you go along, both of you."

Tay laughed. "No, it's a real game."

I tossed down my five of hearts. "Bees shouldn't mock each other."

"We're humans," said Tay.

"We're all bees," I said. "Like the posters."

"Oh, I never thought of that as a real thing. We just call them babies."

I hadn't considered how differently it might be viewed here. Most bees were sent away, so there wasn't the same culture surrounding being a clone. "I guess we formed our own identity around it. We're not the bees they wanted. We're our own sort of bees."

"That'd make me a bee?" he asked.

"If you want to bee."

X elbowed me, but Tay grinned.

"Maybee," he replied.

We waited for Deeny outside the hive. Better this way than meeting her at the boat, so she'd act naturally in the interview.

As soon as she saw us, she ran up and hugged us both. "Zanty! X! It's been too long, I'm so excited and what's wrong."

"Nothing," said X.

"We'll walk you out," I said.

Deeny was oddly quiet. She knew something was up.

Once we were away from the hive, I said, "Okay, now we can talk."

"That message you sent was weird. I don't need to dye my hair that often. I brought it, I got the hint, but what's going on?"

"We found the last bee."

I ran her through the basics of what happened at our interview, the lunch afterwards, and our plan.

"I'll help, of course," said Deeny. "It'll be quite the story to tell my niece."

We reached the house and Julie let us in. Tay waited nervously inside.

"You must be Tay." Deeny moved forward then hesitated. "Do you like hugs? It's so great to meet you! Don't worry about the skirt, I have trousers and things you can wear, and this is so scary, but it's going to be great."

"Er, hugs are okay," he said.

Deeny promptly hugged him and started rummaging through her luggage for things. We had a few days to get everything set before leaving her behind.

The sixth bee had a flower name, just like me. Tulip had been five when she died. A white marble stone marked her resting place and yellow tulips had been planted over the grave.

We'd been shown there by her older brother. George was also a bee, but from a different parent. He was about my height, though ginger and freckled in a way that matched none of my relatives.

"I'm sorry it had to be like this," he said.

"Thank you for showing us. It must be hard."

X stepped forward with the flowers we'd brought. There was a pot in front of the gravestone, so they placed them in that.

"If there's anything you want to know about her, feel free to ask."

"How did it happen?" asked X.

That was a sensitive question to ask, but George remained stoic. "There was a cat on the other side of the road, so she ran out. The car was going too fast to stop."

When I started searching for bees, I thought we could undo any harm, make up for the time we lost from being separated. But we'd never have a chance to get to know Tulip. Those few years where we could have grown up together were gone. Whether that was easier or harder than having known her and lost her, I wasn't sure. I still wished we'd had that option.

"The tulips are all yellow," I remarked.

"Her favourite colour."

The mask fell at that point and George started to cry. He was trying to hold it back, but there was no stopping tears once they'd started. I put an arm around his shoulder. X was more practical and offered him a tissue.

"She was lucky to have a good brother," I said.

George settled enough to say, "Thank you."

"You should keep in touch," said X.

He forced a smile. "I think Tulip would have liked that."

The boat security was remarkably easy. They glanced in our bags and made us walk through the metal detector. The guard offered sympathy for Tay's broken arm. Just like that we were on the boat and away. Deeny would stay hidden for a few days, before contacting the authorities with a sad story about someone stealing her passport.

We were too caught up maintaining the act to think about what happened next. After the boat and train ride, we were back at the flat, as though nothing had happened. Something had, because Tay was still with us.

"You live here?" he asked.

"Yes," I answered. "Well, it's X's place, but I live here too."

"We should order food or something," said X.

Metaphors like crashing waves or sudden blows didn't adequately sum up my thoughts. I knew that all clones technically had citizenship if their parent was a citizen. Everything should be okay. But there was probably paperwork and I had no idea how the system worked. That was before thinking about how to get Tay's information out and what might come next.

"Yeah, you do that. I'm going to call Callie."

It took two years to find the seventh bee. Ashley hadn't initially wanted to be found, but her father had persuaded her that she'd regret it. She was the only bee who lived in the countryside. It was a quiet village that had two buses a day. We'd arrived on the first.

Ashely didn't say a word when we arrived. She'd set up tea and sandwiches outside, so we sat and ate them, and said nice things about the garden. Bees flitted back and forth between the flowers, before returning to the hives in an enclosed area at the side of the garden.

"The sign is a cute touch," said X.

The sign in question read "Beeware of the Bees" and had an angry bee picture on it. The real bees didn't look like they were going to bother anyone.

Ashley smiled, but still didn't speak. We'd been told she might not, as she'd sent a letter first to explain. She wasn't always able to speak. Her first parents had placed her back up for adoption after finding that out, which is when her father stepped in. He was an older bee, so he

293

wanted to help the next generation.

"They look so peaceful," I said.

Ashley giggled silently, so I suppose it did sound a bit simple. I was sure there were exciting times in the hive and bee arguments. But that wasn't the first thing that I associated with bees.

It was the first time I'd really faced the dishonesty of the branding in our lives. The idea of a beekeeper was a kindly one. Someone who cared very much for the bees in their charge. They'd keep away predators. They'd keep the hive warm in winter. It was a homely feel, like old-fashioned farms and harvests and warm golden colours.

The cloning company was none of those things. They weren't kindly. The owners didn't even live on the island. But it made clients feel like there was something wholesome going on. Have a clone baby born the natural way. Never mind that it takes a lot of babies to get one close enough.

I tried not to be melancholy about it. Finding Ashley meant there was only one bee to go. It was time to celebrate. So I drank tea, and ate sandwiches, and talked about bees.

It wasn't that life had settled, but a week in, I was getting used to it being unsettled. Tay was meeting with Callie today. He had an appointment to measure for a new hand tomorrow. The information was out and some places wanted to interview him about it. Somewhere in the mix, I needed to do some food shopping, because X was too busy working overtime. We needed the money more than I needed help with the chores.

My morning routine started with trudging down the stairs to see if anything had arrived for our flat. I was rewarded with one giant parcel, one small parcel, and a couple of letters. The others were in the kitchen by the time I staggered in with the haul.

"Looks like a big one for Tay." I placed it in front of him.

It was probably from George, who'd promised to send some clothes. We didn't have enough to buy Tay a whole wardrobe and most of Deeny's clothes really weren't suitable.

The smaller parcel was addressed to all of us, so I opened it. Inside was a jar of honey from Ashley, to welcome the new bee. "Good news, Ashley sent honey."

"There's also some bad news." X had opened the other letters and was frowning down at them. "It looks like the company is trying to interfere with Jessica's parole. I guess they couldn't come at us directly."

"What are we going to do about it?" asked Tay.

"Jessica says we should keep going. It's the right thing to do."

"Anything from Deeny?" I asked.

X raised the other letter. "She should have her new passport by next week. There's not much they can do about it. They can't hold her hostage."

"My mum's probably spoiling her." He looked a little sad as he said it.

It must be hard being away from home. I wanted to think it would all work out and he could go home to visit, but I knew it might not. What I was sure about is we'd all make it through. Bees work together, and if the company kept trying to come after us, they'd find that bees can sting.

ACKNOWLEDGEMENTS

Anthologies are large collaborative projects, and there are many people without which *Common Bonds* would not exist.

Our first and deepest thanks, however, go to the **451 backers** who believed in this project from the start. Without your generous kickstarter donations, we could never have gone forward with this anthology. Your trust and excitement carried us forward and we will always be grateful for it.

We would also love to thank every publishing professional who has spread the word about the anthology—every tweet, post, like, and retweet count. The queer (and especially aromantic) bookish community has been a tremendous help in bringing this project to life and its support has been truly heartwarming. In particular, we want to thank the book bloggers who have featured and hosted us throughout the Kickstarter campaign and after: we would not have made it without your hard work.

Finally, the whole *Common Bonds* team is grateful for the support of friends and family, who have received their fair share of rants and happy squeals alike, and who are always there when we need them.

Thank you everyone, and we hope you enjoyed the anthology!

CPSIA information can be obtained
at www.ICGtesting.com
Printed in the USA
LVHW050604260223
740430LV00012B/573